# FIREBORN

# FIREBORN

## AISLING FOWLER

**HARPER**

*An Imprint of HarperCollinsPublishers*

Library of Congress Control Number: 2021942267

ISBN 978-0-06-299671-8

Typography by Corina Lupp

21 22 23 24 25   PC/LSCH   10 9 8 7 6 5 4 3 2 1

❖

First US edition, 2021

Originally published in Great Britain in 2021 by HarperCollins Children's Books

*For Ben,*
*My greatest support and*
*inspiration.*

# EMBER

THE
FROZEN WASTES

N

The Heart Grove

THE FROZEN FOREST

THE FANGS

MOUNTAIN CLAN

The Hunting Lodge

Ledge

THE
ENDLESS
OCEAN

The Ilara

The Embrace

Safe Path

GRASS CLAN

RIVER CLAN

FOREST CLAN

Safe Path

THE RIVERLANDS

The Clasp

THE GREAT WOODS

POA

Lake Ilara

The Floating Market

THE SCOUR

Safe Path

NEWT

Safe Path

BOG CLAN

DESERT CLAN

# FIREBORN

# PROLOGUE

*I pledge my life to the Hunting Lodge.*
*I vow to serve all seven clans as my own,*
*To protect them from what lies beyond.*
*I forsake all blood ties and blood feuds,*
*To offer up my name and my past.*
*The Hunters are my family now and always.*
*I swear before them that I will never lower my weapons*
*In the face of darkness,*
*Nor allow tyranny to rise.*

# CHAPTER
# ONE

The sky over the Hunting Lodge was ominously dark and the air smelled of snow. Twelve gazed up at the scudding clouds with storm-gray eyes and huddled deeper into her furs, stamping her feet to stay warm. Her classmates' chatter steamed in the air around her and Twelve watched them moodily, trying to swallow her impatience.

"For goodness' sake!" shouted Weaponsmaster Victory, her eyes sweeping the group. "If you can't even *lift* it, how on earth are you going to swing it? Anyone who can't raise their weapons over their head, return them to the armory for something lighter at *once!*"

Several students scurried away and Twelve's scowl deepened. Losing her temper in battle class never paid off though. Victory was more likely than any of the other Hunters to punish students with night watches or the dreaded dungeons. Plus, the lesson looked interesting if they could get to it: upright wooden stumps covered the snow-dusted training ground, promising something out of the ordinary.

"By the frost!" cried Victory as the students trickled back. "If you can't move faster than that, every creature from here to the Frozen Forest will make an easy meal of you."

A nervous silence fell over the assembled class.

"The brighter among you might have identified today's aim," Victory continued, her disbelief obvious as she spoke. "You'll be sparring in pairs while standing on the stumps to improve your balance and footwork. I don't want to see any feet on the ground."

Twelve almost smiled as anticipation fizzed through her. This would be a challenge.

"If you haven't mastered last week's exercises, then you're going to struggle," Victory said, her eyes lingering on a few of the younger students who were looking distinctly anxious. "Now, form up in pairs and begin yesterday's attack sequence. Remember: constant vigilance!"

As usual, everyone scrambled eagerly away from Twelve into their pairs. She rolled her eyes. If they were too frightened to spar with her, that was their problem, not hers.

Her gaze wandered over the familiar buildings around her instead. The kitchen, dining hall, stables, armory, and resthouse surrounded the octagonal training ground where she stood. All of them were sturdy structures that had withstood the elements for centuries, but all were dwarfed by the defensive walls soaring above them. Even the council house, by far the grandest building with its beautifully carved pillars, appeared little more than a toy beneath those walls. High above Twelve's head, the two skybridges arced gracefully between the ramparts, quartering the distant octagon of sky and allowing patrolling Hunters to see for miles.

"Twelve"—Victory frowned—"partnerless again?" There were a few snickers. The weaponsmaster scowled and stepped closer, lowering her voice. "Practicing alone will only take you so far. You need a decent sparring partner to challenge yourself." Her blue eyes scanned Twelve's face, piercing and expectant.

Twelve's reply was halted by a hand squeezing her arm.

"I'll p-p-practice with you," Seven offered, carefully avoiding the weaponsmaster's gaze.

Victory's sigh as she strode away said it all.

"Keeping the weirdos together," someone muttered. Twelve spun to confront them, her cheeks flaming, but the speaker was already lost in the shifting crowd.

The pale redheaded girl beside her beamed, and Twelve

5

groaned. Sparring with Seven was worse than practicing with a straw dummy. Her attention span was shorter than a snarrow's and her skills with any weapon doubtful at best. On top of that, although she was probably about thirteen years old, like Twelve, her build was that of a much younger girl. Twelve felt like a giant next to her. It made them particularly ill-suited and yet they were often thrown together. Everyone else avoided them: Seven was odd; Twelve was scary.

Most of the stumps were already taken, so the girls threaded their way across the training ground to a less crowded spot.

"W-w-where's Widge?" Seven asked as they walked. "I haven't seen him today."

Widge was Twelve's squirrel, but it had actually been the other girl who had found him as a kit fallen from his nest. Instead of keeping him, Seven had given him to Twelve, something Twelve still didn't understand.

"I'm not sure." Twelve shrugged. "You know he comes and goes as he likes." She bit her tongue to stop herself saying more.

Seven nodded as she clumsily unsheathed her sword. Twelve reached over her shoulders, grabbing the hafts of her two axes. Her confidence surged with them in her hands and she leaped lightly onto the nearest log.

"Shall we?" she asked.

Seven snorted with laughter as she hopped experimentally between stumps. "Wobbly, aren't they?"

"That's the point," Twelve said, unable to keep a snap out of her voice. "Can we start?"

Shouts of laughter, yelps of surprise, and the clash of steel rang out across the training ground, but Twelve had only to wave an axe at Seven and the other girl would drop her weapon or fall off the stumps. In the end, she practiced by herself while Seven sat and watched.

*Whirl, strike, duck, block, lunge, sidestep.* Twelve ran through her routine faster and faster until her axes were a glinting blur. Beneath her furs she was unbearably hot, but she didn't break her flow, enjoying the challenge of keeping her balance on the precarious stumps.

"L-look out!" Seven cried suddenly. This was quickly followed by a yelp and a crash.

Twelve spun around to see a tall dark-haired boy sprawled on the ground. His face was red and furious as he spat out a mouthful of grimy snow. It was Five—her least favorite person in the lodge, despite stiff competition.

"He was c-c-creeping up behind you," Seven said, her face pale and defiant.

Five stood up, towering over her. "It's battle class, you idiot," he said. "*Obviously*, we're supposed to fight." His eyes ran pointedly over her weak stance and incorrect sword grip. "Those of us who are any good at it anyway."

"What, like you?" Twelve snorted.

"We all know I'm the best swordsman here," Five said, shrugging. "I thought I could help you, Twelve. You know, test your reflexes. After all, the dark creatures out there won't announce themselves."

"You weren't trying to be helpful," Seven said, her voice higher than normal. "You wanted to h-h-hurt her. I saw your face."

"Really?" Five said, rolling his eyes. "And did you see inside my head too? You could tell exactly what I was thinking? Who knew we had such a *t-t-talent* among us."

Students nearby snorted with laughter and inched closer as Seven's face crumpled with hurt. Unexpectedly, a dull thud of anger pulsed through Twelve. She stepped off her stump, axes gripped tightly in both hands.

"Speaking of talents," Twelve said, trying to keep her voice even, "do you actually have any besides being awful?" Five's eyes narrowed, but she kept talking. "You're not the best swordsman and you're not nearly as funny as you—"

Five took half a step toward her as a stocky sandy-haired boy shouldered his way through the crowd. "I think you both need to calm down," Six said firmly, taking Five by the arm and pulling him away. He was Five's best friend, quieter and less obnoxious, but Twelve still shot him her fiercest glare.

8

"I'm *always* calm!" she said. It came out a lot louder than she'd intended.

Six grinned at her, his eyes bright with amusement. "So I see."

"What is going on over there?" Victory's voice rang sharp and hard as she strode toward the clustered students. "Get back to practice right now!"

The group couldn't have scattered faster if a winter wolf had pounced among them.

"Thank you," Seven said as Five and Six slipped away.

"What for?" Twelve asked.

"S-standing up for me like that."

Twelve's sharp response faltered—Seven's face was full of warmth, her smile dimpling her cheeks. For an instant, she looked so much like . . . Twelve quickly shook the thought away—it was always a bad idea to think about life before the lodge. Still, before she could stop herself, she felt her lips curve into an answering smile.

She turned away, shocked at herself, and hopped back onto her stump.

"You stood up for me first," she said over her shoulder to Seven. "Anyway, Five should be grateful. Hauling that huge ego of his around must be hard work. If I've managed to shrink it even a tiny bit . . ."

Before Seven could reply, Victory arrived, her

expression thunderous. "Why are you just standing there, Twelve?" she snapped. "Get on with it."

The weaponsmaster stood with her arms folded and her eyes narrowed as Twelve flowed through her routine flawlessly, until a pebble bounced painfully off her temple.

"Ow!" Twelve gasped, wobbling on her stump for the first time.

Victory tilted her head critically and rattled more pebbles in her palm. "You should have seen that coming and reacted. Constant vigilance, Twelve."

Twelve stared. Had the weaponsmaster really just thrown a *stone* at her?

"Five was right, you know," Victory said, her eyes locked on Twelve's. "Dark creatures don't announce themselves and they won't give you a second chance. Now go again." She jerked her head at Twelve's axes.

And threw another stone.

# CHAPTER
# TWO

Twelve felt the sting of a dozen more stones before she could deflect them reliably without losing her balance

"Good! Much better," Victory said, a smile grazing her mouth. She dropped the pebbles into Seven's palm and stalked away, loud criticisms of the next group already streaming from her lips.

Seven's mouth hung open as she gazed up at Twelve. "D-did she just smile at you?"

Overhead, the sky darkened as a wintry evening drew in. Hunters slipped around the dim base of the walls, their feet crunching over the frozen ground to light the torches, their shadows leaping strangely in the corner of Twelve's eyes. High up on the skybridges, braziers flared to life. The temperature dropped and a few tentative flakes of snow drifted down. Breath plumed before cold-flushed faces and fur hats were tugged down to cover freezing earlobes. Savory smells began wafting across the training ground, telling the students that dinner was imminent. The energy of the group dropped noticeably.

"That's enough," Victory called, gathering the class around her. "I can't say many of you have impressed me, so we'll repeat this every day until you do. Return your weapons to the armory and be ready for dinner in half an hour. Remember: constant vigilance." She stared at each student as though she could glower them into greater alertness. She saved her most powerful glare for Seven. "Seven, I want to talk to you."

Glancing over her shoulder as she walked to the armory, Twelve guessed Victory was giving Seven an earful for not taking part. The girl looked upset. For a moment, Twelve considered waiting for her, then shook her head, guiltily pushing away the image of Seven's hunched shoulders, her despondent expression.

The armory was a long, low building and Twelve's favorite place. There was something comforting about the smell of steel, polished wood, and the boiled leather armor they wore in training. Row after row of gleaming spears, swords, and axes stretched away into the gloom, while farther back were more unusual weapons: morning stars, flails, and war hammers.

She took one of the flaming torches off the wall inside the door and made her way past familiar rows of longbows to where her axes were kept, squeezing past her laughing classmates. As she passed a tall rack of arrows, she heard Five's voice on the other side.

"It just makes me sick. She's disruptive and awful every day! If it was up to me, she'd be banished like *that*." He snapped his fingers.

"Well, it's not up to you," Six pointed out. "And you know the Hunters won't do that. Where would she go? Where would any of us go?" There was a heaviness in his tone that made Twelve flinch. "Besides, you started it today and I think you got off pretty lightly."

"Ugh, you're too reasonable," Five groaned. "But does it really not bother you? We've given up our families, our homes, even our names to be here. And in return we have to put up with *her*, the worst girl in all of Ember. Even if she still has a family, they *clearly* wouldn't want her. She's terrible, a total cave-creeper."

"Five!" Six gasped.

The case beside them creaked as Twelve pushed it as hard as she could, her face set, a muscle in her jaw twitching furiously. She would make Five pay for that. The case rocked, squealing as it tipped past the point of no return to crash against a rack of spears.

Five and Six flung themselves to one side just in time. A deadly rain of arrows and heavy shelves missed them by a hand's breadth. Shouts of warning and surprise rang along the rows as each rack toppled into the one beside it. Weapons clanged, wood splintered, and students shrieked.

Twelve's gulp was audible in the shocked silence after the last stack fell. Stretching away from her was a long line of total devastation.

"By the frost, Twelve!" Six hissed, picking himself up. "What is wrong with you?"

"*Twelve* did that?" Five's face appeared next to Six's, his features gleeful in the flickering torchlight. "Ha! You are in *so* much trouble!"

The triumph on his face was more than she could bear. She stepped forward, ready to leap on him across the broken shelves.

"WHAT IS GOING ON HERE?" Victory's roar was a freezing wind, silencing all. Then, in a babble of voices, everyone spoke at once. A moment later, the weapons-master stood before Twelve, vibrating with wordless fury.

Twelve straightened her spine and jutted her chin defiantly.

"I'm not even going to ask," Victory growled, her eyes sweeping over the damage. A blood vessel pulsed unnervingly at her temple. She took a ragged breath and gripped

Twelve's upper arm so tightly it hurt. "Straight to the Elders with you. Again."

"Five called her a cave-creeper," Six said, his face set and resolutely turned away from Five. "That's why she did it."

A scandalized murmuring swept through the press of students and Victory made a sound of disgust. "Five, is this true?"

Five shuffled forward, shooting Six a hurt look before half shrugging, half nodding apologetically. "Yes, but, you know, only—"

"Silence! I don't care why either of you did what you did. Follow me and keep your mouths shut!"

Victory released Twelve's arm and strode away, forcing Twelve and Five to maintain an undignified trot behind her.

Outside the armory, snow fell more heavily and the windows glowed orange, giving the buildings an improbably welcoming appearance.

Something landed lightly on Twelve's shoulder as she passed through the squat doorway and her spirits lifted as Widge, her squirrel, nestled softly at her cheek. His chestnut fur gleamed like copper in the low light, his eyes bright and his tail bushy.

"Hello, you," she whispered. "Where've you been?" He licked her ear by way of greeting and chirped happily when she offered him a handful of nuts from her pocket.

After shoveling them into his cheeks until they bulged, he burrowed down her collar into her furs and immediately began snoring.

"Keep up!" snapped Victory irritably. The new snow squeaked beneath her boots as she hurried across the training ground to the council house, shooting angry glances at the kitchen. Twelve's stomach rumbled and, with a sinking heart, she realized that, unlike Widge, she probably wasn't getting any dinner. Sighing, she returned her axes to the slings on her back and trudged after Victory.

"I don't know what in Ember you're sighing about," Five whispered furiously. "This is *obviously* your fault." Turning, he raised his voice. "And I don't know what *you're* staring at either!"

Seven ducked her head as they hurried past, almost falling off her stump. Victory had clearly told her to keep practicing through dinner. With a rueful groan, Twelve saw the other girl was making about a thousand wobbly mistakes all at once. Even worse, she was imitating Twelve's double-axe routine, ignoring the fact that her weapon was a sword.

*Stand up straighter,* Twelve silently urged her, wincing as Seven tumbled to the iron-hard ground yet again. She opened her mouth to call out encouragement, then shut it abruptly. She wasn't here to make friends—it would only complicate things. Several deep breaths calmed her as she climbed the council house steps behind Victory.

The magnificent double-height doors were ornately carved with battle scenes from legendary hunts. Beyond them lay the Great Hall, the grandest space in the Hunting Lodge.

Its wood-paneled walls were mounted with antique weapons, and the heads of hunted creatures loomed over the fireplaces. Winter wolves, ogres, and other strange beasts glowered down at her, their glass eyes glinting. Twelve blinked as her own eyes adjusted, then she shivered. It was an imposing space, designed to impress their rare visitors with the Hunters' prowess.

Unlike the rest of the Hunting Lodge, the council house was lit with moonstones rather than torches. Set into the ceiling, the tiny stones glowed at night, casting their mysterious silvery light over everything. Before arriving at the lodge, Twelve had barely believed they existed. Moonstones were like witches, often discussed but never seen. The people who mined them rarely sold them. Her stomach flipped at the sudden reminder of the cave clan. It sickened her that they had access to such wonder. She pushed the thought down quickly before unwelcome memories began to surface.

Victory stamped the snow off her boots and led them up a flight of stairs. Soft, deep-piled rugs sent by grateful desert caravans muffled their footsteps. More moonstones gleamed down on a long hall off which each of the three Elders had a room. Twelve's heart sank as Victory marched them to the farthest door. She was taking them to Elder Silver. To distract herself, Twelve examined the gifts from various clans, each hung carefully on the walls: frogskin-bound stilts from the bog folk; an enormous, intricate village-rudder from the river clan; a fur-soft bark cloak from the forest people; and brightly feathered gliding wings from the mountain clan.

Twelve's eyes drank them in even when they stopped outside Silver's room. Inside her furs, Widge awoke. He poked his head out of her collar to take in their surroundings and squeaked disconsolately. Twelve could only sigh in agreement as Victory knocked and the door flew open.

# CHAPTER
# THREE

"Victory?" Elder Silver was an imposing figure, tall and lean. Every movement held a fluid grace that belied her age. Her hair stuck up in downy white tufts that barely softened the features beneath. Her nose was sharp and slightly beaky, her lips thin, and her eyes unnervingly pale, the blue of a frozen lake. Those eyes ran over the group before her and settled on Twelve. "Oh dear."

The disappointment in the older woman's voice was obvious. Twelve bit her lip and pushed away a wave of shame. Widge tucked himself back into her furs, safely out of sight.

"Yes," Victory said, her irritation obvious. "Problems with these two again. Can I come in?"

Silver nodded and stepped aside.

"Wait out here," Victory growled over her shoulder before closing the door.

Five leaned against the wall on one side of the door and Twelve on the other. Both elaborately ignored one another while straining to hear the murmur of voices inside.

"Come!" Silver called eventually. Five shouldered in front of Twelve and she resisted the urge to shove him as hard as she could.

The study was large and sparse, the stone walls almost bare. An arched trio of windows looked down onto the training ground while a fire burned merrily in the hearth. Over the mantelpiece was the mounted head of an enormous Ygrex, its cruel horns and needle-thin fangs gleaming. Two leather armchairs were turned toward the flames, but Silver sat in the uncomfortable, upright chair behind her enormous desk. Twelve knew the Elder well enough to recognize this was a bad sign.

"Quite a story Victory brings me," Silver said shortly, her fingers steepled as Five and Twelve moved to stand opposite her. "You're very lucky no one was hurt, but Victory tells me there's significant damage in the armory."

"Hours of repairs." Victory scowled.

"That was Twelve," Five said quickly. "Honestly, I didn't do anything."

Twelve resisted the urge to laugh. There was nothing Silver hated more than people trying to shift responsibility away from themselves. Five never seemed to learn that.

Silver turned a wintry gaze on him and his defiant pose wilted. "You didn't do anything?" she asked, her voice dangerously quiet. "Victory tells me you openly insulted the cave clan."

Five gulped, his face the color of milk. "Yes," he croaked, "but there were, um . . . reasons."

"Which were?" She sat perfectly still, staring at Five.

"Twelve . . . uh . . . she . . ."

Twelve allowed the corner of her mouth to twitch. She was enjoying this more than she'd expected.

"Look at her!" Five cried, color flooding back into his face. "She's smirking! She sneers at everything, *obviously* thinks she's better than everyone else! She's intolerable and—"

"Silence." Silver didn't raise her voice, but the hairs stood up on the back of Twelve's neck nonetheless. Five made a gagging sound, half choked by his own words.

"So, just to be clear, Twelve's *personality* made you say it?" If Silver's voice had been any colder, the air around them would have frozen.

Five licked his lips and made a noise like a mouse pinned down by a cat.

"Speak the Pledge," Silver commanded, her fingertips white where they pressed together.

Five blinked in surprise and quickly covered it with a

cough. The Pledge was given every morning at breakfast and every evening at dinner, but it was unusual to hear it outside those times. He spoke rapidly, the words automatic after years of repetition.

*"I pledge my life to the Hunting Lodge.*
*I vow to serve all seven clans as my own,*
*To protect them from what lies beyond.*
*I forsake all blood ties and blood feuds,*
*To offer up my name and my past.*
*The Hunters are my family now and always.*
*I swear before them that I will never lower my weapons*
*In the face of darkness,*
*Nor allow tyranny to rise."*

In the silence that dripped off his last syllable, a log in the fire shifted and sparks whirled up the chimney. Twelve suppressed a shudder.

"To forsake all blood ties and blood feuds," Silver said meditatively. "What does that mean to you, Five?"

"To forget which clan we came from and to accept them all as equal," he said, his voice shaking slightly.

"Exactly," Silver said, her tone clipped and precise. "It's the lodge's most important and most difficult rule: never to mention your past lives, never to speak of the clans and families you once held dear. It's the ultimate sacrifice, but one vital to the trust between lodge and clans. You would jeopardize all of that just to throw an insult at a student you don't like?"

Five opened his mouth to speak, but Silver cut him off, her voice shaking with suppressed emotion.

"If word of these incidents spread across Ember, do you think the clans would still invite us to their villages to hunt the dark creatures that plague them? Would they think of us as impartial? Trust us to arbitrate their disputes with neutrality? How long do you think it would be before war broke out again?" Silver shook her head in disgust. "You speak the words of the Pledge without thinking, without considering what they mean. I suggest you remedy that immediately." She took a deep breath. "I'd like a minute to talk to Twelve alone. You can wait outside until I decide your punishment."

Five gulped and hurried out, his face waxen.

"That boy," Victory sighed. "He thinks the world owes him something."

"Reminds me of someone else I know," Silver said, the corner of her mouth quirking up.

Victory looked affronted. "Me? I was nothing like him." She paused, her brow furrowed. "*Was* I?"

Silver shrugged good-naturedly and glanced at Twelve. The humor faded from her face.

"You could have killed someone, Twelve," she said.

Twelve nodded, knowing it was true, unable to meet Silver's or Victory's eyes.

Eventually, the Elder sighed and rubbed a hand over her face. "What are we going to do with her, Victory?"

The weaponsmaster shifted. "If anyone knows the best path, it's you, Silver. By the frost, you've mentored enough difficult youngsters, and I include myself in that."

"Hmm, well. You're my greatest success story." The two women shared a smile, the warmth between them palpable. "This one though . . ." Silver broke off and shook her head.

"Oh, Twelve," she groaned. "What am I supposed to do with you? Punishments that deter other students don't faze you at all and I still receive at least one complaint a day about your behavior toward the Hunters or other students."

Twelve winced, desperately tried to convince herself that Silver's opinion of her didn't matter. "Yes, Elder Silver," she said, her voice shakier than she'd intended.

"I understand . . ." Silver began hesitantly, "why you'd be wary of forming relationships here, especially given . . . well . . . we both know the circumstances that brought you to the lodge . . ."

Twelve stiffened in horror. Silver had promised her, *promised* her when she'd arrived that they would never speak of that again.

"You're not alone though, Twelve," Silver continued. "You're certainly not the only student here to have lost their family."

Twelve's jaw clenched. Her family weren't "lost"—they were dead, murdered by the cave clan in the coldest of cold blood.

Silver must have seen the look on her face. She stopped talking and sighed, glancing at Victory for support.

"You're one of the best students in battle class," the weaponsmaster said, taking Twelve by surprise. "Probably *the* best. But you're also the least likely to pass a Blooding."

Twelve stiffened despite herself. "Why? You just said I was one of the best!"

"She knows what she said," Silver said quietly. "Why do you think, Twelve? What do you know of the Blooding?"

Twelve wished again that Victory had taken her to another of the Elders. Elder Hoarfrost would have roared at her, then given her a night watch on the skybridges and forgotten her immediately. Elder Argyll would probably have just made her write lines. Why did Silver have to care so much? Guilt gnawed at her.

"Um"—Twelve paused, collecting her thoughts—"I know that when they're deemed ready, a team of students goes out together to the Frozen Forest, similar to how a team of Hunters might be called to a real hunt in a village. They're given a task to complete there and, when they

25

return, it's decided whether the students can become Hunters and choose new names."

*If* they return.

Twelve glanced up at the Ygrex head glowering above her and swallowed hard. It leered back at her sightlessly. Ygrex were notoriously difficult to defeat. They got inside your head, twisted your own memories to ensnare you. The story went that Silver had battled this creature in the Frozen Forest during her Blooding at the tender age of fifteen. It was a feat previously unheard of in one so young and the foundation of her fearsome reputation.

"And you don't think you'd struggle with that?" Silver asked, her expressive eyebrows shooting up into her hairline. "There's no part of the task that concerns you?"

"If I have my axes, then I can do anything," Twelve said stubbornly, glad of their reassuring weight on her back. Neither of the Hunters needed to know she had no intention of ever taking her place in a Blooding.

"Do you think I managed to defeat an Ygrex by myself?" Silver asked, jerking her chin at the mounted head. Twelve hesitated. According to the stories, that was *exactly* what she'd done. Silver sighed and shook her head.

"Stories have a tendency to take on a life of their own," she said eventually. "I wouldn't be here without the team I had with me that day. That's the truth. And that's why I worry for you, Twelve. Who will be on *your* team?"

Twelve groaned inwardly as Silver came to the point.

"Fighting is only one of the skills a Hunter must possess," the Elder said carefully "It's necessary against dark creatures of course, but our role in the world is shifting. We spend more time peacekeeping between the clans now than we do hunting. For that you need *teamwork*, patience, diplomacy, an open mind. You have none of these qualities and seem determined to remain that way. Last time you were in here, as I recall," Silver went on, "you promised me you'd make more of an effort with your fellow students. Have you done that?"

Seven's face flashed into Twelve's mind and she quickly pushed it away, examining the floorboards instead.

Beside her, Victory sighed. "No, she hasn't. She's always as good as partnerless in my classes." Her voice rose in frustration. "She should be pushing herself with the toughest opponents out there. She has more skill than even I did at her age."

Shame flooded Twelve, thick and sour. She'd let them both down.

Silver nodded and made a calming gesture at Victory. Raising her voice, she called, "Five, come back in here, please!"

The door opened and Five edged in to take his place beside Twelve.

When Silver next spoke, she sounded determined,

angry. "You've both behaved despicably this evening and your attitudes worry me, to say the least. I think a period of quiet reflection would do you both a world of good." She paused and glared at them. "I'm sending the pair of you to the dungeons for the night." Five's head jerked in horror and Twelve's breath caught in her chest. Beneath her furs, Widge shivered. "You'll have plenty of time to think down there," Silver went on remorselessly, "and I'll expect an *immediate* improvement in your behavior as a result."

Silver nodded, as though convincing herself, and rose to her feet, gesturing toward the door. Too shocked even to jostle one another, Twelve and Five followed.

## CHAPTER
# FOUR

The dungeon entrance lay next to the armory. When Silver creaked the door open, a sucking blackness seemed to slide out, snatching at them with silent fingers. Twelve flinched and Widge, now on her shoulder, squeaked his concern. Behind her, Five's breath caught and Twelve tried to take satisfaction in knowing he felt the same dread as her.

She gazed back to where Seven was still practicing in the training ground. The other girl's eyes met hers, filled with sympathy as she raised her sword in silent solidarity. Twelve nodded once, the weight in her chest lifting slightly. When she turned back to the dungeon, the darkness seemed a little less dark.

Silver's solitary torch threw shadows over the group as

they descended a steeply spiraling staircase to a grim warren of passages below. The Elder led them into a narrow tunnel, past cell after cell hacked out of the earth, their footsteps muffled by the packed dirt. A clammy coolness coiled down Twelve's neck in spite of Widge's warmth, and the smell of damp soil filled her nostrils. Somewhere nearby, water dripped.

"Five can go in here," Silver said to Victory, the torch catching her face in profile. "I'll take Twelve a little farther on."

Behind her, Twelve heard a door clanging shut and a key turning. Grinding her teeth, she threw back her shoulders and took a deep breath. Just because she felt scared didn't mean she had to show it. A few cells farther on, Silver stopped and opened a hefty wooden door with bars at eye level.

"In you go," she said heavily.

Twelve's gaze swept the space as she stepped in. A pile of moldy straw lay under a great canopy of cobwebs large enough to have been made by a deathspinner. In the corner, a bucket stank outrageously. Twelve clenched trembling fingers into fists and turned back to Silver. Shadows danced across the Elder's face and her eyes were pools of regret in the torchlight.

"It's only for one day, Twelve." She spoke softly and her hand found Twelve's shoulder in the gloom. "Use the time wisely. Please. Think about whether you have a future at the lodge. Think about the person you want to be."

She stepped back and locked the door. On the wall opposite the cell was a small alcove. Silver placed the key in it and lit a waiting candle.

"I'll send someone down with your dream milk," she said over her shoulder as she walked away. "I don't want you to suffer any more than necessary."

Slowly, Twelve's fingers unclenched and she stepped forward soundlessly. She pressed her face against the cold metal bars to keep Silver and Victory in view for as long as possible. When they vanished, the silence pressed around her. She couldn't stop herself imagining the huge weight of earth above, waiting to crush her. Panic fluttered in her chest like a moth. Widge sensed it, squeezing himself against her neck and licking her cheek until her thoughts calmed and her breathing became regular again.

She raised a hand to scratch his cheek the way he liked. "Sorry," she whispered. "This is my fault. You deserve better." Widge chirped his agreement, but carried on licking her cheek.

Furious with herself, Twelve closed her eyes and let the warm orange candlelight bleed through her eyelids. If she stayed like this, she could almost imagine she was somewhere else.

"You *obviously* don't." Five's voice broke rudely into her

thoughts. Twelve opened her eyes, the horror of the dungeon crowding in on her again. She didn't speak until she was sure her voice wouldn't let her down.

"I don't what?" she said loudly, pleased by the icy chill in her tone.

"Have a future at the lodge of course," Five called. "If anyone in this place doesn't have the temperament for it, it's you. You'd be terrible at settling disputes among the clans. It's laughable, totally ridiculous."

Privately, Twelve agreed with him: the lodge was a means to an end. That was all.

"You're right," Twelve said. She allowed herself a moment of pleasure at the shocked silence that followed.

"Uh . . . I am? I mean, yes, I am!" Five corrected himself quickly. "Clearly."

"My only consolation is that you'll be worse," Twelve went on, starting to enjoy herself, despite the coiling darkness. "I just can't see the clans putting up with your whining. They'll be hiring a banemage to do away with you before a week is out. I'd last at least a fortnight longer than you."

"Whining?" Five sounded apoplectic. "My *complaints* are solely about you and are all totally valid."

"Try telling that to the banemage," Twelve shrugged.

There was a thud as though Five had kicked his door. Then, mocking: "I heard Silver mention dream milk."

Twelve remained silent, her grin fading. Widge bristled.

"Does someone have nasty dreams? Poor Twelve, trying to be so tough when really she's such a delicate flower."

His laughter was high and forced. Twelve gritted her teeth, backing away from the door until she felt straw under her feet. She sat down slowly, leaning against the back wall and keeping her eyes on the glow behind the bars. Widge flowed down into her lap so she could stroke him, the repetitive motion soothing for them both.

Her thoughts turned to Silver; she wanted to feel anger toward the Elder, but instead she only felt ashamed that she'd let her down . . . again. The same went for Seven—she should have waited for her after battle class. Seven would have done at least that much for her. If Twelve had waited, she wouldn't have heard what Five said, and she wouldn't be in this mess. She hunched her shoulders miserably and tried to turn her thoughts onto safer tracks.

It felt like hours later when she was startled out of her reverie by the sound of someone approaching.

"Hello?" Five's whisper in the dark was painfully hopeful.

Footsteps pattered to the bottom of the staircase and along the passage, past Five and on to Twelve's cell. Briefly, a small, hooded figure was silhouetted against the bars and a glass of pale dream milk was set between them. Next to it, the visitor carefully placed a small package before once again slipping away.

Widge sprang from Twelve's lap toward the door, nose twitching hopefully.

"Thanks!" she called, scrambling eagerly to her feet. Usually, she didn't welcome conversation, but tonight might have been the exception. The figure hurried away though, footsteps vanishing back into the darkness.

She grabbed the glass of dream milk eagerly, hoping it would quell her roaring hunger. In her haste, she knocked the package beside it. It fell out of reach with a heavy thud and Twelve groaned, belatedly realizing it might be food.

Cursing her clumsiness, Twelve carried the dream milk carefully to the back of her cell and sat down again, Widge following closely. She pushed him away gently.

"You've still got nuts to eat," she said, prodding his stuffed cheeks. "And you don't need this stuff anyway." He stared at her, first surprised, then delighted. A moment later, there was a nut in his paws and he was nibbling happily.

She wanted to savor the milk, but ended up gulping it. Its soothing herbal taste was a balm to her hunger and fear. Immediately, she felt calmer, the darkness seemed to recede, and her breath came more easily. A pleasant warmth spread through her frozen limbs and her eyelids drooped. Widge climbed onto her chest and Twelve gave in to sleep willingly.

When she snapped awake sometime later, her heart was racing and she didn't know why. She lay on the gritty straw, blinking and disoriented, wondering if she'd somehow had a nightmare after all. Perched on her stomach, Widge's tail was stiff and upright like a brush, his every muscle taut as he peered into the blackness at the back of their cell.

Then Twelve heard it: the wall was whispering.

She sat up slowly and pushed herself away, hardly trusting her own senses. Were there wraiths down here or something? A few seconds later, she heard it again: a muted mutter, then scuffling and a grunt. It was definitely coming from inside the walls. A clod of earth fell from above, tearing through the gauzy spiderwebs and landing near Twelve's feet.

Her brows snapped together in confusion. Whatever this was, it couldn't be a wraith, not according to her much-thumbed copy of *A Magical Bestiary*. She'd read the whole thing so many times she practically knew it by heart.

WRAITHS *are the lost spirits of those who die violently. Recognition is easy: the shape they had when living will remain, albeit in a gossamer form. As a spirit creature, they can never touch nor alter an inanimate object, but they can interact with creatures containing spirits of their own. Possession of animals and occasionally even people allows wraiths to cause significant damage.*

*A wraith cannot be killed as it is already dead. The only way to release it from this world permanently is to find its bodily remains and burn them.*

*Aggression: 5/10.*

*Danger posed: 5/10.*

*Difficulty to disable: 7/10.*

Twelve stared at the fallen earth. A wraith couldn't do that, and they didn't make scuffling sounds either.

Gulping, she and Widge crept farther away until they were pressed against the locked door. Fear flared in Twelve's gut and she fumbled for her axes. The grunting, scuffling noise sounded again, and more soil fell from above. Terror surged through her so strongly she felt nauseous. She was trapped in the dark. Axes wouldn't save them if the roof came down; they'd be buried alive. A band of panic tightened around Twelve's chest and she struggled to breathe, hugging Widge with one hand and clutching her axes in the other.

The whispering returned, muffled and indistinct as the ground shuddered again. The air grew colder and goose bumps broke out all over her. Something was very wrong. She could feel it with every fiber of her being. There was something dark down here with her.

# CHAPTER
# FIVE

Twelve didn't know which to fear more: whatever creature was down here, or the crumbling ceiling that might crush her at any moment.

"Uh . . . Twelve, are you awake?" Five's whisper was low and urgent, making her jump.

"Of course," she whispered back. She'd forgotten he was there.

"We need to get out of here!" His voice teetered on the brink of panic. "Can Widge fetch your door key for you?"

Twelve blinked at the suggestion. She'd never trained Widge, but he came with her everywhere and she always thought he understood most of what was going on. She hated that the idea had come from Five, but it was worth a try.

"Maybe," she whispered back.

She climbed to her feet, feeling the ground juddering through the soles of her boots, and turned toward the candle in the alcove, burning low but still alight. She saw immediately that the squirrel was small enough to fit through the bars of the cell.

"The key, Widge," she whispered, pointing. "Can you get it?"

She gave him a little push and he sprang lightly between the bars, vanishing to the ground. A moment later, he reappeared triumphantly with the package she'd accidentally knocked away gripped in his teeth.

Forcing her voice to stay calm, Twelve took it from him—heavier than she expected—and dropped it into her pocket.

"The key," she whispered as more earth fell. "Hurry!" Once more, he bounded out of the cell and this time, in the glow from the candle, she saw him scrambling up the opposite wall until he was in the alcove, his eyes bright and determined. He circled the candle warily, the flame flickering as he moved, and picked up the key.

Twelve swallowed a howl of pride and delight as he deposited it in her palm. She hugged him as hard as he would allow and kissed the top of his head.

"Genius squirrel," she whispered as he chirped happily. And then to Five, "I have it!"

Before he could reply, an explosion rocked the passage. A gust of foul, stinking air rushed past. Her candle guttered, nearly going out. The temperature dropped dramatically, and an ominous crack sounded above her.

With her heart in her mouth and the key in her hand, Twelve fumbled with the lock until it clicked open. She had barely taken a step when something made her freeze: an otherworldly green glow bled into the dank corridor between her and the spiral staircase. And, where there had been a muted whispering, now there was clear speech.

"Excellent work," said a low, rasping voice.

A small figure stepped into the pool of strange light, looking over its shoulder so it didn't see her, a ball of green fire in its hand. The glare blinded Twelve and she stumbled back, her thoughts spinning wildly. The lodge's walls had never been breached in their thousand years of history, but somehow, impossibly, a goblin stood only a few feet from her.

A *goblin*.

In the *lodge*.

And, based on the gleaming sword she'd glimpsed in his other hand, she had a strong suspicion they were under attack.

# CHAPTER
# SIX

Twelve gripped her axes so tightly the grain of the wood was imprinted on her palms. She couldn't believe what she'd seen. Goblins avoided Hunters and had done so even before the Dark War.

She bit her lip and risked another glance around the door frame. There were now two of them visible, both shorter than her but powerfully built, their features too large for their faces. Gleaming armor caught the ghoulish green light and their weapons glinted—it was like seeing the pages of her books come to life.

One of them spoke. "You have the plans, Ferrick?"

"I have memorized them, my lord Morgren. I will find her," Ferrick said, his voice breathy, excited.

"Excellent."

"There are prisoners down here," Ferrick said. "Shall I kill them?"

Twelve stifled a gasp. On her shoulder, Widge could have been made from rock.

"No, leave them. Soon there will be no one to bring them food or water. Dehydration is a slower, crueler death than even you could deal." Morgren's laugh turned Twelve's stomach. "Come, Ferrick, we have matters to attend to."

"Yes, my lord."

There was another roar. The stench that accompanied it almost made Twelve retch. On her shoulder, Widge chittered fearfully, his nose wrinkled in disgust. She shrank back into her cell and shuddered in horror; there was an ogre out there with the goblins—she was sure of it. Only an ogre could smell so terrible. A rattling snarl made the hair at the nape of her neck stand up—*that* was the sound of a winter wolf.

Twelve crouched down, pressing her back against the cell wall and closed her eyes, listening as a procession of creatures forced their way through the narrow passage to the staircase. The green glow dwindled as the goblins climbed up.

The fear-freeze that had settled over Twelve lifted slowly. She stood shakily, clutching a trembling Widge to her. She'd always thought she'd look forward to her first real battle; the truth was a brutal shock.

*Think about the person you want to be.*

Silver wouldn't cower in a cell like this, Twelve was sure. Victory certainly wouldn't. Making up her mind, she darted out of her cell and grabbed the candle before hurrying along to Five. Whole chunks of the ceiling had come down outside his cell. Twelve tried to be quiet, but her breath sounded foghorn-loud in her ears as she scrambled over the rubble. Miraculously, his candle was still burning and the key was still in the alcove. When she turned back with it in her hand, his pale face loomed, eyes staring.

"Wh-what in Ember happened?" he whispered, dazed.

"The lodge is under attack," Twelve whispered back, handing him his candle from the alcove. "We have to get up to the training ground and warn everyone."

"You're letting me out?" he asked. His usual arrogance was gone and he sounded much younger.

"Of course," Twelve muttered, shoving the key into the lock. "Are you . . . are you all right?"

He didn't look good when the door swung open. She'd expected him to shove past her and take off, but he stood frozen to the spot. A trickle of blood gleamed darkly on his forehead and soil smeared his clothes. The cell behind him was devastated—he was lucky to be alive.

She grabbed Five's arm and tugged him forward, but he pulled back with a jerk, his familiar supercilious expression returning.

"Warn everyone? That's what the night watch is for!" As if on cue, the deep, dolorous boom of the alarm bell sounded. It shivered through the earth walls straight into Twelve's heart.

It had begun.

Five shrank from the sound. Twelve was unpleasantly reminded of herself only moments before. But, if the lodge was under attack, then she was determined to do her bit in defending it.

"Fine," she snapped, adrenaline making her hands shake. "You stay here. I'm going to help."

Without waiting for his response, she scrambled over the clods of earth and jogged to the stairs, cursing as her candle flame flickered, nearly going out. Widge's claws dug through her furs as sounds of fighting crashed down from above, hurrying her feet. Growls and howls, screamed orders, the clash of metal and the shrieks of the injured all mingled into a terrifying cacophony of battle sound.

At the top of the spiral staircase, the dungeon door had been smashed off its hinges. The scene beyond it froze Twelve to the spot. In the pale light of dawn, a nightmare of violence and destruction spread before her.

The candle slipped from her fingers and Widge chittered his shock.

Four fully grown ogres roared in the center of the training ground, spittle flying from their mouths. Twenty feet tall and armed with morning stars, they swung furiously at the Hunters swarming around their legs. Spears and arrows rained down from the night watch on the skybridges, but they had little effect on the ogres' tough hides.

Twelve hovered in the broken doorway, axes in hand, gathering her courage. "Better get off, Widge," she whispered. "This fight is for real—no place for a squirrel."

Widge gave her a disparaging look while baring his teeth. She couldn't help but snort a nervous laugh. "I'm not sure your teeth will be much good against an ogre, but it's up to you. Better get on my back instead though."

The squirrel obliged.

Twelve took a deep breath and sprinted out into the chaos.

# CHAPTER
# SEVEN

Twelve didn't think, didn't hesitate—just ran straight for the nearest ogre.

She had barely taken three steps before something huge slammed into her—a wall of fur and teeth and meat-stink. She hit the ground hard, and rolled, teeth snapping an inch from her face. The winter wolf's momentum carried it straight over her and Widge. It scrabbled to turn back, blue eyes gleaming, tongue lolling manically.

Cursing, Twelve sprang back to her feet, ignoring the pain blossoming down her side. Her axe hafts were slick in her grip, but if there was one thing she'd learned from *A Magical Bestiary* it was that you never fled from a winter wolf. They were *always* faster. She faced it as it circled her, watching every ripple of muscle, every flicker of its eyes, trying to read when it would pounce. Her life depended on it.

*Now.*

The wolf sprang and Twelve threw herself aside, her axes ready. From nowhere, a Hunter dived in front of her, two sword blades carving a deadly curve across the wolf's throat. An arc of shining blood spattered over the training ground and up the wall. Twelve's heart leaped as Silver spun to face her, eyes wild.

"Twelve," Silver cried, shouting over the cacophony. "You're alive! When I saw they came through the dungeons, I . . ." Her grip on Twelve's arm was very tight. One of the buckles on her armor hung loose and blood smeared her face, but her relief was unmistakable. "You can't be here—you're not trained. Get to the resthouse. I'd never forgive myself if something happened to you."

"Silver!" Victory screamed her name, gesturing across the training ground to where a circle of Hunters was backing another creature against the wall. She was needed. One of the ogres roared again and the ground shook.

Silver glanced from Victory to Twelve, torn.

"Don't worry about me," Twelve said quickly. "I can look after myself."

"To the resthouse, Twelve," Silver said, her grip tightening further. "Don't let me down. Stay in the wall's shadow. Low and fast. Don't attract any attention." There was an urgency to the woman's voice that Twelve couldn't ignore and beneath that something else—fear. Silver was afraid for her. Twelve nodded silently, her heart pounding. The Hunter stared into her face, then was gone, her lithe form racing straight between an infuriated ogre's legs to rejoin her team.

Battle frenzy tainted the air. Twelve stepped back into the darkness at the base of the walls, her breath shuddering. Widge gave a high-pitched squeal of alarm: the splash of wolf blood was right next to them. Her stomach lurched at the sight of it. Then, slowly, the blood seeped into the rock—and vanished.

In the very same spot, the rough stone . . . there was no other way to say it . . . *rippled*. Like the surface of a puddle disrupted by a pebble.

Twelve gulped and backed away, glancing at the carnage over her shoulder. Was this part of the attack? The wall bulged outward, distorting crazily. She flung herself to the ground just in time. With the low rasp of stone on stone, something animal-like ripped free of the rock, bounded over Twelve and into the battle.

On her back, Widge squealed in surprise. Twelve rolled to look behind her and felt her jaw drop. The thing that had jumped over her was a huge stone dog, easily the size of a horse. It sank its teeth into a winter wolf and shook viciously, tossing it away as if it was no bigger than a rabbit.

The Hunters who saw it raised a hearty cheer as it dispatched the other wolves and turned its attention to the nearest ogre. Twelve stared, dumbfounded. Could it be? She'd always assumed it was just a story to entertain the younger students. But here it was: the lodge's Guardian.

Her heart lifting, Twelve ran along the base of the wall toward the resthouse. She would have entered it but for an earth-shattering roar behind her. One of the ogres clawed at its face, an arrow deeply embedded in its cheek. It stumbled, dropping to one knee. The hair on its back almost reached the ground, shaggy enough to climb. Twelve was sprinting toward it before a conscious thought formed. On her shoulder, Widge trilled his outrage.

Silver's face flickered in front of her as she ran. The Elder would be proud if she helped defend the other Hunters, wouldn't she? Wasn't that what the lodge was all about?

Twelve flung herself at the ogre's back just before it hauled itself up. She clung on grimly as the ground lurched away, then began to climb, keeping her focus on her hands and feet, grateful the ogre was too irritated by the Hunters to notice her. Widge knew better than to distract her, but disapproval radiated off him in waves. She breathed through her mouth, but still the smell made her gag.

At the ogre's shoulder, wiry hairs the width of a finger sprouted. She grabbed two and hauled herself up.

Immediately, the creature craned its head around to look at her. Its face loomed unpleasantly close, dull brown eyes goggling at her, teeth as gray and forbidding as tombstones. It opened its mouth and roared. Twelve thought her head might explode as the blast of sound rattled her bones. Strings of saliva sprayed over her. Widge darted into her furs to escape them.

The ogre grabbed at her with an enormous hand and Twelve ducked, hacking furiously at its fingers with her axe. It roared again and made another grab for her, but a spine-chilling shriek from the training ground below distracted it. For a moment, everyone froze and an uncanny silence fell.

On the far side of the arena, a ring of Hunters had backed a very different creature against the wall.

"No. Way." Twelve gasped, shocked to her core as a new terror flickered into view. Widge's head immediately popped up, eyes bright with curiosity.

In the morning light, it was almost translucent. But in the shadows it was clearer—very tall, skeletally thin, almost colorless. Its "face" was a smooth, featureless oval. Immensely long dark hair writhed like snakes behind it. In each palm, a mouth, black and hungry, gaped in a silent scream. There was no doubt in Twelve's mind that it was a Grim.

That changed everything. They hadn't even covered

Grims in creature classes; they were so rare and dangerous it wasn't thought a huntling would ever come across them. Even most of the Hunters had never seen, let alone fought, one.

Forcing herself to take a breath, Twelve remembered what *A Magical Bestiary* had to say on the subject:

> *These deathly creatures stalk the Frozen Wastes of the far north and are thankfully very rarely seen. Few have attempted to study their habits, and those who have rarely survived the experience. Anecdotal evidence suggests a Grim feeds on warmth, can sense a living body from many miles away and uses this heat to track its prey.*
>
> *If faced with a Grim, and you carry weapons made of bronze, then you may have a small chance of killing it in any of the usual ways, although its hide is extraordinarily tough. If not, you must flee and try to lead the Grim to a larger, more tempting prey. Never forget that a single touch from the Grim's hands on exposed flesh means death; all warmth will be sucked out of the body by the creature's abominable mouths. The unfortunate victim is instantly frozen to death.*
>
> *Aggression: 10/10.*
>
> *Danger posed: 10/10.*
>
> *Difficulty to disable: 10/10.*

Twelve adjusted her position and gripped the ogre's hair with both hands as it kicked out at the Hunters surrounding it. But her attention was firmly fixed on the Grim. She saw with pride that Silver and Victory were leading a joint attack.

The Grim was backed into a corner and a shield wall held it in place. Hunters armed with bronze weapons attacked in perfectly synchronized waves, vaulting over the shield-bearers into the circle to attack, then sliding back to safety as the shields shifted to allow them out. It was a move they had often practiced in weapons training, one that Twelve had privately thought pointless. Seeing it in action now almost took her breath away.

The Grim screamed again and Twelve's teeth chattered at the sound. With a chill in her heart, she saw that two Hunters were unmoving inside the shield wall, still standing in battle pose, their weapons readied to strike; statues of ice instead of living, breathing flesh.

The next wave of Hunters readied themselves.

"Advance!" Silver roared, her swords grasped in both hands as she vaulted over the shields.

As one, twenty Hunters landed alongside her in the defensive ring and pressed toward their quarry, weapons ready. Twelve watched in amazement as Victory and Silver attacked together, darting back and forth fluidly until the Grim was so confused it didn't know which way to turn.

It screamed again and the ogre beneath Twelve howled in response.

Then, in the midst of the precise, practiced moves, the unthinkable happened—Victory stumbled, knocking into Silver. Twelve's stomach churned with horror. Silver struggled to regain her balance. The Grim sensed her disadvantage, turning toward her before any of the others could react. Its hair coiled into ropes and darted at the Elder, catching her around the wrist and dragging her toward its monstrous, outstretched hands.

Twelve couldn't move, unable to take her eyes off what was unfolding. On her shoulder, Widge began to shake. Fighting hard, Silver struck again and again at the Grim, but still it dragged her closer.

"Cut that hair!" screamed Victory, scrambling to repair her mistake. The Hunters obeyed, desperately hacking at the Grim. It was no good. Its hands cupped Silver's face in a strangely tender gesture. The color began to leech out of her immediately. Even her armor faded as she turned to ice before her Hunters' horrified eyes. As Silver diminished, the Grim pulsed with life, its outline momentarily clearer in the weak morning light.

Twelve wasn't sure if the screaming she could hear was hers or Victory's. Time seemed to slow and the sounds of battle became muffled. Twelve's breathing felt wrong somehow. It was as though an iron band was tightening around her chest every time she exhaled. Her knees wobbled and her vision blurred. Widge pressed himself against her cheek, his tail twitching with distress.

It couldn't be true, it just couldn't. Silver wasn't dead—that was impossible.

*Not impossible, never impossible,* her thoughts swirled bitterly. *This is what happens to the people you love. Surely you don't need another lesson in that.*

Dark spots danced across Twelve's vision and then she was falling through a hail of arrows. As the ground rushed up to meet her, everything slipped into darkness.

# CHAPTER
# EIGHT

Everything hurt. Twelve's mouth was full of blood, her nose was full of ogre-stink and no matter how many times she blinked, her vision wouldn't clear.

"Widge," she croaked as soon as she could organize her tongue. "Where are you?"

Something moved on her chest and a little nose nuzzled her cheek. Relief flooded her. She moved her hand to stroke him tentatively, amazed that nothing felt broken.

"Twelve, can you hear me?" A familiar voice spoke from beside her.

Twelve blinked furiously, her sight dark and shifting.

"Victory?" she asked as shadows bled slowly into a recognizable shape. The weaponsmaster sat beside her, her face deathly white, streaked with blood and grime.

She was in the small, whitewashed sickroom, the smell of wintergreen and woundwort strong in the air. Five Hunters lay unmoving in beds lined up under the tall, narrow windows. Opposite each bed a fire burned in a small hearth. Improbably cheerful rays of wintry sun striped the scrubbed floors. Someone had draped a bear-skin over her, but Twelve felt chilled to the bone as her memories slowly trickled back.

"Yes, I can hear you," she groaned, trying to push herself up through a wave of pain and dizziness. She ignored Widge's growl of disapproval. To her surprise, she discovered she was still gripping her axes. "What happened?"

"You fell from the ogre's shoulder," Victory said. "You bounced off its leg and one of the Hunters managed to catch you. You're lucky you haven't broken every bone in your body."

"And Silver . . . ?" Twelve asked. She couldn't bring herself to finish the question.

"Dead," Victory said, her voice choking over the word.

Twelve swallowed, furious to find her eyes prickling with tears. Victory's hand found hers and squeezed once, hard. The Hunter's face mirrored the devastation Twelve felt.

"Dead, and it was my fault," Victory whispered. "Constant vigilance, Twelve. Always. It only takes one moment . . . one lapse . . . but the consequences . . ."

She buried her face in her hands, then shook herself and straightened before Twelve could find the right words. This was a side of the weaponsmaster she had never seen.

"I need to know everything you saw and heard in the dungeons before the attack," she said, her voice hers again, if higher than normal.

Nodding, and grinding down her grief, Twelve recounted all she could remember.

"You're absolutely certain they were goblins?" Victory asked when she had finished.

"Yes," Twelve said firmly. "They're easy to recognize."

"They are," Victory said slowly, "but you're the only one who saw them."

Twelve stared in surprise. "What about Five? He was right there!"

"Must have been knocked unconscious in the blast," the Hunter said darkly. "He only came up into the courtyard as we finished off the last ogre. And none of the night watch saw them either."

Twelve absorbed this in silence.

"Are you sure you heard them say they'd find 'her'?" Victory asked. Urgency hummed through the question.

"Yes," Twelve said with a frown, "I'm certain."

Victory stood and paced along the foot of the beds, her jaw tight. "A student is missing," she said finally, her voice strained. "Seven is no longer in the lodge."

"What?" The shock was a physical pain, a thorn tearing the center of Twelve's chest. Widge became very still, barely seeming to breathe.

*Not Seven. Not her too.*

"We think she was taken," Victory continued. The weaponsmaster turned back to Twelve, saw the sudden trembling in her fingers. "Are you all right?"

For a moment, Twelve couldn't speak, could only picture Seven as she'd last seen her, offering a smile of encouragement as Twelve followed Silver down into the dungeons. The kind of smile Twelve rarely returned.

"I . . . yes." Her mouth felt as dry as a desert. "What happened? How did they take her? And where?"

"We don't know," Victory said slowly. "You said the one called Morgren had magic. The goblin mages used to be notoriously powerful, but still . . ." She stopped and shook her head. "I must go and report this to the council. Your testimony is vital."

Before Twelve could respond, the weaponsmaster whipped around and strode away, her boots ringing on the flagstone floor.

Twelve's troubled gaze traveled the room. *Where was Seven?* Worry buzzed like a hive of bees under her skin.

Victory's words echoed in her mind. *Goblins. Kidnap. Magic.*

If what she had seen in the dungeon was so important, then shouldn't she be telling the council herself?

Her eyes met Widge's and she made up her mind. She should. Yes, she definitely should. She threw back the fur and stood unsteadily. The floor seemed to tilt under her, but she made her way to the door and wobbled down the stairs. Widge chittered encouragement on her shoulder, his claws digging in hard when she swayed.

The training ground was a shock, almost unrecognizable after the destruction wrought on it. The ogres and the winter wolves were dead, the smell of blood thick in the air. The only things still standing upright were the Hunters frozen by the Grim and the Grim itself. Twelve's heart nearly stopped when she saw it, until she noticed the bronze sword through its chest. It was dead, turned to ice just like its victims. She kept her face averted from the other slowly melting ice statues, but her grief for Silver still howled inside her.

Choking down a sob, Twelve hunched her shoulders and hurried to the Great Hall. Before she even reached the doors, she could hear voices raised in argument.

"Snickering snarrows!" boomed the unmistakable voice of Elder Hoarfrost. "This ain't the ruddy floating market, Cirrus. No need to yell like that!"

"Excuse me," sputtered Cirrus, "but there certainly is! Victory is right: the Guardian should be tracking the girl right now. Every moment we lose light and she gets farther away! And if *goblins* have taken her . . ."

"Aye," Hoarfrost said. "*If* goblins have taken her. Guardian, what say you?"

"My place is here," a strangely deep and gravelly voice said. "Our walls have been breached. Never before has this happened. There may still be danger."

Twelve stepped closer to the enormous doors, cracking one open just enough to peep inside. The Hunters' backs were turned to her as they gazed at the stone Guardian.

"Send Hunters for the girl," he urged. "I should stay."

Through the mass of bodies, Twelve caught sight of Victory, her face strained. "Guardian, respectfully, I must disagree. Your battle strength is *exactly* what is needed to retrieve our lost student." Her voice rang with authority and a murmur of agreement swept through the assembled Hunters. "You are faster than our snagglefeet and will catch up with the girl before we would. We Hunters are more numerous than you: we can collapse the tunnel and secure the lodge more quickly than you can." An edge of frustration crept into the weaponsmaster's voice. "My logic is sound. I don't understand why you're still here. Nothing like this has happened since the Dark War—our response must be a hammer blow. Guardian, you are that blow!"

Yells of mixed agreement and dissent rose, shivering the wooden door beneath Twelve's fingers.

"SILENCE!" roared Elder Hoarfrost.

The hubbub of voices died down immediately. Twelve inched farther into the room to hear what he said.

"We've got one girl's word there were goblins 'ere. None of ye lot saw 'em. Our Guardian didn't see 'em. None of the *reliable* students saw 'em. Grinkeling gimlets! What Twelve says doesn't make sense. There ain't no more goblin mages—the witches of Icegaard set it so that could never happen again."

Twelve felt a dull flush flood over her face and her hands clenched into fists. Did Elder Hoarfrost really think she was lying? On her shoulder, Widge growled softly.

"Silver trusted the girl," Victory replied evenly. "She would have listened to her."

"Silver is dead," Hoarfrost said shortly.

In the silence that followed, Victory's quiet words rang clear. "*I* trust her."

For a moment, all Twelve could hear was the pounding of her own heart. A warm, liquid feeling spread through her at Victory's words.

"This fits with a pattern of evidence," a voice called out a moment later. "The winter wolves, the snarrows, *all* the supposedly seasonal creatures we meet are now dangerous year-round. Dark creatures are more problematic than ever before and wraith possessions are higher than they've been for centuries. There has to be a reason behind all of this."

A shy voice called out, "Should we send word of the attack to Icegaard?"

Sounds of derision reached Twelve's ears. "The *witches*? What are they going to do?"

The same voice rose again, defensively. "They might know something we don't. They might help us find the girl."

"We ain't heard from the witches in decades," Elder Hoarfrost said, "an' I don't reckon they'll be bothering themselves to help now."

Twelve released a breath she hadn't realized she was holding and stepped back into the training ground, her mind whirling. Horror at Seven's fate coiled in her stomach. The girl had been taken and the Guardian was refusing to go after her. Worse, the Hunters were just sitting in their council house, arguing, and all the time Seven was being whisked farther away.

An idea, bright as a beacon, flared to life, but Twelve pushed it away. She could not abandon her plans for some girl she barely knew. She turned away and stomped across the training ground toward the resthouse.

"I don't care. I *don't* care," she whispered to herself. But the lie tasted foul and the frozen Hunters stared at her in silent judgment.

Widge listened with his head cocked to one side, unconvinced, then gently nudged her cheek and licked her earlobe. He always knew when she was upset. Twelve ran her fingers through his fur and remembered when Seven had given him to her.

"I'm not good at taking care of things," Seven had said, her smile strange and twisted. "But I think you might be."

Widge had been small enough to fit into the palm of her hand. His eyes were barely open, his fur barely there, but he was beautiful even then. It had been obvious that Seven wanted to keep him, but she'd given him to Twelve instead and never asked for anything in return.

The girl's face rose in Twelve's mind, the warmth in her smile so like how Poppy used to look at her.

*Poppy*. The name jolted through her and Twelve flinched from it.

No. This was about Seven, not *her*.

A voice echoed in her memory. *Think about the person you want to be*.

Twelve steeled herself and glanced across the training ground at the frozen figure of Silver, her stomach roiling with the pain of it. Would the Elder have approved of the plan she was forming? Twelve had a feeling that she would.

Her fists clenched and her mind made up, Twelve jogged to the resthouse with renewed purpose. She would have to be quick. In the gloom of the boys' and girls' corridors, Twelve could see the dormitories were locked to keep the students inside. She hurried to the nearest door, drawing back the bolt and throwing it open.

"The Hunters say we can come out now," she called brightly into the gloom. Dimly lit faces peered hopefully at her.

"About time!" a boy howled, bursting past her toward the training ground. "Are the ogres still out there? And the winter wolves? Did the Guardian really appear?" The other students rushed after him and Twelve unlocked the other doors until the halls and training ground were full of overexcited shouts of amazement and disbelief.

Twelve ducked into her dorm, relieved to see it was empty. She changed quickly into her warmest clothes: two layers of woolen leggings—waxed waterproof but soft on the inside—three pairs of socks squeezed into fur-lined boots, three thick tunics under her bearskin, her warmest fur hat, muffler, and gloves. Over everything, she buckled her knife belt and the two axes in their slings while Widge fought to drag a dusty canvas bag from under her bed. She shoved blankets and oilskins into it along with her copy of *A Magical Bestiary*. Without pausing for breath, she hurried back to the training ground and couldn't contain a grin as she stepped out into the daylight again.

It was chaos. Students milled everywhere, climbing over the ogres, prodding the dead wolves. A couple of Hunters were trying to round them up, but it was like herding bees.

After so long locked in their rooms, the children were in no hurry to return.

Twelve jogged lightly to the kitchens and ducked inside, her eyes scanning the neat, long shelves of labeled jars and bottles. On her shoulder, Widge's interest noticeably sharpened, his nose twitching hopefully. There were trays of yesterday's bread beside the ovens and she grabbed two loaves along with some dried meat, a small bag of raisins, and three apples. She emptied a jar of nuts into her pocket for Widge, then added a box of matches and some candles to her pack. Trying not to attract the Hunters' attention, she slipped out of the kitchen and hurried to the armory.

Inside, order had been restored. The shelves stood once again in neat rows, the weapons carefully organized and gleaming. Twelve pulled down one of the torches from inside the door and made her way past the swords, long-bows, and axes, past even the rarely used flails and war hammers, until she reached the back of the building. Here, tucked away as if the Hunters hoped it would be forgotten, stood a large steel-mesh cage with a padlocked door.

Twelve's axes made short work of the lock and she stepped inside, breathing as quietly as she could. Widge gave a frightened squeak and vanished into her bearskin. In front of her stood a single stack of four shelves and on each shelf, at perfectly spaced intervals, sat three plain wooden boxes no bigger than Twelve's handspan.

Not allowing herself time for second thoughts, Twelve picked up the nearest box. With trembling fingers, she flicked the lid open. There was just time to make out three curled, glowing forms before a pair of eyes snapped open and Twelve slammed the lid closed again. Beneath her fingers, the wood grew warm, then cool again. With a sigh of relief, Twelve tucked it at the very bottom of her bag and hurried back to the training ground.

Outside, more Hunters had emerged from the council house and the students were rapidly being returned to their dormitories. There wasn't much time. Hugging the wall, Twelve slipped around the base of the fortress to the dungeon. At the threshold, she paused and took a deep breath, then, resisting the urge to look back, she stepped out of the pale light of day, and into the yawning darkness.

# CHAPTER
# NINE

Twelve hurried down the steps and night gathered around her, as smothering as an unwanted hug. She fished out the matches and struck one, its flare momentarily blinding her as she fumbled for a candle to light. Beneath her, the spiraling stairs appeared, shadows dancing over them strangely.

Swallowing her misgivings, Twelve descended to where she'd seen the goblins, marveling at the destruction she'd stumbled over earlier. In places, whole sections of the ceiling had fallen. Pale roots trailed obscenely from above, brushing Twelve's face like the damp hair of a drowned child. Shuddering, she ducked into the cell the goblins had emerged from.

The back wall had exploded inward. In its place stood

the gaping mouth of a tunnel entrance. An evil, ogrey stench was wafting out of the passage and the blackness pressed close, hungry and malevolent. Twelve took a deep breath and stared into the hole, crushing her dread into disgust.

*Victory wouldn't be afraid. Think of Seven. Think of Silver.*

She swallowed, even though her mouth was dry, and climbed over clots of earth into the tunnel beyond. Widge ran along her arm to within a whisker-length of the candle flame, his eyes searching the shadows beyond. Four eyes were better than two. Hot wax ran over Twelve's fingers and the only sound was her own ragged breathing as she began to walk, her eyes straining ahead into the black. The tunnel was perfectly round and arrow-straight, every inch proclaiming its unnaturalness. Magic had made this, Twelve was sure.

She walked for hours, until the candle was only a stump and her imagination battered her with an army of terrors. What if the tunnel didn't lead straight out? What if she was lost underground? What if she and Widge weren't alone?

Clenching her teeth, Twelve sped up until the gradient of the tunnel shifted and a speck of daylight appeared in the distance. Widge flicked his tail with delight, bounding from her wrist to her shoulder and back again. Swallowing a cry of relief, she broke into a run until the tunnel spat them into the soft light of late afternoon. She took a deep lungful of bitingly cold fresh air and allowed herself a moment of triumph.

Young, leggy pines surrounded her, their shadows striping the snowy ground. Between the trees, the winter sun was diving behind the Fang Mountains, its dying rays tinting the earth gold. Twelve's breath steamed as she turned on the spot, trying to orient herself, but the lodge was nowhere to be seen. The tunnel had sent her out somewhere farther into the mountains. Trees and snow stretched on as far as she could see. The silence was absolute. On her shoulder, Widge grew still and somber, their shared elation fading.

Fear leaped in her gut and instinctively she began scanning the ground around her, keeping her thoughts focused on interpreting the tracks there, anything but the enormity of the task she had set herself.

There were a multitude of prints, but as Twelve examined them a story began to emerge. The creatures had all arrived from different directions, but had entered the passage together. Three sets of prints traveling in the opposite direction caught her eye and she heaved a sigh of relief. There had been no guarantee the goblins had left the way they'd come, but here were two narrow sets of goblin footprints with an unmistakably human one between them.

"Seven," Twelve whispered, gazing at the print. Still alive and able to walk.

*For now.*

Twelve shook her head, pushing away all the goblin atrocities she'd learned about in class, wishing she didn't have quite such a good memory. She would find Seven and bring her back. She had to.

"Better get going," she muttered to Widge. His whiskers tickled her nose as she checked her axes and started forward. "We've only got a few hours of light left." Her voice seemed unnaturally loud in the vast silence around her.

Beyond the clearing, the trees grew closer together, their trunks glittering with frost. The tracks weaved through them until they broke out onto a gently sloping snowfield. In the distance, the Fangs scratched the sky. Twelve skidded to a stop, her eyes darting over a muddle of marks in the snow. Three sleds and at least four more goblins had waited here for their counterparts to return.

She scowled into the setting sun and took a deep breath to calm her pounding heart, angry with herself that she hadn't seen this coming. These goblins had orchestrated several seemingly impossible feats: of course they'd planned their getaway just as carefully.

A soft crunch in the snow behind her made Widge's tail bristle. Twelve's axes were in her hands in an instant, but there was nowhere to hide. She turned back to the trees, determination and fear pounding through her as a dark shape shifted in the distance, moving toward her with the confident gait of a predator.

Twelve's heart thrummed a frantic rhythm, but she stood her ground.

Only as it moved closer did she realize what she was looking at: the lodge's Guardian. She didn't lower her axes as he approached. Widge, in agreement, bared his teeth, fur standing on end.

Twelve had seen many strange things since she'd arrived at the lodge, but the Guardian was easily the strangest. He was the reddish stone of the lodge walls and so lifelike that he could have passed for flesh and blood, except for his enormous size. One of his ears was badly torn, giving him a dangerous appearance. With a flicker of horror, she remembered how he'd thrown a winter wolf aside as if it weighed nothing. Her fingers gripped the hafts of her axes more tightly and she gave him her fiercest scowl as he halted in front of her, his ears pricked, expression serious.

"What are you doing here?" he asked, his voice grating like millstones. His eyes flicked from Twelve to Widge and back again. "Return to the lodge at once. The Hunters will worry."

Twelve couldn't contain her snort. "Like they're worrying about Seven? I think I'm better off out here." She resisted the urge to flinch as he loomed over her, taking in her clothing and bulging canvas bag.

"You try to track the huntling yourself," he said, his disapproval obvious.

"I'm not *trying*, I'm doing it," she said, jutting her chin. Her expression, and Widge's bared teeth, dared him to contradict her.

His bark of gravelly laughter caught her off guard. "But I am here now," he said, his tail wagging slowly as he regarded her. "You must go back."

His amusement was infuriating and Twelve's anger roared inside her. "You don't even want to be here," she said, her voice much louder than she'd intended. "I heard you in the Great Hall. I don't believe you'll even *try* to get Seven back."

The Guardian's tail stopped wagging and a low, ominous growl sounded at the back of his throat. Clenching her teeth, Twelve turned away from him, back to the prints at her feet.

"I spoke the truth to the council," he said from behind her. "This plan is not sound. The Elders command me to find the child regardless. Therefore I must do it." His growl grew more pronounced. "Return to the lodge. *Now*."

Twelve spun back to face him, her hands still clutching her axes. "No!" The word rang with determination. In the silence that followed, the Guardian's expression shifted from annoyance to concern, then back to annoyance again.

"You waste time," he growled, glancing at the deepening shadows spreading across the snowfield. "The girl is getting farther away."

"Then you'd better get moving," Twelve said. "I'll be right behind you."

The Guardian stared at her in amazement. "You have no snagglefoot. How will you cross the Fangs?"

Widge stared at the Guardian, then turned to hear Twelve's answer, expectant down to the very tips of his whiskers.

Twelve winced. She would have brought a snagglefoot to ride if there had been any way of getting it across the training ground unseen. "One foot in front of the other," she replied with more confidence than she felt. "Just like you."

Widge gave her a rather dark look, his tail sagging with disappointment.

The Guardian barked another laugh, this time humorless. "Ridiculous child."

Twelve bristled. "I know what to expect and I can look after myself." She glanced pointedly at the sun diving behind the mountains. "Shouldn't you be going?"

Instead of bounding past her as she expected, the Guardian began to pace, his agitation clear in every movement.

Twelve turned back to the tracks in the snow, trying to block him out as she examined them more carefully. Seven's trail became more confused the closer they got to where the sleds had been. Her footsteps led toward a sled, then were scuffed and smeared before racing away again. Drag marks implied she had been pulled back to where she started. The last clear footprints caught Twelve's eye—facing away from the sled, with the outline of Seven's toes visible. It looked as though the girl had almost escaped, but then been hauled back by her captors, losing her boots in the struggle. Three sets of sled tracks raced away across the snowfield into the distance, heading straight into the mountains.

Twelve turned around and almost collided with the Guardian. He didn't look happy.

"We travel together," he said without preamble, an icy wind rippling his stone fur. "I cannot leave one student in favor of another. If I take you back, I will lose the last light. You must ride on my back though. It will be uncomfortable but faster. You will be safer than on your own."

Whatever Twelve had expected, it hadn't been this. The Guardian sat sphinxlike in the snow before her and nodded for her to climb onto him. Her mind raced. She didn't want a travel companion, and this one obviously thought she was a helpless irritation. And yet . . . Twelve's eyes flicked over the jagged peaks and a tiny, traitorous part of her admitted she didn't want herself and Widge to face the dangers alone.

"I'm in charge," Twelve said, her voice ringing with more authority than she felt.

She swore the Guardian raised his eyebrows. "You are Unblooded," he said. His tone bordered on disdain and Twelve took grim pleasure in his affront.

"It's that or leave me here in the wilderness"—she gave a shrug—"with only a squirrel and my wits for protection. . . ."

A glint of something like admiration appeared in the Guardian's eyes. "You are as wily as a veiled fox. But I cannot agree to your terms." His expression grew serious. "Everything I do will be to find the girl. To bring her back alive. If we share that aim, we shall have few disagreements."

Twelve narrowed her eyes suspiciously at him, but could find nothing objectionable in his face. After a moment, she held out her hand.

"Shake on it," she said.

He laughed a laugh like pebbles rattling in a glass. "My first handshake." Carefully, he lifted a paw and placed it on top of Twelve's hand, the weight of it enormous. "You should call me 'Dog.' It is simpler than 'Glorious Guardian of the Hunting Lodge.'"

Twelve snorted, then saw that he wasn't joking. "People actually call you that?"

"Yes," he said. "But Dog will do."

"Well, I'm Twelve," she said, scrambling up onto his back. "And this is Widge. But I'd prefer you call me 'Stupendous Student of the Hunting Lodge.'"

Dog gave her a definite *look* over his shoulder. Then, without another word, he sprang along the sweeping tracks.

Twelve clung on fiercely as, with ever-lengthening strides, they raced toward the glowering mountains.

# CHAPTER

# TEN

They streamed across the snowfield and through a narrow, deeply shadowed gorge. Beyond that, a broad, pine-filled valley spread before them. The ridge of the First Fang reared into view, its face scored with indigo shadows, snow-kissed in shades of lilac. The moon carved an upward path through a deepening velvet sky and the first valiant stars peeped out. Night was closing in, and Dog ran as though he could outpace it.

The temperature dropped steadily and the wind scoured Twelve's cheeks, freezing her snot and whistling down her neck. Her eyes streamed and the tears froze on her lashes, but she kept quiet, determined not to complain. The only warm part of her was over her stomach, where Widge was curled up beneath her furs, apparently fast asleep. At least one of them was snug. Dog hadn't lied—riding him was uncomfortable: his back was hard, cold rock and he leaped across the snow in huge, flurried bounds that bounced her mercilessly.

The good news was they were moving fast. Twelve's heart lifted as icy air whipped past. Maybe they had a chance to catch up with Seven after all. Hope bubbled in her chest as they sped through a dense stand of pine.

When Dog stopped, it was so sudden that she was thrown off, narrowly missing a tree trunk.

"What the . . . ?" Twelve spat snow furiously. Beneath her furs, incredibly, it seemed Widge was still asleep.

"Something is following us," Dog growled. His hackles stood up in stony ridges as he looked back, his head cocked to one side.

Twelve strained her ears, but could hear nothing. "Are you sure?"

It was dark between the trees, but his look of outrage was obvious. His response was cut off by the unmistakable sound of a twig cracking. A feathercoo cried its alarm and exploded into the darkening sky, its wings ghostly in the moonlight.

Twelve held her breath and reached for her axes with frozen fingers.

"Hide in the trees," Dog whispered, his eyes fixed on the tracks behind them.

Twelve set her teeth and forced calmness into her panicked thoughts the way Silver had taught her. "No," she whispered fiercely. "We face whatever it is together."

Dog flinched as though she had hit him and broke his unblinking stare into the trees. Before she could say another word, he pounced on her and hauled her by her axe slings back into the gloom between the thickly needled branches.

"You are troublesome," he growled as he dragged her struggling form effortlessly. "Listen to me in the future."

Twelve fought him furiously and silently, her fury a boiling, living thing inside her. How dare he?

Suddenly awake and mightily offended by it, Widge darted up onto Dog's nose and tried fruitlessly to bite him.

Another twig snapped, much closer this time, and the wind whirled a fragment of jumbled conversation to them. Paws crunched through the snow, approaching steadily. It sounded like there was more than one and they were big.

Twelve froze.

In an instant, Dog sprang away from her, and onto whatever was lurking beyond.

# CHAPTER
# ELEVEN

A shriek ripped through the trees, followed by a stream of curses and Dog's yelp of shock. Twelve scrambled to her feet, her heart sinking: no dark creature had made those sounds.

She shouldered her way through the tangle of branches and, sure enough, there were Five and Six. Both were mounted on shaggy snagglefeet, armed to the teeth and dressed in their warmest furs. The two groups stared at one another, weapons drawn, eyes wide. Widge fled from Dog's shoulder back to Twelve's.

Charger, Five's gray snagglefoot, rolled his eyes wildly. His short, curved horns gleamed in the watery moonlight and his bearlike snout puffed panicky breaths into the crisp night air. Six's snaggle, Surefoot, was calm in comparison. Her long nut-brown fur rippled in the breeze, powerful claws hidden beneath the snowcrust.

Twelve was the first to relax, returning her axes to their slings and glaring at the boys. "So, which one of you has that high-pitched scream? Five? Bet it's you."

Neither boy responded, both too busy gawping at Dog.

"I told you," Five muttered to Six. "*Told* you it was awake!"

"It?" Dog growled, his lips drawing back to reveal razor-sharp canines.

"Did it just talk?" Five gasped, his eyes huge.

Six elbowed Five hard. "Sorry about him—he babbles when he's nervous."

Dog snarled, glaring at Five.

"What are you two doing here?" Twelve demanded.

Five quickly regained his composure. "The same thing you are, *obviously*," he said, looking down his nose at her. "Rescuing Seven."

"Why?" said Twelve. "What do you care about Seven?"

"We have our reasons," said Six, his face pale in the gloom. There was an urgency and sincerity there that took Twelve by surprise. He'd always treated Seven with the same disregard as everyone else.

"Your reasons do not matter here," said Dog. "You must ride back to the lodge."

Six turned to the stone Guardian, ignoring his command. "I'm glad you're here. We thought the Hunters weren't doing anything."

"They sent me," Dog said. "You huntlings make my task more difficult though."

"We won't slow you down at all," Five said, his eyes running over Dog admiringly. "We picked the fastest snagglefeet."

"You will not slow me down," Dog agreed, lowering his head to peer at the tracks in the gathering gloom. "You will be elsewhere. Return Twelve to the lodge."

His tone was so confident and commanding that Twelve wondered if he ever hadn't been listened to.

"No!" Six's and Twelve's voices sounded in unison. They both stared at each other in surprise.

"We're coming with you," Six added quickly, his voice every bit as determined as Twelve's had been.

"Yup," Five said, glancing at Six. He grinned at Twelve. "If you're staying, then *clearly* you'll need our protection anyway."

Twelve made to leap at him, Widge bristling on her shoulder, but Dog stepped solidly between them.

"Quiet!" His bark was flinchingly loud. "You waste precious time with your bickering." Twelve felt small as he shook his head at them. "I will find the girl alo—"

"Seven," Six interrupted. "Her name is Seven."

Dog yelped, his frustration becoming more obvious. "I am fastest alone. *Go. Back.*"

"I won't," Six said with finality. "It's too dark to follow the trail any farther tonight. You don't have to babysit us if you don't want. We'll camp here and keep going at first light. You can do whatever you like—pretend we're not here if you prefer."

Equal parts admiration and dismay swept through Twelve. Six had handled Dog without even raising his voice, but the idea of traveling with Five was unthinkable. Even a minute of his pompous sneering made her want to gag him. Six was right though: night had now truly fallen. The sky was a fathomless black behind an explosion of stars, and the snow between the trees glowed with a ghostly sheen.

"Madness," Dog muttered to himself, pacing back and forth. "Madness and insubordination."

Six ignored him, turning instead to untack Surefoot, a mulish expression on his face.

"We're staying, then," Five grinned, dismounting a restless Charger.

Twelve frowned at Five's sidling snagglefoot. Charger wasn't one of the Hunters' regular mounts—he was still too green. She rolled her eyes. "Did you really bring a half-trained snagglefoot with you?" she asked.

"We're here, aren't we?" Five snorted. "So *obviously* I can handle him."

"Like you handled the dungeons?" she asked. She smiled grimly as his shoulders stiffened.

"Enough!" Dog growled, sitting down. The ground shuddered beneath him and pine needles rained around them. "Tonight we camp. Together. Tomorrow you all return to the lodge."

Twelve stared at him. "I am not camping with them!" she exclaimed, her horror rising.

"You are," Dog said evenly. "Danger lurks. I cannot protect two campsites."

"I don't need to be protected," Twelve snarled.

"Of course not," Dog said dryly. "You have your squirrel and your wits."

Five smirked.

Her face burning, Twelve stalked away, biting her tongue to stop herself screaming. This was not what she had imagined when she set off. She took several deep breaths to calm herself and shoved her fists into her pockets. Her knuckles sank through Widge's stash of nuts to connect solidly with something larger and she remembered the mysterious package from the dungeons. Already that felt like a lifetime ago when really it had only been a day.

The object was slightly larger than her fist and tightly wrapped in linen. She squeezed it curiously as Widge sniffed at it, then tugged one end of the wrapping to let it unravel under its own weight. A smooth, milky stone dropped into her hand. She stared at it, confused and disappointed, until it began to glow.

It started so slowly that Twelve thought she was imagining things, then gained momentum until a fierce silvery-blue light erupted from it. Twelve threw up her other hand to protect her eyes as Widge shrieked in alarm. The others crowded around her with exclamations of surprise.

"What in Ember . . . ?" Five's voice was very close and Twelve blinked furiously until her eyes adjusted. He was staring at her, an expression of amazement on his face. "Where did you steal that from?" Then, over his shoulder, "You've got to see this! I've never seen a moonstone so big!"

*A moonstone?*

Twelve squinted at the glowing object uncertainly, so surprised she barely registered Five's insult. Moonstones were the tiny lights in the council house, their pale glimmer barely enough to see by. This seemed something else entirely. It blazed like bottled lightning, burning away shadows, bleaching everything with clean, bright light.

"Where did you get that?" Six demanded, his face bone white in the moonstone light. Even Dog was looking askance at her. Defiance straightened her spine and confusion sealed her lips. Twelve glared at them all in reply.

"I don't think you stole it," Six said, taking a deep breath, "but where did it come from?"

Twelve relented. "Someone brought dream milk to the

dungeons last night and they put this next to . . ." She broke off. With a sickening lurch, she realized she'd forgotten to bring dream milk. Her mouth felt suddenly dry.

"Who brought it?" Six asked as Twelve's mind whirled. She would just have to make sure she didn't fall asleep tonight. Doubt crawled through her though; she was so very tired.

"Must have been a student; they were too small to be a Hunter," Five answered for her. "But it doesn't make sense. No student would have something like this. We're not allowed to keep anything from before, not even our names. This is *clearly* worth an absolute fortune. Why give it to her?"

"Hold it up," Dog growled. He peered into its swirling depths and then stepped back and shook his head, half blinded. "Flawless," he said simply. "It is priceless."

"That's ridiculous!" Twelve sputtered, outrage quelling her rising fear and uncertainty.

"Flawless moonstones are incredibly rare," Six said, his eyes still fixed on the stone in her hand. "Maybe one mined every century, if that."

"I have only ever seen one," Dog nodded. "During the Dark War."

Five's and Six's jaws dropped and Twelve blinked in amazement. That would make him hundreds of years old, perhaps more.

Dog kept on talking, oblivious. "I have heard stories

though. Moonstones like that may do more than provide light."

"More?" Five asked. He looked as baffled as Twelve felt.

"A regular moonstone provides light," Six said, frowning, "but a flawless one can pierce illusions, show the truth."

Five wrinkled his nose, but Dog nodded again, looking thoughtful. "That could be useful." He glanced at Twelve. "Maybe there is more to you than I thought."

The compliment was so meager that Twelve almost laughed. Widge, on the other hand, preened.

Six's face lit up. "It could be useful right now! With this light, we can follow their trail in the dark. We might catch them asleep. We could get Seven back tonight!"

Excitement fizzled through Twelve. He was right. "Then what are we waiting for?"

Six was already saddling Surefoot when Twelve turned to Dog. He looked utterly dismayed.

"Go back." His tail wagged hopefully. "Please?"

Twelve shook her head slowly. "I can't," she said, "for the same reason you can't. I have to find her."

Dog made a sound that was half sigh, half groan, but finally he nodded and let her climb onto his back again.

Twelve's heart soared twice: once for Dog's acceptance and once for the jealousy on Five's face when she jumped onto the Guardian's broad back.

Then they were off.

# CHAPTER
# TWELVE

Dog and Twelve raced ahead, the moonstone held high to reveal the trail. Her heart pounded as the group sped onward, excitement and disbelief mingling with disgust that Five and Six were now with her.

"This is brilliant!" Five called, his voice jarringly loud above the crunching snow and ragged breathing.

"Shh!" Twelve hissed. "Do you want to tell *every* goblin where we are?"

"Not just the goblins," Dog offered darkly as his paws pounded the ground. "Quiet is preferable. Silence better."

"He means 'shut up,'" Twelve clarified.

"How *very* lucky Dog is to have you translating for him," Five said waspishly. Then to Dog, "Do you mind her patronizing you?"

"Quiet," Dog growled as his great body sprang forward, the snagglefeet racing on either side of him. "Please."

From then, they traveled in silence, darkness swirling behind them like a cloak. Twelve tightened all her furs, pulled her hat low and her muffler high. Only her eyes were visible, but still the icy air stung as it froze the inside of her nostrils. Widge retreated to the relative comfort of her bearskin, only his eyes and ears visible above the collar.

Seven's trail drew everyone's gaze forward, and the moonstone was a beacon, filling their hearts with hope. They sped between snow-laden pines, sending clouds of orb moths whirring above them, their jeweled lights making Five gasp.

"So beautiful!" he sighed. "I've never seen that many together."

"There is more of everything farther north," grunted Dog.

A tingle of anticipation ran through Twelve. North of the Fangs was where all the best stories and worst monsters came from. It wasn't a place for students until they'd passed their Blooding in the Frozen Forest. Despite her common sense screaming the dangers, Twelve was excited.

Eventually, they raced out into the open and the sky yawned overhead. Twelve's breath caught in her throat—there wasn't a single cloud to dull the diamond-studded brilliance of it. The sickle moon smiled down on them, as ragged peaks, too steep for snow, melted into the blackness above. The wilderness welcomed them hungrily, its beauty shining with hard edges and teeth.

Unbidden, Dog slowed to a walk and stopped. They were in a wide valley, the slopes thickly forested but the bottom flat and open. The broad, snow-covered expanse shone in the starlight.

"We will camp on the slope," he said. "We can pick up the trail again at dawn."

In unison, the three huntlings began to protest, but Dog was immovable. "Exhaustion creates mistakes," he said. "Even I need to rest. You are all dead on your feet."

"Dead on our bums more like," Five muttered, wriggling on Charger's back.

Twelve's arms were so tired and her eyelids so heavy. Sleep was out of the question without dream milk, but to lie down quietly for an hour or two sounded like bliss. Then she thought of Seven, the warmth of her smile, the dimples that reminded her so much of Poppy, and all thoughts of rest faded. They *had* to keep going.

"We can't stop now—we could be so close!" Six's voice broke into her thoughts.

"And we're not tired anyway," Twelve lied quickly.

"Speak for yourself," Five muttered, shooting her a dark look.

Dog shook his head. "They are half a day ahead of us.

Even if we caught them, we would be exhausted. They would not."

Twelve frowned, trying not to admit he was right.

Six's face looked haggard as he gazed along the trail, then up at the sky. He sniffed the air. "The sky's clear, I suppose," he said finally. "The tracks will still be there in a few hours. I just hope . . ." He shook his head and the group stood in silence, each desperately hoping Seven was all right. Admitting she would have to spend the rest of the night as a prisoner made her plight more terrifyingly real.

"Come," Dog said, his tone gentler than Twelve had expected. He led them away from the trail and into the trees, the scent of pine sharp despite the cold.

Half dazed with exhaustion, Twelve and Six each used an axe to cut wood for a fire. Twelve examined Six from the corner of her eye as they worked. Her dislike of Five was so all-consuming she'd never paid any attention to the boy constantly beside him before. She decided Six wasn't what she'd expected. Unlike Five, he was quiet, but anything he did say appeared thoughtful and deliberate. It made him almost the opposite of Five, and Twelve couldn't help but wonder what he saw to like in the other boy.

When the logs were crackling merrily, the three hunt-lings settled onto their oilskins and furs, nibbling their rations appreciatively. Widge perked up at the promise of food, then scampered off to explore. Twelve lay back against her canvas bag with a sigh, stretching her aching limbs. Dog sat sphinxlike by the flames, watching everything at once.

"Want some?" Twelve asked, holding out a slice of her dried meat to Dog. Everyone was eating except him.

The look he gave her was amused. "I am made of stone. I have no need to eat."

"Oh." Twelve put the meat back in her bag, feeling stupid as Five smothered a grin.

"It is kind of you to ask," Dog added, catching Five's expression. "My sense of smell is very sharp, but I have no sense of taste. I would love to be able to eat though. Chicken pies smell delicious." The sigh he gave was full of longing.

Twelve stayed silent, not sure what to say.

"Do you sleep?" Six asked, intrigued.

"No. But I have spent hundreds of years inside a wall," Dog said dryly. "Does that count?"

"What about pain?" Five piped up. His eyes flicked to Dog's maimed ear. "You *must* have felt that."

Dog stared into the fire. "Not as you would," he said finally. His tone made it clear the conversation was over.

Five shrugged and started chewing noisily. "By the frost, it's all a bit mysterious, isn't it?" he said, wiping his fingers on his furs. He rolled his eyes at their stares. "You've all forgotten the woods because you're too focused on one tree. The lodge walls were breached for the first time *ever* and out of everyone they took Seven. Why?"

Twelve frowned and risked a grudging glance at Five. It was a good question, one she should have asked herself. The group mulled it over in silence.

"During the Dark War, the goblins often kidnapped enemies," Dog said eventually. "People who could reveal information when tortured." Everyone winced, but Dog carried on talking. "Clan leaders, witches, and Hunters were all targeted." He paused. "Sometimes their families. The daughter of a cave clan leader was taken to force his cooperation. He complied, but she was still returned in pieces."

"We're, uh . . . talking emotionally, I hope?" Five asked. "She was in figurative, emotional pieces?"

"No. Actual pieces," Dog growled. "Legs and arms and . . ."

"All right," Five said quickly, looking ill, "I get the idea."

Twelve's stomach curdled at the mention of the cave clan. "I'm surprised they had to take his daughter at all," she said, her voice harsh. "The cave clan were collaborators."

"No," Dog said with authority. "It was never that simple."

"Really?" Twelve asked, anger hot in her veins. "I can't have been listening properly in Elder Hoarfrost's lessons, then. Didn't the cave clan shelter the goblins after the Battle of Breakneck, allowing them to escape capture? Didn't the same goblins later attack a river clan village, sinking it completely?" Her voice rose as she spoke until she was almost shouting.

"Some sympathized with the goblins," Dog said, his expression far away as he remembered. "Most of the cave clan did not. They were horrified by the goblin atrocities. And afraid. The type of fear that changes people. You cannot understand the darkness that reigned back then. Terror stalked the world. Much was sacrificed to banish it."

A deathly silence had fallen over the group as they listened, and the hair prickled at the nape of Twelve's neck.

"Battle lines were drawn in the caves. The fiercest fighting was there. And it was where I spent most of the war." A strange shiver passed over him and he stood up suddenly, shaking himself. "You cannot judge a whole clan based on the actions of a few." His voice was brusque. "You should know better, Twelve."

Twelve snorted. She judged them all right.

Before she could speak again, Six interrupted. "We're getting off the subject." His voice was tight. "The Dark War is ancient history. Let's talk about *now*. How did the goblins get inside the lodge without anyone knowing?"

Dog stared at him for a moment, his expression unreadable. "Ancient history for you perhaps. I remember it like it was yesterday."

"Yes," Five said, "but you're hardly normal."

"Shut up, Five," Twelve muttered. Dog had turned away, tension thrumming through him.

"What?" Five asked, his face a picture of innocence. "What did I say?"

"This attack should not have been possible," Dog said abruptly, turning back to the group and pointedly ignoring Five. "The witches of Icegaard laid protections on the lodge when it was built. Even the elementals helped." He sighed and frowned. "But that magic is very old now. Perhaps it is weakening. A goblin mage could exploit that." Dog paused and shook his head. "A goblin mage should not be possible since the war either."

He sounded worried. Twelve pulled her muffler up higher, suddenly chilled. The Hunting Lodge could never be home, but it had provided her with food and safety for the last two years, taught her how to survive. The thought of it vulnerable, besieged by enemies, made her stomach twist.

"Maybe that's how they got in," Five said from the other side of the fire, his face distorted in the rising smoke and heat, "but it doesn't explain why in Ember *Seven* was taken instead of Elder Hoarfrost or someone."

Silence.

Dog nodded. "That is true," he admitted. "What do we know of the girl?"

Unbidden, an image of Seven rose before Twelve. Her swirling dark hair—no, that was Poppy. Twelve shook her head. Settled on the right memory. "She's always alone," she told him, thinking hard. "Most of the huntlings ignore her. She's a bit . . . odd, always distracted. She's atrocious with every weapon she's ever tried."

Six shot her a dark look across the fire.

Twelve shrugged. It was true, though it felt wrong to describe Seven like that. She hesitated, then went on. "There *is* something quite strange about her, although it's difficult to explain. Something in her manner. But, if there's anything that sets her apart from everyone else, it's that."

"Could she know something useful?" Dog wondered aloud. "Perhaps she has family connections?"

"She's a huntling," Five pointed out, "so chances are they're dead. If they *are* alive, they must be incredibly poor to have sent her to the lodge." He chuckled. "Or maybe—maybe they just couldn't stand her!" He guffawed then, a laugh that was met with stony stares. He cleared his throat awkwardly. "Just thinking aloud."

"Resist that," Dog growled. He shook his head. "Is she good at anything?"

Twelve thought back over her interactions with Seven. "Not that I can think of."

"Anyone?" Dog asked, looking at the boys.

Another silence.

Dog sighed and lowered his head onto his paws. "When we catch the goblins, we will demand answers."

96

Twelve lay back as well, wrapping her blankets around herself and tucking another oilskin over the top to make a sleeping bag. She hugged her knees to her chest and stared into the fire, thinking of Seven, hoping she was all right, wherever she was.

Beyond the sphere of firelight, a movement caught her eye in the trees. She bolted upright and stared into the darkness. A strange, creeping fear curled in her stomach and she instinctively grabbed one of her axes.

Dog had leaped up at her sudden movement and the boys were sitting up too, their weapons already in their hands.

"What is it?" Dog asked, by her side in an instant.

"I . . . something moved," Twelve said, her certainty fading. Dog peered into the darkness with her. Widge sprang out of the nearest tree and bounded over to her, fur stiff with alarm.

"That thing's going to get itself killed," Five huffed, shoving his sword back into its sheath. Six lowered his bow and arrow with a sigh of relief. Dog relaxed and turned to them.

"Sleep," he said. "I will patrol."

"Excellent," Five yawned "You're *so* useful, Dog." A moment later, he was snoring.

Twelve lay back down, unsettled, sure it hadn't been Widge she'd seen. In her arms, he shivered as she stroked him, his eyes fixed on the darkness between the tree trunks.

"Did you see something too?" she murmured, wishing, not for the first time, that he could speak.

She gripped her axes even tighter. Her thoughts were whirling, but she welcomed them. The last thing she needed was to fall asleep without dream milk.

Across the fire, Six's breathing became deep and steady. The flames crackled comfortingly and Dog paced quietly around them. Widge relaxed and slowly Twelve's thoughts calmed. Her eyelids began to droop.

*Don't fall asleep!*

The desperate thought snapped her eyes back open. Fear prickled her scalp. She gritted her teeth and stared up into the dark branches laced above her. Dog paused beside her, his face quizzical. Then understanding dawned.

"You have no dream milk," he said quietly.

Twelve winced, hoping the firelight hid the color flooding her cheeks. "No," she said finally, her voice as stiff as her back.

Dog hesitated, then said, "I have heard much about nightmares. They cannot kill you. Lack of sleep can. You must be on sharp form tomorrow, Twelve."

Twelve didn't have the energy to argue so she settled for silence. When he continued his patrol, she forced her eyes open, wide and unblinking. She would not allow herself to fall asleep.

# CHAPTER
# THIRTEEN

*T*welve's eyes snapped open and immediately she knew she was in trouble. She was lying on a ground cushioned with thick, springy grass and beyond the branches the sky was the bright, welcoming blue of a summer's day.

She swore and pinched herself hard, her breath hitching.

A warm breeze lifted her hair and carried voices from nearby. Easy chatter and laughter, the kind never heard at the lodge. The hairs stood up along Twelve's arms and her heart began to pound.

"Starling?" a woman's voice called through the trees.

Twelve stood, the voice a knife twisting in her gut. When she was awake, she could barely remember her ma's voice. Here it was still vivid though.

The woman retreated and a man's deeper tones mingled

with hers, their words almost discernible. A girl's laugh burbled.

The sounds were a bittersweet agony that Twelve couldn't resist. Slowly, almost against her will, she walked toward them. Her eyes drank in the details around her greedily. Interspersed with the grass were wildflowers: yellow suncups and tiny pink babwinkles. Poppy had once made chains of them for her.

Poppy.

Her pace quickened and she broke unexpectedly into sunlight. A man and a woman sat together on a bright hand-woven blanket while two small girls played nearby.

None of them saw her.

The man was powerfully built, his beard thick and dark, his eyes a stormy gray. The woman next to him was tall and solid. Everything about her was firm and capable, except her hair, which was almost ethereal: a gleaming blue-black cloud floating around her strong-featured face. Her quick, clever fingers wove dried grass into a basket while the man lovingly sharpened a pair of axe blades.

Twelve drank the pair in hungrily, stepping so close that she could have reached out and touched them.

"Well, what should we do, then?" the woman said, glancing toward the children and lowering her voice. "If we don't sell the wheat crop, then we won't have enough to see us through winter."

"I know," the man said heavily, "but there's trouble all across Ember and the safe paths aren't safe anymore. The forest clan is raging over burned home-trees; their tree whisperers say the fires were started on purpose. Chief Torrent has withdrawn all her floating villages to the riverlands. The mountain gliders haven't been seen beyond their own lands and the desert folk have pulled right back into the Scour's sandstorm. Everyone's uneasy about what might be . . . beneath us." He glanced down at the ground and his face darkened, a thundercloud crossing the sky.

"If we can't use the safe path, travel up the Embrace or through the forest, then we're cut off," the woman said, biting her lip. Birds trilled and swooped, chasing insects across the clearing as she thought. "We'll have to sell to Rifkin," she said a moment later. "He won't give us a fair price, but he'll be the one taking the risk, not you."

"Rifkin?" the man snorted, his nostrils flaring with temper. "We won't get half of what it's worth!"

"The girls need both their parents." Her voice was severe. "And half is better than none."

The man nodded slowly and ran his hand through his hair.

"Can I go to the stream?" a breathless voice asked from beside Twelve. She looked down at the small girl who had spoken: bright cheeks, gray eyes, a mischievous smile, and their ma's cloud of dark hair. Poppy.

The woman smiled. "If Starling goes with you."

*The older girl skipped up, her eyes eager. "Of course I'll go!"*

*"Take care of her or we'll trade you to the cave clan," her da said, a twinkle in his eye. "I wonder how big a moonstone we could get for you?"*

*Starling snorted a laugh and looped her arm through her little sister's.*

*"I don't need minding," Poppy muttered crossly as the girls walked away. "I'm big now!"*

*"I know that," Starling whispered, "but Ma and Da don't!"*

*Poppy beamed at the taller girl, her cheeks dimpling.*

*Twelve reached for Poppy without even meaning to, but it was Starling who turned with a gasp. Their eyes met and Twelve felt a vicious tug deep in her chest. The world seemed to tilt and slide around them, colors bleeding, shapes smudging into one another.*

*Only Starling remained in an otherwise empty void of featureless gray. Twelve blinked hard, trying and failing to find something other than her to focus on.*

*Somewhere behind her, a crow carked low.*

*Slowly, ever so slowly, the hairs on Twelve's arms stood up. The back of her neck prickled, and her breath jarred into ragged, fearful gasps. She knew that sound.*

*Starling was walking away. She looked different, older, dressed more warmly. Her footsteps were sure and quick, despite the doe carcass slung over her shoulders. Starting from her, the world pulled back into focus.*

*A cart track through rolling hills spread out from her feet. Green and gold grass grew up to her thighs on either side of the path. Cobwebs spun between the stalks glittered with dew. The air was fresh and cool; the world felt new. But Starling hurried, biting her lip.*

*Twelve tried to walk the other way, but found she couldn't. Dread choked her. The world pulled her after the girl, drawing her on against her will. Together, they crested the hill and a valley split into fields before them. A sparkling stream coiled through the middle and on the other side sat a grass clan village.*

*"Poa," Twelve croaked, drinking in the sight. The breeze caught the word and threw it back at her.*

*Poa, Poa, Poa.*

*Starling half turned with a listening frown, but her eyes passed over Twelve, unseeing. She hurried on, dragging Twelve with her.*

*It was a small, neat place. The houses were set around a large green, comfortably shaded by three ancient plane trees. The buildings were made of intricately plaited, lacquered grass. Each one was unique, their owners proud to demonstrate their ingenuity. In the fields, ripe wheat swayed, rustling in the breeze. Swallows darted and swooped, their beaks full of insects.*

*Starling paused as she descended the slope, something catching her eye. A fence now ran alongside the path and* there was an arrow embedded deeply in the wood. It definitely hadn't been there when she left. Its shaft was made of unusually dark wood, a slice of night against warm chestnut. The fletching was strange too. Instead of feathers, bats' wings granted the arrow flight. A cave clan arrow, just like in the stories. Her fingers brushed it, as if to make sure it was real, and her expression changed to one of fear as she turned to look properly at Poa.

It was still early, but the village was very quiet, unusually still. No smoke coiled from the chimneys; no voices carried on the breeze; nothing moved. Even the animals in their barns were silent. Starling drew a shuddering, fearful breath, and the doe slipped from her shoulders. The air smelled wrong.

Twelve tried not to look.

With the scratch of talons on wood, a crow landed next to them. Its black eyes watched Starling slyly as it shuffled on the fence, its beak razor-sharp and smeared with red. The girl's eyes flicked from the bloodstained bird to the eerily quiet village, and back again.

"No!" she whispered, shaking her head. With a cry of terror, she began to run, arms and legs pumping, already knowing she was too late.

The fish-hook tug in Twelve's chest wiped the world away again, and when it re-formed she was standing in Poa at the edge of a deep pit on the village green. Starling was six feet below her, digging mechanically, fresh earth clotted around the great hole like blood. Sweat and mud mingled on the girl's face, but she never broke her rhythm to wipe it away, even when it ran into her hollow eyes.

The houses stood empty and silent, their roofs black with greedy crows, prickly with arrows. The girl's gasped breaths tore the quiet, the slice of her shovel and the soft thwack of flung earth the only sounds as the sun dropped below the horizon.

Icy-cold dread fingered its way up Twelve's spine and she turned away, sickened and faint, her heart hammering in her chest. She didn't want to see any more, not of this. Everywhere she looked, there were the same dark arrows resting triumphant in the hush they had wrought.

Starling climbed from the pit and fetched a wheelbarrow. Twelve squeezed her eyes shut.

Tug.

Nighttime on the green. With a cry of relief, Twelve saw the grave was filled in, the awful crows gone. A small fire burned on the grass in front of her and Starling was silhouetted there, cross-legged, in front of it. Her spine was very straight and, apart from the rise and fall of her chest, she didn't move. Silence cloaked the place like a shroud.

Twelve took a slow, deep breath, trying to quell her nausea as memories broke over her in a drowning wave.

The girl by the fire shook as she picked up her father's axes with trembling fingers. A sob tore from her throat, then a scream—a raw, visceral sound, more animal than human.

*In the space between heartbeats, the world around her was suddenly ablaze. Every house, every tree, the fields, even the grass roared with inexplicable flames.*

*In the center of the inferno, untouched, sat Starling, still screaming.*

# CHAPTER
# FOURTEEN

"Twelve . . . TWELVE!"

"Wake UP!"

Twelve sucked in a breath like a person half drowned, and snapped open her eyes. Slowly, the screaming receded and the world swam into focus.

She was sitting bolt upright, her blankets twisted around her ankles like ropes. Five, Six, and Dog were crouched in front of her, their faces variously pale and shocked. Widge was clawing one side of her face and the other side stung like she'd been slapped. Her breath was shuddering and tears spilled over her lashes. Emotions ricocheted through her seemingly at random, churning her guts and muddying her thoughts. But one quickly engulfed the others: humiliation.

"What are you all staring at?" she gasped. She'd been hoping for defiance, but what came out was a rasping squeak.

Dog nudged her gently with his nose. In unison, Five's and Six's expressions slid from fear into pity. The humiliation shifted and gathered into a roaring flood of fury. Five only just managed to dodge her fist.

"What the . . . ?" he yelped, picking himself up and jumping farther back. "What in Ember is *actually* wrong with you?"

There was a familiar sensation coursing through Twelve's veins, one she'd thought the dream milk would prevent her ever feeling again: trapped panic, a butterfly in a killing jar hopelessly trying to escape. Her limbs felt shaky, her mouth was dry, and her heart pounded. Worse than that, worse even than the dreams, was the thought of someone knowing about them and feeling sorry for her. Anything but that.

"It's all right, Twelve," Six said gently, his pale brow furrowed with concern. Summoning up her strength, she swung at him too. He was ready for her and dodged nimbly out of reach, but his infuriating expression remained. "I understand," he said, "I really do. I used to use dream milk too. The first night off it is the most difficult. Five thinks so as well."

"Hey!" Five yelped. "Shut up! *Obviously*, that's private!"

Six winced.

Twelve's breathing was finally starting to feel easier and her heart was beating at a normal rate. She managed to wrestle her face into what she hoped was an expression of revulsion.

"Are we supposed to bond over that or something?" she said, her voice colder than the snow beneath her fingers. "I'm not interested in your sob stories."

Six's face dropped. The look of disgust Five gave her would have shamed most people, but Twelve jutted her chin at him defiantly. He sloped back to his oilskins and began packing up. Six was harder to read: a series of emotions, too quick to identify, flashed across his features and were gone again.

"Well," he said eventually, his expression neutral, "sun's coming up. We should get moving."

Widge was licking the salt from her cheeks. If they'd been alone, she would have buried her face in the familiar warmth of his fur, but she settled for stroking him instead, the repetitive action slowly bringing her back to herself.

Dog's shadow loomed over her. "You are not the first huntling to be haunted by their past. I have known many over the years. I am here if you want to talk."

The anger, simmering just under the surface, flared

hot again. "Why would I want to confide in a stone dog who doesn't sleep and doesn't even know what pain or fear are?" Her voice was a whiplash.

Dog regarded her steadily until she looked away. "I never said I felt no fear," he said quietly.

"Anyway, it's hardly a competition," Five muttered, shooting her another glare and turning back to saddle Charger. Six's lips formed a thin white line.

Twelve fumbled her oilskins into her bag, trying not to feel guilt, trying not to feel anything. Widge licked her cheek again, his worried eyes on her face.

"It's all right," she lied, patting him gently. His was the only attention she could bear.

The group that assembled a few minutes later was pale from lack of sleep, silent and grim. No one met Twelve's eye, not even Dog as she climbed onto his back. Without a single word being exchanged, the group set off, following the goblin trail as the sun rose beside them.

Try as she might, Twelve couldn't keep herself focused. Her thoughts kept drifting back to the dream. The details of her parents' faces were clearer and sharper in her mind than they'd been in two years. And then there was Poppy. There was a pain in her chest that throbbed when she thought of her little sister. She remembered again the dimples in Poppy's smile, the warmth of their arms linked together. How she wished things had stayed like that between them. A metallic taste filled her mouth and she realized she'd bitten her lip too hard.

Clenching her jaw and wiping her mouth, she shook herself. This wouldn't do. This was exactly why she needed the dream milk, to stop her moping like this. If a goblin had attacked in the last few minutes, it would have decapitated her before she'd even realized it was there. Then she'd never find Seven. With difficulty, she forced her attention back to the sled tracks.

The landscape around them was changing and the trail was leading them ever higher. They were above the tree line now and in every direction the jagged vista was blindingly white. The peaks were much closer and twisted fingers of ice and rock beckoned to the blazing sky. Despite a bright morning sun, it was bitingly cold. Frost crystals hung about them in the air, glittering like diamonds. Above Twelve's eyebrows the fur of her hat was frozen solid and there were frost flakes on her eyelashes, haloing the edges of her vision into a rainbowed blur. Even with her muffler pulled tight, each breath tingled unpleasantly, and, on the rare occasion she opened her mouth to speak, the freezing air made her teeth ache. Widge returned to her furs, only his head poking out of her bearskin to take in their surroundings.

It was more beautiful than anything she'd ever seen: a raw, brutal, unforgiving sort of beauty, and one that seemed to be tolerating their presence for now. Twelve wasn't fooled though; she knew the mountains were mercurial. She checked the sky and sniffed the wind every few minutes, searching for a sign of change in the weather, forcing herself to concentrate.

*Constant vigilance.*

The thought of Victory made Twelve sit taller. The weaponsmaster would never allow herself to be distracted like this.

Behind her, the boys were talking quietly, their words indistinguishable. Their snagglefeet matched each other's strides perfectly so the boys could lean in to speak. Twelve scowled—they were probably talking about her. She turned to glare at them, but something else caught her eye in the distance. It was difficult to see clearly—the ice in the air caused a kind of haze farther away—but in the glittering mist, just for an instant, something shifted. Furrowing her brow, she stared harder.

"What's up, Twelve?" Six asked, urging Surefoot closer to Dog. His pale features were fixed on her face, his expression concerned, but underneath was a kind of eagerness that Twelve instinctively flinched from.

"Nothing," she said, glaring. "But if you think there's something to see, you should look yourself. I'm not the only one with eyes here."

For an infuriating moment, Twelve was sure she saw a

flash of amusement on Six's face. How did he stay upbeat even when she snarled at him? She shook her head, determined not to acknowledge the flicker of warmth she felt toward him.

Dog had turned around and was staring unblinkingly into the distance. "I see no enemy," he said eventually. "But we must all be on our guard." Under his breath, Twelve distinctly heard him mutter, "They must have *some* skill among them."

"Well," Five said, his eyes flinty, "thank the frost we have Twelve on it. If her eyes are anywhere near as sharp as her tongue, or as quick as her fists . . ."

Six groaned. "Can we focus on what's important here? We're going to have to fight together, probably sooner rather than later. We should be building bridges, not burning the few we have."

Five shrugged.

"Whatever," Twelve said. "I'm here to rescue Pop—" She cut herself off just in time, shocked. What was wrong with her? "I'm here to rescue Seven, not make friends."

"Obviously," snarled Five, his cheeks flushing pink. "You're unbelievable—no wonder everyone hates you so much."

The venom in his voice caught Twelve by surprise and her throat tightened. Not trusting herself to speak, she kept her back to him and her eyes firmly on the tracks. A muscle in her neck spasmed painfully from how stiffly she was holding herself, but she ignored it. On her shoulder, Widge licked her cheek and squeaked softly.

Six muttered something to Five, but Five didn't bother to lower his voice in response.

"No, it's not!" he cried, indignation threaded through every syllable. "She's just embarrassed because we saw her crying and she's acting like it's *our* fault. It's so obvious and so pathetic. I'm not going to put up with it just because she's forgotten her stupid dream milk."

Twelve's fingers twitched toward her axes.

"Enough," Dog yelped, coming to a standstill, his hackles rising. "A flock of glintwings took most of my ear. Yet I preferred their company to yours." Five and Six glanced at one another ruefully as Dog went on. "If your words are not useful, then remain silent."

With that, he turned and bounded along the trail, snatches of furious mutterings audible. "Slower than snails . . . attention span of a snarrow . . ."

Twelve might have grown irritated by it if Five hadn't discovered the goblin camp.

# CHAPTER
# FIFTEEN

T hey were still in the realm of the peaks when Five spotted tracks ahead veering to the left. Twelve was almost impressed, despite herself. She had thought *her* eyes were sharp. Following the trail, they came quickly to the goblins' camp. A mass of footprints spread over the whole area. There were no trees or rocks to provide cover, and Twelve shivered at the thought of how cold a night Seven must have spent up here. The remains of a fire were still smoking gently and she hurried straight to it, her eyes scouring the prints for signs of Seven as she went. Widge scrambled out of her furs to stare around too, nose twitching at the new smells.

"Nice sheltered spot they chose," Five said, leaping off Charger lightly.

"Is sarcasm useful?" Twelve mused out loud. "I don't think so." She was stirring through the fragments left in the fire and tugged off her glove to feel the heat coming off them. "An example of a useful contribution would be something like: 'These ashes are still warm, so they must have a maximum four-hour head start on us.'"

Twin spots of color appeared on Five's cheeks. "Finding the camp was a pretty useful contribution."

Widge flicked his tail dismissively. Twelve began to say something back, but glanced at Dog and remained silent, focusing on the ground instead.

"I make it eight goblins," Five said a few minutes later.

He looked at Six but Twelve answered. "Same here but—" She broke off and scanned the ground, fear growing in her. "I don't see any sign of Seven."

"Over here," Six said. He was crouched a little way off, his fists clenched. "What does this look like to you?"

The others crowded around to peer at the marks in the snow.

Five hissed out a breath through his teeth. "Looks like someone was wriggling around in the snow. Maybe they were tied so they couldn't get up. Maybe they were trying to make a snowsprite. They've got the wings totally wrong though."

Five's attempt at lightness fell flat. The snow was tinged red. Perhaps Seven hadn't even survived the night.

As if reading her thoughts, Dog spoke. "She has value. They would not let her perish."

"Maybe she gave them what they wanted," Five said doubtfully.

"Which would be what?" Twelve asked, frustration bubbling.

Six stood up, looking sick. "If she was dead, surely they'd leave her? Why carry a corpse?"

Widge shivered, made himself small on her shoulder.

The sight of Seven's blood filled Twelve with a creeping dread. She imagined her lying here, freezing while they'd been warm by their campfire. Last night she'd thought of the other girl and hoped she was all right. Obviously, she hadn't been. Unbidden, Seven's face formed in her mind: the same dimples as Poppy, the same smile she couldn't ignore.

Twelve stood up abruptly and paced the rest of the site, scouring the ground for clues they'd missed. Her heart pulsed with fear; there had to be *something* that would tell them Seven's fate.

Goblins had tramped everywhere, their footprints crisscrossing one another around the fire. Twelve stiffened as she spotted the eight deeper impressions around the embers. The goblins had slept in the warmth, leaving Seven to freeze. Just as she was about to give up, she spotted a trail of larger, shallow prints heading back toward the sled marks.

"Here!" she called, her voice high-pitched with relief. Widge wriggled with delight and Six was by her side in an instant.

"Yes," he said, his face splitting into a huge grin. "That's her. Definitely human and her size. You've got sharp eyes, Twelve!"

The compliment warmed her more than she'd expected, and she almost smiled back. Why did he have to be friendly? It just made everything more difficult.

"Let's make sure they don't get farther away from us," he called, his voice high with excitement as he hurried back to Surefoot and leaped into the saddle.

A minute later, they were away again.

The shock of seeing the blood and the subsequent relief at finding Seven's footprints helped Twelve focus properly on their mission. She was more determined than ever to find the girl.

Farther on, the trail led them lower again, the gradient so steep they had to zigzag. Down and down they went, the mountainsides closing around them like a trap. At the bottom, the way was so narrow that their path fell into shadow and the sky became little more than a blue ribbon, winding high above them like a weird, inverted river. The slopes here were more like cliffs, so sheer no snow rested on them. They gleamed blackly in the dim light, giving off vicious waves of cold.

Widge burrowed back into Twelve's furs when ice crystals began to form on his ears, something he hated.

"I do *not* like this one bit," Five said eventually, his voice echoing off the exposed rock.

"Really?" Twelve asked. "The rest of us are having a wonderful time."

"Useful words only!" Dog growled back warningly at them.

Twelve clenched her jaw and scowled into the gloom. Her skin was crawling. This place gave her a very bad feeling. Widge was clearly uncomfortable too, shifting and wriggling beneath her bearskin until she prodded him to stop.

"Do you smell that?" Six asked a minute later, crinkling his nose.

Twelve sniffed and nodded in agreement. A foul odor was wafting on the air.

"Ugh, smells worse than ogre," Five grimaced.

"Worse than you," Twelve said, unable to resist.

"Twelve!" Dog growled, but his voice had dropped low and the group drew to a halt.

On both sides, the cliffs were drawing closer, the ground before them narrowing like a wedge. Twelve squinted ahead, wondering if she should get the moonstone out of her pocket. Longingly, she glanced over her shoulder to where the light filtered down more plentifully. She flinched. Silhouetted unmistakably against the sunlit snow was a figure. Twelve blinked and it was gone. Goose bumps broke out along her arms and the hairs on the back of her neck rose.

"Uh, this could *clearly* be a trap," Five whispered. "We should go back and find another way around."

Twelve cleared her throat uncomfortably. "That might not be a good idea," she said carefully. The others turned to her quizzically. "I'm almost certain there's something following us."

The boys' heads whipped around in unison.

"I don't see anything," Six said uncertainly. "What was it? What did it look like?"

"Humanoid," Twelve said apologetically. "But definitely not human. And tall, so not a goblin."

"Pfft, not much to go on," Six sighed.

"We are deep into the Fangs. That could describe many things," Dog agreed.

Silence fell as each of them mentally ran through lists of dark creatures and tried not to give in to panic.

"I suppose we're all hoping it isn't another Grim," Five said lightly, his voice belying his sudden pallor.

Six winced and Twelve's stomach dropped. An image of Silver, dead and frozen, slipped across her vision.

"And when you say you're 'almost certain' . . . ?" Five added. He was very pale, his brown eyes wide in the gloom.

"Very certain," Twelve corrected herself. "On the mountaintop earlier, it was too far away to be sure. Just now it was clear, only for an instant, but there's definitely something there. Also . . ." She broke off, suddenly feeling like an idiot. She should have mentioned this before. "Also, I think there might have been something around our campsite last night. It wasn't Widge I saw."

Inside her furs, Widge chirped his agreement.

Everyone looked at Dog. He let out a low growl. "It is possible."

Five's shoulders slumped. "Great. So something's stalking us?"

"It seems likely," Dog admitted.

Six licked his lips and glanced behind them again. "We're really stuck between a Grim and a glimmer, then," he muttered.

"Well, we can't just stand here," Twelve snapped, sounding angrier than she'd meant to. "We have to keep going. Either way, I suspect we'll meet something we'd rather avoid. At least if we move forward we're still on Seven's trail."

"Agreed," Six said resolutely. He squared his shoulders. "And there's no guarantee there'll be another way around anyway. We'd risk losing the trail altogether if we go back."

Even through her fear, Twelve felt another flicker

of irritation. There he was agreeing with her again. She wished he would behave more like Five: it would make it much easier to dislike him.

She pushed the thought aside as Dog turned toward the narrow gorge. Unwillingly, the little group moved deeper into the darkness.

# CHAPTER
# SIXTEEN

"I think I'm going to be sick," Five groaned, pulling his muffler higher up over his nose. "Let's take our chances with whatever's behind us and pray it's less stinky."

He was only half joking. The smell had become so overpowering Twelve could feel it coating her tongue, sliding down her throat like a slug. She tensed against a rush of bile. Behind her, Six retched quietly and, inside her furs, Widge shuddered.

As the stench grew, the light diminished. Far above their heads the cliffs leaned lovingly toward one another, blotting out the sky. The gorge was now more of a cavelike tunnel and it was setting Twelve's teeth on edge. She took the moonstone out of her pocket.

Their faces were strange in the silver-blue light, all

smooth-bone whiteness and shadowed hollows. The cold was a physical thing, beating at them, crawling under cuffs and up sleeves. Snow cracked beneath Dog's paws and their mufflers dripped with icicles.

Six pulled an arrow out of his quiver and dragged it lightly across the gleaming black rock. A thick, gelatinous substance trailed off it and he groaned in disgust, flicking it away.

"Not ogres, then," Twelve said darkly, catching his eye.

"No," he gulped. "The smell, the darkness, the slime. It's got to be cliffcrawlers."

"Maybe we'll get lucky and it'll just be one or two of them," Five said. But his forced jollity only made him seem more scared.

Six kept his mouth tightly shut. Unconsciously, the group moved closer together.

Twelve was racking her brains, trying to recall everything she could about cliffcrawlers. Then, in a moment of inspiration, she remembered that she'd packed *A Magical Bestiary*. Eagerly, she rummaged through her bag and pulled out the heavy tome.

"You brought a *book*?" Five gaped. "What in Ember are you going to do with that? Throw it at a goblin?"

Twelve shot him a withering glare and flipped to the pages on cliffcrawlers. There were some vivid sketches she tried hard to ignore, focusing instead on the summary at the bottom of the page. She read fast and out loud, all too aware there was another unknown creature behind them.

"*Cliffcrawlers are relatively common creatures. They usually reside underground, making them a particular problem for the cave clan or those venturing through cave systems. However, there are documented instances of them being found elsewhere and any dark nook from which a foul smell emanates should be treated with caution. . . .*"

Five snickered. Dog cut him off with a low, warning growl and Twelve continued:

"*The creature itself is little more than a mouth containing innumerable fangs, and a tail carried on four squat legs. Commonly, they live in large groups—a surprising number of these creatures can pack themselves into a limited space. The bog clan village of Newt famously reported a hundred and fifty crawlers in one small cupboard.*"

Twelve cleared her throat and swallowed, glancing at the space before them. The darkness snatched at the moonstone-light and gave every impression of not being small. Five stopped laughing, looked a little pale.

She read on: "*This author advises avoiding all contact with cliffcrawlers where possible. They are foul, filthy creatures. However, if it is inevitable, remember that cliffcrawlers are sightless. Their forked tongues 'smell' the air and are incredibly accurate when detecting blood, but relatively insensitive to anything else. The simplest solution to maintaining the upper hand is stealth and ensuring no drop of blood is spilled. They are strongly repelled by fire and in a tight spot this can be used as a deterrent.*

*"Aggression: eight out of ten. Danger posed: eight out of ten. Difficulty to disable: nine out of ten (assuming an average-sized congregation of two thousand individuals)."*

"An *average* of two thousand?" said Six. "Did you misread that, or . . . ?"

"No," said Twelve. "It's what it says."

"Right," Five said slowly, eyeing the ever-narrowing space before them. "So, do we think this is an average-sized congregation, or . . . ?"

"Bigger," Six said firmly, nodding at the oozing walls. "Look how much slime there is."

Beneath Five, as though sensing his discomfort, Charger snorted and tried to shimmy away toward the light. Five pulled him up with a scowl. His hands were shaking, but his voice was light when he next spoke. "You know, being eaten alive by cliffcrawlers has *really* never appealed to me. Not before I've passed my Blooding anyway."

"Well, we'd better avoid getting bitten, then," Twelve said, tucking the book back into her bag and shaking her head. There'd been one picture in particular she wished she hadn't seen.

"Great idea," Five said, rolling his eyes. "And how do you propose we achieve that?"

For a moment, the three huntlings and Dog all stared into space, thinking.

Twelve's eyebrows shot up and she plunged her hand into the very bottom of her bag, triumphantly pulling out the wooden box she'd taken from the armory.

Five gave an amusingly high-pitched squeak when he saw it. Widge poked his head above her collar to see what was happening, made a remarkably similar sound and vanished.

"That is *not* what I think it is?" Six gaped, backing Surefoot away.

Dog craned his head around to see and yelped in shock.

"I think," said Twelve, weighing the box, "that it's *exactly* what you think it is."

# CHAPTER
# SEVENTEEN

"*Firesprites?*" said Five.

"Firesprites," Twelve confirmed, ignoring their reactions and feeling quite pleased with herself. "I brought them for emergencies."

"Them being here *is* an emergency!" Five exclaimed. "Are you mad?"

"I agree with the boy," Dog said, disbelief written over his face. "To the firesprite, destruction is . . . play!"

Twelve frowned. "They can't be that bad or they wouldn't be in the lodge."

"They are that bad," Five snapped, "and, if you studied your history, you'd know the debate about keeping them inside the walls lasted years."

"Although," Six said slowly, catching Twelve's eye, "they *can* be controlled if you hold your nerve."

For the second infuriating time that day, Twelve found herself wanting to smile at him.

Five stared, aghast. "You can't be—"

"But they *can*," Six insisted. "You must remember the demonstration Elder Hoarfrost gave us. It was before you arrived, Twelve."

"What I remember is how many Hunters and buckets of water were on standby," Five said, staring darkly at the box in Twelve's hand. "And that Hoarfrost was wearing full battle armor. Which it *obviously* turned out that he needed."

"We're wasting time," Twelve said, glancing behind them again. "Does anyone have a better idea?"

Silence.

"Then we're doing this. Six, give me your dagger."

From within Twelve's furs came a squirrel-yowl of despair.

Six's confused expression only grew more pronounced when Twelve leaped off Dog and stabbed his blade into the frozen ground. Then, before she could change her mind, or be talked out of it, Twelve flipped the catch and opened the lid of the box. The others shrank back instantly.

Three tiny figures whirled up and out, their brightness increasing until darts of flame fell from their fluttering wings. Fire glowed under their skin and they glared around with sharp-featured faces, their tiny fists clenched, noses wrinkled in disgust at the smell.

Twelve resisted the urge to pull back as her cheeks began to burn in their heat. If she showed any weakness now, she was done for—and probably the others as well.

"My name is Twelve," she said to them. She had read that courtesy was vital when dealing with sprites and that flattery rarely went amiss either. Though she wasn't sure how she would know if it was working. But she plowed on. "And it's me that has brought you out of the lodge, because only you can help us. A student has been kidnapped and we're the rescue party. She's in mortal danger."

The sprites let their fiery gaze wander over the others and began to laugh. There was something cruel in the sound that made Twelve's skin crawl. Pressed against her heart, Widge shivered.

She spoke quickly. "We've come this far, but now we've hit a problem. We know how exceptionally talented you are at controlling fire. . . ."

Behind her Dog snorted, but the sprites seemed to inflate before her eyes, puffing their chests out and chattering excitedly to one another.

". . . And we can't go any farther without your assistance."

The sprites flew closer to her, all in a line, their heads

tilted at the same angle. The effect was disconcerting. Twelve tried to ignore how the icicles were melting off her hat.

"Be careful," Six whispered. "They're too close to you."

As if Twelve hadn't noticed that herself when it was *her* eyebrows that were being singed. The urge to roll her eyes was almost overpowering. Instead, she explained the situation quickly, and what she wanted the firesprites to do, then showed them the knife in the ground. They glanced at it, back at her, and then retreated into a huddle to chitter at one another.

Twelve was pretty sure this was a bad sign. Usually, sprites did something or they didn't; they rarely talked about it.

Six waggled his eyebrows at her hopefully, but Five moved Charger even farther away, muttering darkly to himself.

One of the sprites detached himself from the group and flew back to her as the others watched.

"Why can't you light the fire yourself?" His voice was painfully high but clear as a crystal bell.

Twelve's jaw dropped. Five nearly fell off Charger and Six gaped. Even Dog looked surprised.

"You . . . can talk?" Twelve asked. "To me, I mean?"

The sprite didn't respond, but stared at her expectantly, one eyebrow raised.

"I have an *extremely* bad feeling about this," Five hissed from behind her.

"You have a bad feeling about everything," Twelve said, trying to order her thoughts. The sprite wasn't making it any easier by flying closer and closer to her. His eyes were burning embers that seemed to look straight through her.

"We can't make fire quickly enough," Twelve said, twisting her head to keep an eye on him as he circled slowly around her face until he was level with her ear. To her amazement, the sprite crossed his legs to land seated where Widge usually perched. He rested his chin in his hand and considered her as the other two flew to join him, trailing sparks.

"Uh . . . Twelve, are you all right?" Six muttered. "Your shoulder's smoking."

"Yes, fine," Twelve said, her voice slightly more high-pitched than normal. She could feel Widge vibrating with fear and outrage.

"Fire is the work of a moment," the first sprite chimed at her.

"For you maybe," Twelve said, "not for us. Why do you think we need you in the Hunting Lodge and out here with us? *No one* makes fire as fast as a firesprite."

The three of them looked at one another and began to laugh again.

"Twelve . . . ," Dog said, a warning in his voice.

With a single swipe, Twelve brushed the three of them off her shoulder and ducked the retaliatory fireballs they threw at her. Their faces became more pointed in their anger and their teeth visibly lengthened.

"Enough," she snapped, her patience at an end. Being nice to sprites obviously didn't work. She pointed imperiously at the knife handle in the ice, shooting her most threatening glare at them. "Show me what you can do."

To her immeasurable relief, they actually obeyed. Almost lazily, they flew over and unleashed white columns of fire onto the dagger, their hands vanishing in the flames, their wings shooting sparks into the ice around them. The blade of the dagger glowed red-hot and the handle crumbled to ash.

The ringleader smirked at her and she released a breath that she hadn't even realized she was holding.

"Good," she said. "Thank you. Could you do that again if we need you in there?" Twelve pointed to the darkness before them.

"The shadows with teeth," he said, his voice like glass breaking. "They fear us like that boy does." He gestured dismissively at Five. "We can destroy them."

Twelve frowned. "I'm sure you can, but *will* you?"

The sprite eyed her with interest. "Clever girl," he said slyly. There was something wolflike in his smile.

"Sharpspark, Brightfire, and Burnfoot at your service. We will defend you when you ask it of us." He swept her a low, mocking bow. Warm air rolled off him, smelling of hunger and destruction.

Twelve nodded, not trusting herself to speak. To her discomfort, the sprites settled on her shoulders again, looking vastly pleased with themselves.

Widge popped his head out of her collar, saw they were still there, and disappeared again with an alarmed squeal.

"Sorry, Widge," Twelve whispered. She jumped back onto Dog and cleared her throat, trying to look nonchalant. "Happy?" she asked, turning to the others.

Five scowled at her. "Emphatically not."

Six grinned and rolled his eyes. "Come on, Five, this is brilliant. Three firesprites have just agreed to protect us! Look at what they did to my favorite knife. . . ." He trailed off, gazing at it sadly for a moment before brightening. "Well, at least they're up to the task. And they can talk! Who knew that?"

"I have heard of rare instances," Dog said, twisting to give Twelve an odd look. "There are specific—"

"Look, can we just crack on?" Five snapped, his voice tense. "We're either going to be torn to shreds by cliff-crawlers or incinerated by firesprites. I can't *wait* to find out which."

"Oh, I disagree," said Twelve.

"Well, I'm glad someone's confident," said Five, a bit less sarcastically.

"No, it's just that there are loads more ways we could die," said Twelve. "We might be caught by whatever's behind us, for example."

"Or murdered by goblins," Six grinned.

Five sighed. "Right, whatever. Can we just go?" His manner was annoyed, but Twelve could see his hands were shaking harder now, one on Charger's reins and the other on the pommel of his sword.

"Let's go," Twelve agreed.

Together, they moved forward, into the narrowing canyon.

# CHAPTER
# EIGHTEEN

"Be careful, everyone," Six said, serious again as they stepped slowly forward. "In the words of our weapons-master: constant vigilance."

"Of course," Twelve said, holding the moonstone up again. Then to Five: "Just make sure you keep Charger under control—you two are the weak links here."

Five made a sound like a kettle boiling over, but Twelve and Dog were already walking away, the firesprites warming her ears with their glow.

She was grateful for their warmth the farther they went. The cold became more powerful and the darkness seemed to push back against the moonstone, its sphere of light shrinking around them. Beyond that, the black was absolute. But Twelve knew they weren't alone. She could feel it in the way her skin crawled and in the soft rustling that seemed to be all around them at once. She fixed her eyes on the tracks ahead—Seven had come this way and every step brought them closer to her. The thought focused Twelve, but fear still buzzed under her skin.

Dog's voice was barely audible when he next spoke. "Quickly. Quietly."

"Agreed," Twelve murmured, signaling to the boys behind.

Charger caught her eye again and her stomach knotted. He was rolling his eyes and tossing his horned head. With a spurt of speed, he ran into Surefoot's rump, terrified of being left behind. Five was struggling to control him. Surefoot tossed her head, but was too well trained to fully express her annoyance. The little group proceeded silently with the walls pressing ever closer.

"It may become too narrow for the snagglefeet," Dog breathed, voicing Twelve's concern. Already, if she stretched out her arms, she could touch both sides at once.

"All we can do is keep going and hope it's all right," she whispered.

On her shoulders, the firesprites shifted and Twelve only just managed not to flinch. Their heat was burning through her furs and acrid smoke plumed behind her. She relaxed a little as they rose off her, flying higher and pointing. What Twelve saw made her gasp. Just above the reach of the moonstone-light, the walls were dense with cliffcrawlers. They slithered over each other with the occasional flash of claws, but it was their mouths that filled Twelve with fear. Every now and then, one of them would pause and spread its jaws wide, much wider than should have been possible for a relatively small creature. From the splayed maw, a bright red tongue flickered, tasting the air. In each mouth, there were an awful lot of teeth.

Widge, who had poked his head up as soon as the sprites left, gave a tiny mewl of terror.

"It's all right," Twelve breathed, scratching his cheek to soothe him. "They can't see us."

*They can only hear, and smell blood.*

Behind her, Charger snorted loudly and Five muffled a yelp. The rustling above fell silent. Eyes wide, Twelve turned to look back, and what she saw chilled her to the core.

Charger was trying to bolt. He plowed into Surefoot again, desperate to barge past her, but there wasn't room. Five was hauling on the reins, but Charger tossed his head and slammed Five's legs into the wall, trying to unseat him. Five's face was sheened with sweat, but nothing he did calmed his snagglefoot.

Twelve saw what was going to happen an instant before it did. Charger threw back his head and bellowed his terror into the darkness. Above her, the rustling redoubled.

The cliffcrawlers knew there was something there, but they weren't sure where. They seethed downward, jaws snapping hopefully.

In an instant, Twelve had her axes in both hands, adrenaline pumping through her. Behind her, Six held his bow and arrow poised and ready. Five wasn't so lucky: he needed both hands just to stay on Charger. Twelve watched with mounting dread, her throat seemingly sealed shut. A cliffcrawler dropped off the wall and landed on Charger's neck. Its jaws snapped once and chaos broke out.

"He's been bitten!" Five yelled, the snagglefoot's blood spattered on his pale cheek.

A terrible chill swept through Twelve. Above them, the cliffcrawlers' forked tongues flicked in and out frantically, tasting the air, working out where their prey was. Then they began to drop, mouths gaping wide.

# CHAPTER
# NINETEEN

Five abandoned his attempts to control Charger. He ripped his sword from its sheath and swung furiously at the black shapes dropping around him. The cliffcrawlers hissed and shrieked, but another managed to land on Charger and take a second deep bite.

The scent of blood mingled with the crawler stench.

The walls above were a surging mass of teeth, and two crawlers landed on Dog's neck. Twelve hacked them apart and turned back to the boys. She could barely see Five through a maelstrom of whirling black. Six was firing arrows indiscriminately and Charger was bellowing. Even Surefoot was starting to panic.

*Do something.*

Dog growled furiously beneath her. "I cannot turn

around! Too narrow!" He tried nonetheless, and Twelve swallowed a cry as he half crushed her leg against the slimy rock.

Five screamed and his sword clattered to the icy ground.

In an instant, Six was off Surefoot's back. He scooped up the weapon and carved a path through the scrum of crawlers without hesitation. "The sprites, Twelve!" he yelled over his shoulder.

Through Twelve's pain, her brain clicked into gear. The firesprites were directly above her, flame billowing strongly off their wings. To her disgust, she saw they were laughing again.

"Don't just hover there!" she screamed, swinging a furious axe at them. "Protect Five and Six!"

The laughter stopped abruptly and the ringleader, Sharpspark, narrowed his eyes. Before she could react, he had flung a fireball at her, almost hitting Widge.

"TWELVE!" Six screamed.

The fire burned through her furs and blistered her arm, hurting so much she nearly dropped her axes. The pain, coupled with the threat to her squirrel, added to her rage. She felt on a precipice, fury and desperation propelling her toward a dark edge. There was a pressure building inside her, white-hot and screaming to get out. The feeling tore through her until she was burning beneath her furs and her fingertips throbbed with it. Her vision was red with the sprites' smirking faces above her. She lunged for Sharpspark and a shower of molten-gold sparks appeared in the air between them, engulfing him entirely. When they died back, he looked dazed.

Widge's tail lashed triumphantly.

"Protect them!" Twelve roared, the heat of her anger juddering and twisting inside her to get out.

Sharpspark stared back at her for an instant, then gestured to his companions. Together they flew to Five and Six, diving into the fray. The effect was immediate. The sprites cast a protective dome of sparks over the two huntlings. It fizzled on the crawler slime and the creatures flinched back from the heat, circling beyond it, trying unsuccessfully to find another route to the boys.

Twelve's heart dropped when she saw them. Charger was dead and Five was bleeding freely from a wound on his cheek. He seemed barely conscious, leaning heavily on his friend. Six's face was as pale as dough, Five's sword still clutched in his hand, black with crawler slime.

Twelve scrambled off Dog and squeezed past Surefoot to help. The ice was slippery with Charger's blood, but somehow they managed to hoist Five up onto Surefoot's back. He slumped dangerously to one side and would have fallen straight off if Six hadn't leaped up behind to support him. Twelve kept glancing at the sprites, her trust in them gone, but they seemed to be obeying her for now.

The crawlers seethed outside the defensive cage of sparks, desperate to get to their meal.

"Hurry up," Dog cried, his frustration at being unable to help obvious. "We must leave!"

"No argument from me," Six called, his voice shaky. "Will the sprites stay with us though? Five's bleeding a lot. The crawlers will smell him for sure."

"They'll stay," Twelve promised darkly, her eyes meeting the ringleader's. He nodded once and the sprites flew closer around them, drawing the shawl of fire tighter. Stomach-churning sounds reached them as Charger was left outside the circle of protection. Twelve was glad she couldn't see through the bright curtain.

Dog surged forward. Surefoot and the sprites kept pace and together they raced between the narrow walls, the crawler stench growing stronger, the gnawed bones of past victims cracking beneath them. Twelve thought of Charger's fate and shuddered. Five would have been dead too if it wasn't for Six. She was furious at herself for her slow reaction. Victory would have been horrified—she'd frozen, allowed the attack to take her by surprise, just like in the dungeons. It couldn't happen again.

Twelve set her jaw. She'd never *let* it happen again.

# CHAPTER
# TWENTY

The darkness seemed to stretch on forever. Twelve lost track of how long they rode for, but finally, high above their heads, the first chink of daylight appeared between the leaning cliffs. Slowly, the walls peeled apart until the blue sky stretched clear above them, its brightness a shock after the horrors they'd faced.

But panic drove them on. They didn't slow until a bright expanse of snow spread all around them. Only here, bathed in glorious daylight with the gorge far behind them, did they feel safe enough to finally halt.

The sprites had long ago ceased their protection and now they darted overhead, throwing fireballs at one another. Twelve's eyes narrowed at their carefree manner. Her breathing was ragged, her heart still pounding, great gouts of breath steaming in front of her. Widge was digging his claws into her skin where he was hiding, pressed against her, but she barely felt it. Behind her, Six and Surefoot were in the same state, but Five was terrifyingly still, his head lolling back against Six's shoulder.

Twelve leaped off Dog's back and they both hurried over to the boys. Her squashed leg hurt, her arm was agony, and her fingers felt burnt, but together they managed to lower Five from Surefoot's back. He half slithered, half fell to the ground.

Dog peered down at him, tension humming through him. "By the stone, that should not have happened," he said. "You are only huntlings." He turned abruptly and paced away, his lips drawn back in a silent snarl.

"He's alive," Six said, his voice juddering as he struggled to catch his breath. "That's the main thing."

Together, Twelve and Six laid Five on his back, checking him for other wounds.

"I think it's just his face," Twelve gulped, her nerves jangling at the deep, ragged wound over his cheekbone. Six swallowed hard.

"If blood bothers you, stand back a bit," Twelve said. It wasn't meant unkindly, but her voice came out rough.

Six glanced sharply at her. "I'm fine," he said, staying where he was. "Or at least I should be. I've seen enough of it in my life." He shook his head angrily.

Twelve nodded briefly. "It's different when it belongs to someone you care about. Do you have anything we could clean his face with? Did you bring woundwort? I . . . I think I forgot." Color flooded her cheeks. Woundwort was one of the first things she should have packed. How many times had she heard Hunters declaring they owed their life to it?

Six winced. "I didn't bring any." He rummaged through Five's bag and shook his head. "None in here either and we don't have anything clean. I'm wearing all my clothes."

Twelve groaned. "Me too."

In the end, they cut strips off their middle layer of tunics—which they hoped were the cleanest—and bound Five's cheek tightly.

"Do you think he'll be all right?" Six asked, his eyes wide as he looked between Twelve and Dog.

Twelve winced, thinking of the pictures in *A Magical Bestiary*. "Their bite is poisonous," she said carefully. "Sometimes it's . . . serious." Dog looked like he wanted to add something, but thought better of it. He resumed his pacing.

Six ducked his head, but Twelve saw his expression.

"He'd be dead if it wasn't for you," she said hesitantly.

"He'd do the same for me," Six said, his eyes overbright. Something in her gaze must have shown her doubt. Six shook his head emphatically. "You don't know him like I do."

There was such certainty in his expression that Twelve felt a tingle of doubt run through her. She thought she *did* know Five, and what she knew she happily loathed. For the first time, it occurred to her that she might only see one side of him, and that she could be as much to blame for that as him. She nodded slowly. "We should make a stretcher for him," she said finally, standing up. "Dog or Surefoot can drag it and it'll be easier than you holding him; that must have been hard back there."

"What in Ember are you implying?" Five groaned, shifting painfully and opening one eye. "There's not an ounce of fat on me!"

Twelve's heart leaped.

"Five!" Six yelped. "Are you all right?" He knelt next to him.

"I've been better." Five winced, trying to get up and falling back again. Six batted his hand away as he reached to touch his cheek.

"You were bitten," Six explained quickly. "Best not touch it."

Five's face paled even further. For his sake, Twelve hoped he hadn't seen the images in her book.

"Is it bad?" Five asked.

Twelve, Six, and Dog didn't even need to look at one another. They all shook their heads forcibly.

"B-barely a scratch," Twelve said, her tongue stumbling over the lie.

"The bandages were more of a precaution," Six added.

The effect was not what they'd desired.

"By the frost," Five groaned, closing his eyes again. "So half my face is gone."

Twelve shifted and caught Six's worried eye.

"It's my admirers I feel sorry for," Five said, sighing theatrically. "I mean, *clearly*, it's my sharp wit and sparkling intellect that they're interested in . . . but my ravishing good looks never hurt."

Twelve couldn't help it—a bubble of desperate laughter burst out of her.

"Things must be really bad if Twelve is *actually* laughing," Five went on gloomily. There was a sparkle in his eye though.

"Think of the tale you'll have to go with the scar," Six grinned, nudging him.

Five nodded with faux modesty. "You make an excellent point." He winced and closed his eyes again, his face losing more of its color. "It does hurt though," he muttered, almost too quietly for them to hear.

Overhead, the firesprites shrieked with laughter, the sound pulling Twelve away. A dull throb of anger pulsed through her. She stomped from the others, yelling for the

sprites to come to her. To her surprise, they obeyed immediately, swooping in front of her face, their wings a hot
blur.

"What happened?" she demanded, crossing her arms
and scowling at Sharpspark. Everything seemed confused
now, her memory no more than a jumble of conflicting
images. There had been rage, a burst of fire, but where had
it come from?

*Just like in Poa.*

Twelve shook the thought away and refocused on
Sharpspark.

"We saved you," he said, his eyes challenging. Flames
licked across his hands.

"Barely," Twelve growled. Out of the corner of her
eye she could see Dog watching them, his snarl revealing
daggerlike teeth.

Fire-darts flew from Sharpspark's wings and a sly
smile flashed across his face. "Our agreement was for your
protection, not theirs. It is you who changed the terms, not
us."

A low hiss escaped from Twelve's lips. "You tricked me."

"No," the sprite said, "we took you at your word. Why
would we agree to protect *them*?" He gestured at the others contemptuously, sparks flying from his fingers.

"Well, why did you agree to protect me?" Twelve cried.
She had the strong sense that Dog had been right. The

sprites were devious, dangerous—she'd been a fool to put her trust in them.

Sharpspark regarded her coolly and she had the wooden box out and open before he deigned to reply.

"You are different from them," he said finally. "There's fire in you."

Twelve snorted and held the box out, but Sharpspark shook his head and backed away with the others.

"No," he said, "not like that. We will serve you—but on our own terms." With that, the trio sped away, their fire dimmed in the bright daylight. As soon as they were gone, Widge emerged from Twelve's furs, chattering furiously after them. It would have made Twelve smile if she wasn't so angry.

She clenched her trembling fingers and swallowed the urge to scream as Dog appeared beside her.

"What happened in the gorge?" he asked, watching the firesprites vanish into the distance through narrowed eyes.

Twelve shrugged. Her hand throbbed painfully again and when she glanced down she saw the fingers of her gloves were singed. Unease whispered through her. "Are you all right?" she asked Dog. "You haven't stopped pacing."

He shook his head. "I thought bringing you was safer than leaving you," he growled. "Grave misjudgment."

Twelve scuffed her boot in the snow. "We would have

followed the trail with or without you," she said eventually. "What happened back there wasn't your fault. Don't feel bad."

"Feel bad?" Dog yowled, making Twelve jump. "I feel furious! You should have listened. The Hunters should have listened. Tracking is not my strength. Protecting huntlings is not my strength. Fighting is the thing I'm good at. Fighting under command. When I make my own decisions, it always . . . I always . . ."

Twelve was startled by the anguish in his voice and grasped blindly for the right words. Suddenly she longed for Silver. The Elder had always known what to say to make someone feel better. Tentatively, Twelve reached out and put her hand on Dog's shoulder. "It wasn't your fault," she said again. She turned, quickly walking back to the others, hoping she hadn't made things worse.

They'd stopped for long enough and every moment carried Seven farther away. The girl's dimpled smile flicked into Twelve's mind and she pushed down a wave of fear for her. She reminded herself that the tracks had continued through the gorge and out the other side. There was no reason to think Seven hadn't passed through unscathed, but the fear didn't abate.

"Can you ride Surefoot with Six?" she asked Five. Her voice came out harsher than intended.

"Definitely, since the only other option is riding Dog

with you." He scowled at her. "I *told* you the firesprites were a bad idea. You can't trust them."

Their high-pitched laughter at Five's plight came back to her and she knew he was right. She nodded slowly. "They're still the reason we're standing here though. Without them, we'd have been shredded."

"I agree," Six said, helping Five to his feet. "And without you they never would have helped us at all. You have a way with them."

Five snorted. "No friends, but the firesprites like her. Why doesn't that surprise me? And what happened to her hair?"

Twelve blinked and raised a hand to her head. A hank of hair fell away at her touch. "Widge!" she groaned. The squirrel curled his tail around himself, ducking his head in shame. "He chews it sometimes when he's scared." Twelve sighed, dropping the hair onto the ground.

"*Brilliant* taste in pets too," Five muttered.

Six rolled his eyes as he helped his friend into the saddle. "Ignore him, Twelve."

"I always do."

He caught her eye and grinned. Twelve felt the traitorous corners of her mouth twitch in response and turned away quickly.

"We must move on," Dog said, rejoining the group. "Whatever follows us may also survive that place."

"And Seven is only getting farther away," Twelve added, checking her axes and climbing up onto his back.

"So, what are the chances that we catch the goblins without meeting anything else nasty?" Five asked.

"Zero," Dog said bluntly. "They are moving fast. We will reach the Frozen Forest soon."

Twelve nearly fell off Dog's back and Widge was almost thrown off her. *What?*

"The Frozen Forest?" Six said, urging Surefoot alongside him.

Dog nodded. "You are Unblooded so you will not yet know this. All paths north lead to the forest. There is no way around it. Even witches cannot avoid it on foot."

"Wonderful," Five said. "Just wonderful."

Six's face was pale but resolute. "Well, we knew there'd be danger when we decided to leave the lodge. No point crying over it now."

"Yes," Five grimaced, "except I don't *actually* remember deciding to leave. You did, and I followed like an idiot."

Six winced at this and opened his mouth to reply.

"No, no. Don't." Five cut him off. "I'm sorry, all right? My face really hurts, I'm frozen, and I think we're probably all going to die out here. But I shouldn't have said that."

Twelve saw Six's fingers tighten on Five's shoulder. She looked away, something akin to loneliness echoing through her.

"Come on," she said gruffly. "Let's go. Seven needs us."

The group sped along the trail through a landscape that opened around them like a lily. All the hard edges were smoothed away and snow lay in great sparkling mounds, as soft as sugar. The sun melted the ice from the air until Twelve almost felt warm. Nothing moved behind them and she prayed whatever she had seen had met a sticky end. If there was any advantage to the cliffcrawlers, it was that they were unfussy eaters.

As the sun began to scythe a downward path, the tracks dived over a steep escarpment and zigzagged down to the flats far below. The little group gathered at the edge of the drop and took in the view in silence. A pale, tangled forest stretched to the horizon in every direction, its frostbitten canopy gleaming in the late afternoon light.

No one spoke. Twelve swallowed a lurch of fear and excitement as her eyes drank in the sight.

The Frozen Forest—a place of monsters and legends, where Hunters earned their names or died trying.

And somewhere in there was Seven.

# CHAPTER
# TWENTY-ONE

The journey down the ridge took several nerve-racking hours: the slope was horrifyingly steep and icy. No relief met them at the bottom though; the Frozen Forest waited with a glare, its trees cloaked in twilight shadow.

Twelve was certain Widge had chewed off some more of her hair, but she couldn't find it in herself to be cross with him; this place was terrifying. She had tried to be matter-of-fact; she'd told herself over and over on the journey down that a forest was just a collection of trees, nothing more. But there was something in the air here that stuck in the back of her throat. Up close, the trees looked strange—taller than normal, their shadows a little darker, frost-rimed branches bare and as sharp as claws.

The group hung back, pressing themselves longingly

against the slope they'd just descended.

"So, here it is in all its dubious glory," Five croaked. His skin had taken on a gray cast and his eyes seemed to have sunk into his skull. He looked awful. "Not feeling too great," he admitted, catching Twelve's look and shrugging it off.

"You'll feel better after a rest," she said quickly. She glanced between him and the forest, biting her lip. He couldn't have looked less ready to enter the most dangerous place in Ember. To her surprise, she found that it bothered her, that she was actually worried about him.

Six came to stand beside her, seeming to read her mind. "If we stop now, we're saying Seven has to spend another night in danger," he whispered. "But . . ." He looked back at Five, leaning heavily against Surefoot, his expression agonized.

Twelve frowned up at the sky. The sun was on a downward dive and the forest's shadows crept menacingly toward them. Every instinct screamed that it would be madness to brave the forest in the dark, especially with Five in such a state. But to leave Seven with the goblins for another night? Everything in her railed against it—they should have found her by now.

Dog looked equally torn until a thump made them all turn. Five's knees had given way and he was sprawled in the snow, looking faintly surprised.

"You know," he said, struggling into a seated position and waving Six away, "I'm *really* starting to think you've all told some fibs about this cliffcrawler bite."

Twelve and Dog stared at one another while Six became very interested in a patch of snow by his boot.

Five sighed impatiently. "Twelve, brutal honesty is practically a hobby of yours. How bad is it?"

There were times when hearing the truth was helpful and times when it wasn't.

"It's deep but clean," she lied, offering him a strip of dried meat from her bag. "You lost a lot of blood and need to keep your strength up." That part at least was true.

Something flickered across Five's features: fear.

"You trying to be nice is actually scarier than the forest," he said tonelessly, swiping the meat from her hand and stuffing it into his mouth. Every bite sent a shudder of pain through him.

Twelve watched him with a sinking heart. "I think we should stay here tonight," she said unwillingly to Six and Dog. "We can go into the forest at first light, give Five time to gather his strength." It took a moment, but eventually they nodded in agreement. Part of Twelve wished they hadn't, that they'd insisted the group press on.

Surefoot and Dog began digging a cave into the packed snow of the slope, as far from the tree line as they could get. The Guardian muttered to himself as he worked. "Bossed around . . . low point . . . never in centuries . . ."

"You know we can hear you when you do that?" Twelve asked, mildly offended.

Dog coughed, looking embarrassed. "Oh." The muttering stopped.

When the work was finished, Surefoot was settled at the back of the dugout with a nosebag. Five, Six, and Twelve laid their oilskins in front of her and leaned back against her steaming side, trying to get warm. Dog stayed outside, pacing, his eyes scanning the forest and slope. A fire was out of the question: burning forest wood was said to have unpleasant consequences and none of them wanted to risk it.

Five fell asleep almost immediately and Twelve felt something akin to jealousy prickle her. The dread of her dreams was back in full force—there was no rest for her, not even in sleep.

Six was chewing mechanically beside her, staring out at the forest as the first stars appeared above it.

"Worried about the dream milk thing?" he asked, without looking at her. There was a studied indifference in his voice that should have annoyed Twelve, but she was too tired to react. Instead of giving him a piece of her mind, she shrugged.

"Do you think Seven'll be all right tonight?" she countered, nodding toward the forest.

Six considered her, his chewing paused. "I didn't know that you two were close," he said eventually.

"I could say the same about you," Twelve responded.

Six nodded slowly. "Fair point," he said. Then, "What do you think about Five?"

Twelve winced. "Cliffcrawler venom is powerful," she whispered. "I think he'll get a lot worse before he gets better."

"If he gets better at all," Six said unsteadily, voicing what they both feared.

"We need to keep him eating and drinking," Twelve hurried on, aware of a sudden humming tension in Six. "We won't let him fade away."

"I don't need much to keep me going," Six whispered. "He can have my rations."

"And mine," Twelve agreed quickly.

"Thank you," Six whispered, reaching out to squeeze her arm. "I'm glad you're here."

A rush of emotion flooded Twelve, stealing her breath and prickling her eyes. It had been two years since anyone had said anything like that to her. She hesitated, then whispered, "I'm glad you're here too."

It was so dark that they couldn't see each other's smile.

Twelve stared at the stars outside as Six's breathing deepened. Widge snuggled into her neck, chirruping softly, and she reached up to stroke him. She hoped they were wrong about Five. She hoped they would find Seven unharmed, and that the Frozen Forest's reputation had been vastly exaggerated.

When had she started hoping for so much?

Twelve hadn't realized she'd fallen asleep until a voice filtered through the gloom.

*"Starling!" A whisper. And then: "Shh, don't wake your sister."*

*"Da?" A voice in the shifting dark.*

*Twelve looked around, confusion sharpening into a fear that made her muscles tense and her heart pound.*

*"It's all right, just me! I want to show you something though. It won't take long."*

*"All right, Da, I'm coming." A stifled yawn.*

*Twelve stood blinking in the darkness, willing her eyes to adjust, although she knew this room like the back of her hand. Two narrow beds swam into view, both with a small bedside table holding an unlit candle. Between the beds lay a lovingly plaited rug, its familiar bright colors muted in the gloom. From one bed Starling rose and in the other Poppy slept on, her cloud of dark hair fanned across the pillow.*

*Twelve couldn't resist moving closer, savoring each moment of the deep rhythmic breathing.*

*Poppy.*

*Her bright, curious, infuriating little sister, Poppy.*

# CHAPTER
# TWENTY-TWO

*T*he smell of her own home almost made Twelve cry out with longing: sweet dried grass, beeswax, the lavender-scented soap her ma made to trade. She wanted to stay here forever, listening to her little sister sleep, but the fish-hook tug in her gut forced her to follow Starling down the stairs. She trailed after her, running her fingers along the smooth plaited-grass walls. Her very earliest memory was of her parents building this house.

In the living room, dying embers in the fireplace revealed another bright rug, this one unmistakably from the desert clan and her ma's pride and joy. Very occasionally, the caravans ventured away from the Scour to trade, bringing the bright dyes and desert glass that her ma and Poppy adored. Around the rug, several beautifully carved chairs were angled toward the grate. The smell of beeswax polish was strong, needling at Twelve, trying to draw out the thousand little memories tied to it, but she resisted. Instead, she shadowed Starling as the girl opened the lacquered front door and slipped outside.

"Da? Where are you?"

"Over here," he whispered from the side of the house.

Twelve paused to drink in the familiar outline of Poa. Candles burned in windows and animals shifted in their stalls. The village might be slumbering, but it was undoubtedly alive. Her heart swooped and soared, the joy and despair dizzying.

Her da was sitting on the big log, head bowed over his two axes as he rubbed a nutty oil into the gleaming hafts.

"What are we doing up so late, Da?" Starling asked, plonking herself on the log beside him. Twelve hung back, feeling awkward and resentful, unable to take her eyes off them.

"Waiting for a shooting star," he said mysteriously, waggling his eyebrows at her.

Starling did not look amused. She gazed up at the clear, star-filled sky with a scowl and pointed a moment later. "There's one!"

Her da snorted and rolled his eyes. "Not just any old shooting star, a special one."

Starling pulled her knees up to her chest and wrapped her arms around them, her expression skeptical.

"This one appears every fifteen years," her da explained, "and it's supposed to be lucky for those who see it."

"Oh!" Starling looked more interested now. "How will we know which one it is though? They all look the same."

"Your ma says this one is unmistakable," he grinned. "She saw it as a girl and the next day she met me, thus proving its luckiness!"

Starling laughed and threw her head back to stare at the sky unblinkingly.

"Doesn't she want to see it again?" she asked as her eyes began to stream.

"You think she could get luckier than meeting me?" her da exclaimed in mock outrage. "Impossible! No, this is just for us."

"Not Poppy?" Starling asked, glancing at her da out of the corner of her eye. Spending time with him alone was a precious rarity.

"She's still little," he said. "We'll let her rest."

"Just me, then," Starling grinned, unable to keep the triumph from her voice.

The smile faded slightly from her da's face as he gazed at her, frown lines appearing between his brows.

"Yes, just you," he said. "Your ma suggested this might be a good opportunity for us to talk."

"Talk about what?" Starling asked breezily. There was a new tension in her posture though. Her eyes, still upturned, no longer scanned the sky.

"The way you've been treating Poppy recently," her da said carefully.

Starling scowled and kicked her legs away impatiently, folding her arms across her chest. "She's annoying. Always following me, pestering me, copying me . . . !"

"You used to not mind that," her da replied, his scowl mirroring Starling's exactly. "She looks up to you. She's your little sister, your family—you should treat her with respect."

Starling made an undignified snorting sound. It was the wrong response—her da's gaze hardened.

"You should be a little kinder and more forgiving of the faults in others," he snapped, "since you're hardly perfect yourself . . ."

He broke off at the look of shock that passed over Starling's face.

"I . . . I'm sorry, I didn't mean that. You're my daughter and I love you unconditionally, but I love Poppy the same way and it pains me to see you make her so unhappy. She's more sensitive than you. . . ." He broke off again, searching for the right words. "I want to see you making more of an effort with her from now on. No more mean comments, no more jokes at her expense. I want you to spend time with her. Be the kind of older sister you'd like to have yourself."

Starling was frowning openly and mutinously, but her da ignored her.

"Your eleventh birthday is coming up. I'm spoiling the surprise, but I don't think you'll mind; we got you a hunting bow."

Starling's frown vanished into an excited squeak of delight. Her da smothered a grin.

"Yes, it's a real beauty," he said proudly. "Traded for it at the floating market and the bartering went on for over an hour. Worth it though. Beautiful egret-feather arrow flights—you'll love it."

"Egret feathers," Starling breathed. "From the bog clan."

"Yes," he grinned. "Sure you wouldn't have preferred king-fisher from the river folk? Eagle from the mountains? There were some cave clan traders there too. . . ."

A shiver of delighted horror ran through her and Starling threw her arms around his neck. "No," she said, her voice muffled. "Egret is perfect."

"Your first deerstalk would normally be when you're older," he went on, "but your ma and I have decided to let you go early. You have the skills, and it's safe enough still in these parts, thankfully."

Starling's jaw dropped wide open in amazement.

"There is one condition," her da said, holding her at arm's length until he'd finished. "Take Poppy with you."

The effect of his words was immediate. The joy and excitement faded from Starling's face to be replaced by a sullen glare. "But Poppy's useless at hunting," she said moodily. "She'll ruin everything."

Her da took a deep breath to control his impatience. "This

*is exactly what I'm talking about, Starling. Poppy isn't 'use-less'—she's just younger than you. And she's as good a tracker as you were at her age."*

*Starling sniffed at this.*

*"With you helping her, she'll learn faster and maybe you'll even enjoy teaching her. What do you say?"*

*Starling shrugged. "So, I can't go without her?"*

*Her da sighed. "No, you can't."*

*"Well then, I'll have to take her, I suppose," Starling said grudgingly, flopping back onto the log next to him.*

*Her da shook his head slowly, his disappointment obvious. "Think about the person you want to be, Starling."*

"Twelve! TWELVE! WAKE UP!"

She gasped. Her eyes opened.

*Think about the person you want to be.*

Dog and Six were crowding around her, their faces too close in the dark. Widge was patting her cheek with an insistent paw.

"By the frost," Six snapped, his green eyes wide, "you're hard to rouse."

"What is it?" Twelve said, relieved to find no tears on her cheeks, despite the ache in her chest.

"The forest," Dog growled, his bulk looming into the snow cave. "It has moved."

Twelve blinked uncertainly and Dog stepped back. Immediately behind him was a tree where before there had been open snow.

With a gasp, Twelve crawled out, limbs stiff from the cold, and struggled to her feet. For a moment, she was unable to speak. The slope was still there behind them, but now it was densely forested.

Tired of waiting, the forest had come for them.

# CHAPTER
# TWENTY-THREE

Twelve turned on the spot, heart pounding.

*Impossible.*

"What happened?" she gasped.

"I do not know," Dog said. "A moment ago, the moon was high. Now it is almost dawn." A low growl sounded from him. "By the stone, I hate this place and its magic."

Twelve gulped and Widge squeaked his agreement. The stifling sensation of the previous night was back again, even stronger; the air was catching in her throat, crushing her lungs. The sun hadn't risen yet, but predawn light splintered strangely off the ground, causing a sort of haze. Some of the trees shimmered at the edge of her vision, only solidifying when she looked straight at them. Others seemed to vanish, only appearing when she looked away.

Where she could see them clearly, the trunks were knot-ted and twisted, their growth gigantic and torturous. The ground was clotted with thorns and vines and everything gleamed with a steely frost.

Then there was the noise: a low, constant sound that was impossible to ignore. It was almost like whispering, except no matter how hard she strained she could hear no words. There were none of the sounds usually associated with a forest. No birds flew; no squirrels scampered; no breath of wind disturbed the frost-rimed branches high above them. But Twelve felt they were being watched nonetheless; a chilly, implacable attention pressed around them.

"You *obviously* fell asleep," Five's voice accused Dog.

"He doesn't sleep," Twelve snapped, feeling her nerves fray.

She turned back to the others and was brought up short by the sight of Five being dragged querulously out of the snow cave by Six. His skin was like parchment and black circles encompassed both eyes. His hands were shak-ing, and he didn't seem able to move his legs at all. Six didn't look much better himself, his eyes wide with shock, whether from Five's appearance or the forest's Twelve couldn't say.

"The tracks are still here at least," Six whispered, pointing to the ground. "That's something."

Dog nodded. "We must move fast. Nothing good comes of lingering in this forest."

"Careful!" Twelve hissed as Dog stepped back. There was a plant just behind him that had begun waving its fronds though there was no breeze. Its leaves were lush, untouched by the frost that coated everything else. "Strangler vine," Twelve pointed out, remembering it from class.

Dog leaped away as more tendrils quested toward him.

They moved on as quickly as they could, but first had to tie Five onto Surefoot's saddle. He was far too weak to hold himself upright unaided and Six needed both hands free for his bow and arrow.

"Outrageous," Five muttered, a slight slur in his voice. "Trussed up like a prisoner."

"Stop using all your energy talking." Six tightened the final rope and leaped up lightly behind him. He dug a slightly shriveled apple out of his pocket and cut a slice off with Five's sword. "Here, eat this."

"Can't," Five scowled. "Hurts."

Widge's nose twitched hopefully toward the fruit until Twelve handed him a few nuts.

"Talking must hurt too so just eat instead," she said to Five. The look he shot her was venomous, but he raised the apple to his lips and took a painful nibble. Behind him, Six nodded gratefully at her.

Twelve felt a little better once they were moving, but the ache in her chest was hard to ignore. Another dream of her family. Would it be like this every night? She forced herself to concentrate on the things she could actually see, trying to peer through the haze to discover what lay before them. She was here to find Seven, she reminded herself firmly. That, at least, was something she had control over, something she could succeed in. Her eyes followed the tracks in the snow and her heart lifted slightly.

In the shifting mists behind them, something moved. Widge stiffened on her shoulder.

"Did you see that?" she muttered to Dog, not wanting to alarm the others.

"No," Dog whispered back. "The haze makes it hard. We could be surrounded and not know."

Hardly reassuring. Twelve huffed out a breath and peered into the distance, but everything was still. She sensed rather than saw the sun rising above the trees. The quality of the light around them subtly changed, but the gloom never shifted and no ray of sunlight pierced the tightly woven branches overhead. On instinct, Twelve took the moonstone out of her pocket and held it up.

"Hey," Six muttered disapprovingly, "we're trying to sneak thr—"

His voice trailed off abruptly as he caught sight of the tree trunk nearest him. By the moonstone-light, the many

knots and whorls in the wood were still visible but shifted and altered. The features were craggy and the mouth barely a gash, but it was undeniably a face. When Twelve lowered the moonstone, it vanished.

The group froze.

"What is that?" she whispered, a slight tremor in her voice.

"I think it's the moonstone," Six whispered, nodding at the glowing gem. "It's flawless, remember, so its light shows things that are normally hidden."

Dog nodded, looking around. "Much is hidden in this place," he growled. "Hold the stone up high. Better that we see everything."

He was right. Almost always the moonstone revealed details of their surroundings that they hadn't seen before, some of them quite deadly. One innocuous-looking shrub was revealed to have wicked red thorns by moonstone-light, a sure sign of poison. Surefoot had been about to barge right through it.

They wound between twisted boughs, keeping their eyes open for the sinister strangler vines and anything else that moved, but all was deathly quiet. The goblin tracks sliced through the snow, deep and easy to follow, and the group moved swiftly, eager to be out of the forest as soon as possible.

Constantly, the feeling of being watched tugged at

Twelve. Her eyes probed every shadow, every low-hanging branch, every swirl of the shifting mist. The others evidently felt the same thing.

"Might be all those faces in the trees," Six whispered, grimacing at a particularly unpleasant one.

"Could be," said Twelve. Widge glanced up at her, doubtful.

"Did you see that?" Five asked a while later, making them all jump. His voice was almost unrecognizable, thick and garbled. He raised his arm unsteadily to indicate a dense stand of trees. He giggled and then noticed the ropes that bound him. "Why'm I tied up?" he slurred. "Lemme go!" He tugged at the ropes, jerking Surefoot's head in the process. She snorted uneasily and slowed, uncertain how to interpret the mixed signals from her back.

The cold drew closer around them and frost sparkled in Twelve's condensed breath.

"It's only so you don't fall off, Five," she said over her shoulder. She glanced at him and flinched. The whites of his eyes had darkened. Black pits stared back at her, devoid of recognition. The hairs at the nape of Twelve's neck stood up.

"Who're you?" he growled, his fingers creeping toward his sword. "Where're you taking me?"

"Six," Twelve said warningly. "*Six*," she cried again, too late. Five snatched the blade from its sheath and jabbed it behind him. Six managed to throw himself back just in time, then tried to wrestle the sword from Five.

Surefoot bellowed her dismay, the sound heart-stoppingly loud in the silent forest. A strangler vine wormed across the ground to wrap around one of her paws and the brave beast panicked. With another great bellow, she ripped herself free of the vine and bolted, Five and Six still struggling in the saddle, and disappeared into the depths of the forest.

Dog surged after them and the movement took Twelve by surprise. She fell heavily to the ground, twisting to avoid crushing Widge.

"I'm fine!" she cried as Dog half turned to her. "Make sure Five and Six are all right. I'll be here when you get back."

He hesitated. Then he nodded, once, and was gone.

# CHAPTER
# TWENTY-FOUR

Silence closed around Twelve like shackles. Widge pressed himself against her cheek, his fur a welcome patch of warmth in the relentless cold. Ice cracked underfoot as she stood and they both winced at the sound. Heart jolting, she pulled the axes off her back, immediately feeling better with them in her hands.

Through the frost-flecked air, Twelve caught a glimpse of movement between the tree trunks.

"That was fast," she called, relieved. "Everyone all right?"
Silence.

Widge scampered to the ground toward the movement, then froze, one paw raised, bushy tail stiff as he stared into the gnarled trees.

Slowly, Twelve realized all the hairs along her arms were prickling with goose bumps. Then Widge shrieked—a high, sharp alarm call she'd never heard before. He turned and fled back to her shoulder, where he shrieked again and again, his gaze fixed on the trees ahead. She could feel him trembling even through all her layers.

Twelve's heart began to pound, and she tried desperately to focus through her dread. Silver wouldn't panic, she berated herself, and Victory wouldn't either. That knowledge sharpened her mind and Twelve turned slowly on the spot, forcing her gaze into every bush, every shadow, every shifting haze. Her senses were on high alert and adrenaline fizzed through her veins.

*There.*

Twelve spun to face the movement, but it was already gone. Cursing softly, she resumed her slow, steady turn, Widge acting as eyes behind her, his tail brushing her cheek. Everything was silent; even the ice under her feet didn't make a sound. A sheen of sweat broke out over her forehead and she clenched her jaw, fighting down her rising fear.

Another movement. Almost too quick to see. A shape flitting between trunks.

The outline shifted again, its movements slower and easier to follow now. Twelve scowled into the mist, adjusting her sweaty grip on the axes. With slow, deep breaths, she steadied her heartbeat as the shape moved closer to her, appearing only for an instant between trees.

"Starling?" *A whisper.*

Twelve's breath juddered and the axes slipped in her hands. She scrabbled to hold on to them.

"Starling!" *Insistent.*

From between two twisted trunks, a silhouette emerged, moving hesitantly at first, then with more confidence, coming closer until Twelve could finally see it clearly.

Slight build. Gray eyes. A cloud of dark hair.

Shock froze Twelve to the spot and her lips moved soundlessly.

Standing in front of her was her little sister, Poppy.

# CHAPTER
# TWENTY-FIVE

A distant part of Twelve knew that she should move, speak, anything. But she couldn't. She just stared, fragments of thoughts whirling uselessly around her head, a strange pressure building in the front of her skull.

This wasn't possible. She had buried Poppy. Buried her with everyone else. Yet here she stood, her dark hair floating around her face, eyes mischievous, her expression heartbreakingly wary but hopeful.

"Are you all right?" Poppy asked, tilting her head slightly. The voice was so familiar it hit Twelve like a slap.

"I . . ." Twelve shook her head. Words refused to come.

Poppy's small shoulders slumped.

"Why don't you talk to me anymore, Starling? I . . . I've missed you." Poppy scuffed the snow with her toe, shoving her hands into the pockets of her favorite blue dress. Her lower lip wobbled dangerously.

"How are you here?" Twelve gasped. Each word and gesture from the little girl tore at her like a sword through riversilk.

"I don't know." Poppy shrugged, sniffing and looking up. "I was just at home, then there was lots of shouting, then darkness for a long time. When I woke up, I was here."

Hope, intoxicating hope, began to pulse through Twelve, flooding her limbs with a delicious warmth. No one understood the Frozen Forest; no one had even managed to map it. Impossible things happened here, so why couldn't Poppy be one of those things?

"So . . . will you play with me?" Poppy asked, her eyes wide.

Twelve nodded mutely, afraid to blink in case the vision of her sister disappeared. On her shoulder, Widge patted her cheek with his paw, trying to get her attention. She brushed him away gently.

The dimpled grin that Poppy gave her was like sunshine. With a rush of joy, Twelve saw her life open up before her. She would leave the Hunting Lodge, of course, and together she and Poppy would return to the grasslands to build a new life for themselves. Twelve's fighting skills would be useful—maybe she could hire herself out to other villages. . . .

"You're not even listening to me!" Poppy cried, stamping her foot.

"I am, I just—just can't believe it's you," Twelve stuttered. "I thought you were dead. No, I knew you were dead." Her voice broke and Widge shivered. "I *buried* you."

Poppy shifted, looking uncertain for a moment. "But I'm not," she said. "I'm right here!" She held out her hand to Twelve. "I've so much to show you. I found a veiled-fox den yesterday and there are two kits in there!"

The excitement in her voice was infectious and Twelve reached for her hand. The younger girl drew back with a yelp. "What are those?" she cried, pointing an accusing finger at Twelve's axes.

"My axes," Twelve explained, "so I can protect us."

Poppy shook her head decisively. "You can't bring them," she said. "And you don't need them anyway, not if you're with me. I know the right paths."

Twelve hesitated, then set the axes down gently in the snow. On her shoulder, Widge shrieked his alarm again and both girls winced. Twelve pushed him off her firmly. He gazed up at her, eyes wide.

"Enough, Widge," she said sternly. "This is Poppy, my sister." Words she'd never thought she'd say again. "Poppy, this is Widge."

"Come on," Poppy grinned, bouncing on the balls of her feet. "For once, I'll be the leader!"

Twelve followed willingly as the girl broke into a trot, then a flat-out run, sprinting through the undergrowth and leaping over obstacles.

"Keep up, slowworm!" Poppy called over her shoulder, her hair catching in her mouth to be brushed away impatiently.

Poppy had always been fast and Twelve rejoiced that this was still the case. Whatever hardships the girl had faced—and there must have been many—somehow, she'd survived, maybe even thrived on them. Widge was speeding behind her, squeaking madly, but Twelve couldn't risk taking her eyes off her sister.

"Keep up, Widge!" she cried, hoping he'd catch up.

Her heart was thundering in her chest and her breath was coming in great burning gasps, but still Poppy sped on, her feet barely seeming to touch the ground.

"Wait," Twelve panted. "Too fast . . . slow down . . ."

To her relief, Poppy pulled up, laughing, and waited for Twelve to reach her. She stopped thankfully, doubling over and resting her hands on her knees while she caught her breath.

They were in a small clearing, the trees woven tightly together around them, the canopy very low and dense. There was an unpleasant smell in the air, like rancid meat. Twelve wrinkled her nose.

"It stinks here," she said.

Poppy pursed her lips and said nothing, but stepped closer, her expression serious. "I think we need to talk, Starling."

Twelve blinked, her old name sending a shiver through her. Poppy didn't wait for her to respond, but plowed on, her fingers balled into determined fists.

"I've had a lot of time to think while I've been here and I want to know why you did it," she said. Her lips pressed into a line, just as their da's had when he was annoyed.

"Did what?" Twelve's heart was sinking.

"Why didn't you take me hunting like you promised?" Poppy asked. "If you had, none of this would've happened. I wouldn't have been there when the cave clan came for us. I'd have been safe, with you."

They were the same words Twelve had said to herself a thousand times, but hearing them from Poppy broke her. Her throat closed and tears stung her eyes.

"Poppy," she choked, "I'm sorry. I'm so, so sorry."

The younger girl stepped closer, seeming taller suddenly.

"Is that really good enough, Starling?" she asked softly, her eyes burning into Twelve's. "You left me there to die."

"No," Twelve gasped, sobs racking her. "I didn't know. I was so stupid. I shouldn't have left you. I wish every day that I'd stayed."

"Excuses," Poppy hissed, suddenly angry, her features

contorting. "How can you talk about being sorry when you wanted me gone all along? Admit it, you were happy when you thought I was dead!"

"No!" Twelve cried, shaking her head furiously, feeling her knees give way. "Never! I never wanted . . . AAAARRGGHH!"

Widge flew out of nowhere and landed on her shoulder, his teeth sinking deeply into her tearstained cheek. Bright, vivid pain cut across her vision and, for a confusing instant, the scene before her shimmered and changed.

It was so dark, and the smell! Twelve gagged and pulled the moonstone out of her pocket. It blazed to life, blinding her completely.

Poppy screamed and Twelve tried to shield the light so she could see. Widge was out of control though; he ran down her arm, scrabbled her furs away from her wrist, and sank his teeth into the flesh there too. With a gasp, the moonstone fell from her grip and rolled away, still blazing blue-silver light.

"Stop it!" Twelve cried, shaking Widge away. Poppy was cowering with her back to Twelve.

"Put it out!" her sister shrieked. "Put it out!"

Twelve's fingers scrabbled in the snow—or was it? She paused, confused. The texture was strange under her fingers, soft and slimy. And that awful smell again. A wave of nausea made her gag.

When she opened her eyes, it was as though a veil had been lifted. Everything was altered. She was in some sort of underground nest, tall enough to stand upright in and several yards wide. A single narrow tunnel in front of her wormed its way up through the earth. Pale roots trailed down from above and dead things covered the floor. Rib cages rose like shipwrecks from the filth and empty eye sockets stared balefully at her.

Twelve's shoulders shook as she took this in at a glance. Widge gazed up at her from the muck, his eyes wide, urgent.

"Why did you do that, Starling?" a voice whispered behind her. "We were having such a nice time. You always spoil everything."

Twelve shuddered, a tidal wave of horror breaking over her. Whatever it was standing behind her, it couldn't be her little sister. Could it? The tunnel was in front of her; she and Widge could have fled. It took all of Twelve's strength to turn around, but she had to know, some part of her brain still hoping, still trying to believe.

She turned—and recoiled in horror.

# CHAPTER
# TWENTY-SIX

A wail tore from Twelve's lips as her heart broke all over again. Standing in front of her was not Poppy but an Ygrex, the creature from Silver's room, the dream-stalker who invaded your memories, twisted them to trick you. Its spell broken, it stood before her in all its horror: taller than her by a head, horns gleaming and fangs dripping with venom.

With an enraged squeal, Widge sprang toward it, bounding onto its shoulder and sinking his teeth in deeply. The Ygrex swiped him off with barely a glance, then lunged at Twelve, its clawed fingers reaching out hungrily. She dived aside on instinct, but, as its talons raked past her and Twelve spun away again, a new emotion boiled to life inside her: rage. This monster had worn her sister like a costume, spoken with Poppy's voice and copied her gestures. And it had just tossed Widge, her best friend, to the ground. Cursing her idiocy in leaving her axes behind, Twelve swung her bag at the creature hard, catching it in the face and knocking it back into the damp wall while she scrabbled her dagger free from her belt. It was a short, curved blade but sharp enough. And it was all she had.

"Widge, are you all right?" she gasped, her eyes searching the shadows for him. Horror beat through her until she saw him behind the Ygrex, dazed but shaking himself awake.

The Ygrex snarled at her as they weighed each other up.

"Starling," it whispered in Poppy's voice. The scene shimmered before Twelve's eyes as the Ygrex tried to re-exert control, but she'd already seen through its trick. With a howl, she threw herself toward it, the blade a blur in her hand. The Ygrex surged forward to meet her and caught her wrist, halting the downward plunge of the knife. They struggled in the center of the den, the bones of the nightmare creature's previous victims cracking under their feet, its teeth snapping dangerously close to her face.

Determined to help, Widge sped forward again, springing onto the Ygrex's back to bite and scratch frantically there. It was enough to distract the creature. With a superhuman burst of strength, Twelve managed to knock the Ygrex aside so it stumbled back, tripping over the moonstone. The howl it let out when it touched the stone rang in Twelve's ears long after it had ended and, with grim satisfaction, she realized she had another weapon after all. The stone lay a few feet away, if she could just get to it.

Beside her she could feel the gentle touch of fresh air trickling down the tunnel. Just for a second, the idea of grabbing Widge and running crossed her mind, then Silver and Victory flashed through her thoughts, lending her strength. Just because she might not win this fight didn't mean she was going to hide from it. That would never happen again.

Gritting her teeth, she braced herself as the Ygrex threw itself at her again, head lowered to catch her with its horns. Widge was still clinging furiously to its back, black blood smeared across his nose. Dodging to one side, Twelve shoved the creature past her with all her strength and dived for the moonstone, rolling to her feet with it triumphantly clasped in her hand. An instant later, Widge bounded back to her shoulder, ready to help in any way he could.

The Ygrex screamed and flinched away. For a moment, Twelve thought the simple act of picking up the stone had driven it back, then she saw the arrow piercing its side. For the first time, she became aware of sounds from outside: a ululating howl that made her teeth chatter and voices.

"Twelve! We're coming! Hang on!"

Another arrow, another screech from the Ygrex, and

suddenly Dog was forcing his way into the space, the tunnel too narrow for him, his shoulders streaked with mud. And, behind him, Six with Twelve's axes in his hands.

Their wide eyes drank in the sight of her, and Twelve read both terror and relief there.

"You dropped these," Six said, somehow managing to sound casual as he tossed her the weapons. She released the dagger and moonstone and caught them. Nothing had ever felt so good. On her shoulder, Widge trilled his relief.

The Ygrex lunged for Six, and Twelve leaped forward with her axes. Dog was faster though: in a single bound, he landed on the Ygrex and had it in his jaws. Its scream tore through Twelve's mind and she flinched, covering her ears. Dog shook it like a rag doll until it was silent, then dropped it to the floor, his expression one of disgust as he gazed around.

"Filthy creatures," he growled, turning to Six and Twelve.

The terror and heartbreak caught up to Twelve in a rush and her knees began to shake so hard she had to lean on her axes to stop herself from falling.

"We must get Twelve out," Dog growled, at her side in an instant. "Climb up," he said to her gently, lowering himself into an awkward crouch to make it easier.

Later, she became aware that she was propped up against a tree trunk outside with extra furs over her, Widge pressed protectively to her throat. Dog was sitting in front of her, his face close as he peered hopefully at her. "Can you hear me?"

Twelve nodded. The effort felt enormous. Six looked up from where he was slumped nearby and the relief on his face was even greater. Through the numbness, a thought flitted into her mind as light and beautiful as a butterfly: they had come for her. She didn't know what to say, just stared at them. Her every muscle felt like it was in the process of dissolving and she doubted she could have spoken even if she'd wanted to.

She closed her eyes, just for a moment—and blackness swallowed her.

". . . find the trail again."

Twelve blinked, swimming slowly back to consciousness.

"She needs rest."

"I know that, but we have to think of Seven too. We can't let her spend another night with those *things*: we *have* to catch them."

"You know that is unlikely. We have lost too much time today. Let her rest. Five needs it too."

Groggily, Twelve opened her eyes and the horror of the Ygrex flooded back. She pushed it away, forced herself to see only what was in front of her.

"I'm awake," she said, her voice barely a croak. "And Six is right: we must keep going. For Seven."

Six looked guilty.

At the sound of her voice, Widge stirred, placing two paws on her cheek to examine her more closely.

"I'm all right, thanks to you," she whispered to him. "You were so brave." Satisfied, he gave her cheek a quick lick, then set about grooming himself.

The furs over her had done their job and Twelve felt warmed through. On the other side of the impromptu camp, Five was asleep with his back to her, his head resting on Six's pack. Surefoot was pawing through the snow to the ground beneath, looking much calmer than the last time Twelve had seen her.

Six crouched in front of her. "Are you all right?" he asked gently, his green eyes worried. "I only saw the Ygrex for a moment, but that was bad enough. You though . . . how did you . . . why did . . . ?" He broke off, looking awkward.

"It pretended to be my sister," Twelve heard herself say, though she hadn't consciously decided to speak. "Her name was Poppy and it's my fault she's dead. The Ygrex reminded me of that. As if I could forget."

All the color drained out of Six's face as he knelt in front of her. Suddenly she found her face pressed into his shoulder as he lunged to hug her. Dog moved forward, his step hesitant, then nudged Twelve gently with his nose.

Neither of them spoke and for that Twelve was grateful. There was nothing to say.

They rode back in heavy silence, following the bounding trail that Twelve had made as she rushed after the Ygrex.

But another nasty shock awaited them where they had separated. The goblin tracks had vanished, and with them any way of finding Seven.

# CHAPTER
# TWENTY-SEVEN

The group stood huddled together in shock, until Six leaped off Surefoot's back and began pushing aside the undergrowth, frantically searching for the sled tracks.

"Careful," Twelve warned, remembering the strangler vines.

Six straightened up and let out a low, humorless laugh as he gazed around. "They're really gone," he said hollowly. "Just . . . gone." A muscle was twitching in his jaw and his fists were clenched.

Exhaustion made Twelve's thoughts sluggish, but Six's anguish forced her to focus. They'd come too far and been through too much to fail now.

"We should split up, search a wider area," she suggested, trying to sound hopeful.

Dog's hackles rose and the low growl was back. "This place!" He shook his head. "We must not venture too far apart. Shout if you see anything suspicious."

Six nodded eagerly, swinging himself onto Surefoot behind Five with renewed purpose.

"Not sure how I feel about shouting in here," Twelve said darkly. In the moonstone-light, the slumbering faces in the gnarled trunks were visible again, sending a shiver through her.

"We have made a lot of noise already," Dog pointed out. "We can only hope it goes unnoticed."

They fanned out. Twelve pushed aside bushes, looked with and without the moonstone, and narrowly avoided being ensnared by a strangler vine. But the tracks had vanished completely.

"Over here!" Six's voice called distantly. Twelve was sprinting before he'd even finished his shout, her axes out and ready, her heart pounding. Had he found the tracks again? Spotted some sign of Seven? Widge clung on as she ran, squealing with surprise as Dog sprang from the undergrowth in front of them.

"I'm all right," Six called, "but there's something very strange here." He pointed up and Twelve slowed, peering into the canopy, Dog beside her.

The trees were taller here, the straight trunks unbroken by branches for most of their height. A long way above their heads, just beneath the thick dark canopy, something hung, glimmering in the low light. At first glance, it was difficult to tell what it was, but, as Twelve shifted, light slid along the filaments like water down a thread, and the image began to make sense: a spider's web, the largest she'd ever seen. It hung enormously above them, sinister and spectacular, its silk the width of a thumb and dripping with icicles.

"What could have made that?" Six breathed.

"Must be a deathspinner," Twelve said slowly, her flesh beginning to creep. At intervals across the web hung silk-wrapped packages, some as large as her. She didn't want to think about what was in them or how they'd gotten up there. Widge's tail twitched with alarm and he buried his face in her hair.

"It's way too big!" Six exclaimed. "I know death-spinners are large, but not like this—look at it!"

"Move away," Dog growled, echoing Twelve's thoughts exactly. "We do not want to meet it."

It was as they were leaving that they heard the voice.

"Help," it called weakly. "Please help me!"

It was so quiet that Twelve thought she'd imagined it, until she saw the same hesitation in Six's stride. Dog's ears pricked and Widge twisted around to gaze behind her. For a moment, the group stood frozen, listening.

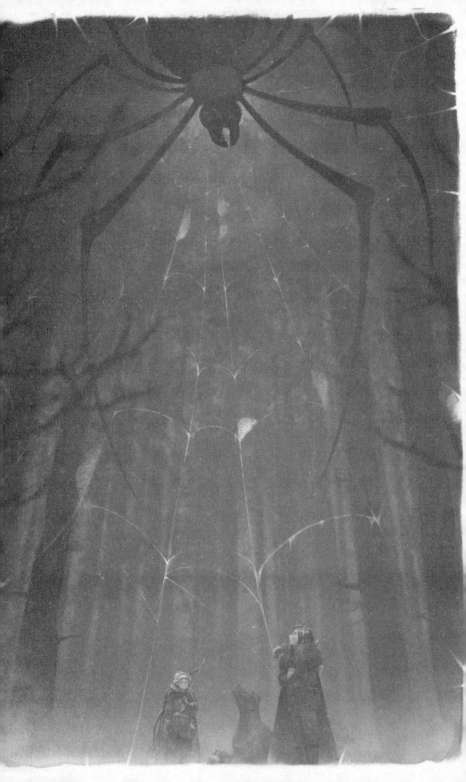

"P-please!" the voice cried again, its words muffled. "I don't want to be alive when it eats me. You have arrows—it would only take one. Surely that's not too much to ask?"

Six caught Twelve's eyes. "Could it be a trap?" he whispered.

"Of course," she hissed back, sudden terror breaking over her in a wave. Hadn't the Ygrex been enough? She pulled herself up furiously. They were in the Frozen Forest: of course there were going to be other creatures. Fear wasn't rational though. It flooded her body, screaming at her to run and not look back. Six looked the same as she felt, his face pale and a sheen of sweat on his brow.

Twelve saw one of the bound shapes wriggling furiously, sending ripples across the web.

Dog nudged them both with his nose, a growl building in his throat. "Keep moving."

"No," the creature cried. "Please! My name is Foxpaw. I—I can't get out—I've tried everything! I just . . . I just don't want to be awake when it comes back again. Please don't leave me like this! I've been here for days." A shiver rippled across the taut threads, away from his bound form.

Twelve's eyes widened. "Days? Did you see goblins come this way? And a girl with red hair?"

"No, I'm sorry."

Dog growled a warning, but Six's face had softened. "What are you?" he called.

"I'm a moxie," the muffled voice called back. "From the Winterdown set." A sob broke its voice. "They're not expecting me home until next week. The deathspinner will have eaten me by then."

Nausea rolled in Twelve's stomach. The memory of the Ygrex flying at her with teeth bared was too fresh. It would have eaten her alive too. Its poison brought death quickly, but not quickly enough. She felt her resolve harden. Almost before the thought had formed in her mind, she was swinging her bag off her shoulder and fishing out her copy of *A Magical Bestiary*.

Six knelt next to her. "What do you think?" he whispered.

Slumped on Surefoot's back, Five mumbled something incoherent, his gaze full of malice as he watched them.

"I think we need to find out what we're dealing with," Twelve replied, fingering through the pages until she came to the entry on moxies. Widge placed both paws on the page, examining the drawings with interest.

Foxpaw's muffled chatter washed over them, his terror evident as he poured entreaties down on them.

Heads bowed together, Twelve and Six read:

*Little is known of moxie habits. They are private creatures and avoid people assiduously. However, it is believed they live in extended family groups called sets with a hierarchy based on age. They are rumored to be experts in herb-lore and have a weak latent magical ability. More research is needed on these creatures.*

*Aggression: unknown.*

*Danger posed: unknown.*

*Difficulty to disable: unknown.*

"Danger posed: unknown," Six said. "What good is that?"

Widge chirped his agreement.

Twelve bit her lip and flicked instead to a hair-raising entry on deathspinners.

*There are two known species of deathspinners, the tree and trapdoor varieties. The trapdoor deathspinner resides in the south and is much feared by the forest clan of the Great Woods, while the tree-dwelling variant is found in the cold climes of the Fang Mountains. The tree-dweller is by far the larger of the two. Despite spinning a traditional web, it rarely catches enough prey to sustain itself from this source alone, therefore it also hunts on the ground. It is capable of great stealth and surprising turns of speed.*

*Adults of both variants are heavily armored, rendering most forms of attack useless. However, where the armor plates meet at joints, there seems to be a weakness that may be exploited.*

*These creatures should not be engaged directly as the chances of success are negligible. At least two teams of Hunters are recommended if contact is unavoidable.*

*Aggression: 8/10.*

*Danger posed: 9/10.*

*Difficulty to disable: 9/10.*

Twelve closed the book, and glanced around nervously.

Six cleared his throat, looking every bit as worried as Twelve felt. "I think," he said, "that we really don't want to meet one of those."

# CHAPTER
# TWENTY-EIGHT

"What are you doing?" Foxpaw cried high above them, his voice raw. "I can see you have arrows. Please just do it. Right through the heart. It would be a mercy."

Twelve exchanged another glance with Six, who was suddenly looking purposeful. She knew what he was going to suggest before the words left his lips.

"Look," he said, pointing up. "That branch is lower than the others. I could fire an arrow with a line attached over it easily."

"You want to climb up there and cut him loose," Twelve said. It wasn't a question.

"Absolutely not," Dog snapped, trying his best to herd them away from the web.

Six stood his ground and nodded. "I can't just kill him.

But we can't leave him either. '*I will never lower my weapons in the face of darkness,*' remember?"

The words of the Hunter's Pledge usually seemed pompous to Twelve, but somehow, from Six's mouth, they sounded right.

Dog half sighed, half growled. "Of course. The Pledge."

The mummified shape of Foxpaw had fallen silent above them, but Twelve could feel the prickle of his eyes upon her. He had a name, a family, and, although *A Magical Bestiary* hadn't exactly been full of information, it didn't sound like moxies were dark, dangerous creatures. Again, the Ygrex lunged through her thoughts and fear shuddered inside her, but this time it galvanized her. She could almost hear Victory's voice in her head. If she let fear stop her from doing what was right, she'd be no more than a coward.

"You fire the line, I'll climb up," she said decisively to Six. From her shoulder, Widge made a sound of despair. Dog began to pace and mutter.

"What?" Foxpaw's voice was tiny.

"We're going to try and get you down," Twelve called up to him. "Do you think the web will hold my weight?"

For a moment, there was silence, and when Foxpaw spoke again he sounded stunned. "Aren't you Hunters?"

"Huntlings only," Six called as he carefully looped and tied a fine rope through the fletching of an arrow.

"Then you're on the quest known as the Blooding?"

"No," Twelve said. "Something else."

There was a pause, then the moxie called, "The web will hold your weight, but it's sticky. You should move quickly over it."

Twelve nodded and turned back to the others.

"It should be me to climb," Six said firmly, looking up from his knotting. "You've been through enough today already."

"And you haven't?" Twelve asked, raising an eyebrow. "No, I want to do this. I think maybe I even need to."

Six nodded slowly, his gaze penetrating. "All right," he said, allowing a grin to spread cheekily across his pale features. "I suppose I can always rescue you again if you get in trouble."

A few hours ago, that would have enraged Twelve. Now she shot him the kind of superior look that Five would have been proud of. "I had it under control."

"Uh-huh," Six grinned. He nodded at Widge. "By the way, I think he's eating your hair again."

"Oh, Widge!" she said, pushing him off her. A small clump of hair fell into the snow beside him. "You have to stop doing that!" But he looked so worried that she had to forgive him straightaway.

Six took aim and fired the threaded arrow. It looped perfectly over the branch and fell back to the ground, carrying the rope with it.

Twelve checked her axes, tightened her furs, and settled Widge next to her bag on the ground. He tried to follow her, but she sent him back firmly, unwilling to endanger him on the web. He'd had more than enough excitement for one day. Slowly and steadily, hand over hand, she climbed the rope until she was able to throw an arm over the branch to haul herself up. She sat astride it, facing toward the web.

"Be cautious," Dog called. He gazed up at her, unblinking, his concern obvious.

Twelve nodded but didn't look down.

"Remember: constant vigilance," she whispered to herself. She could feel her senses sharpening and imagined Victory nodding her approval.

One of the web's anchor threads was attached to her branch where it narrowed. Gently, she shifted her weight toward it, listening for telltale creaks or cracks in the wood, but there was nothing. It held firm.

Foxpaw had fallen silent, but she heard him gasp with the others when she reached for the silk on the underside of the branch and swung down onto it. For a dizzying instant, her stomach swooped as the silk creaked under her weight. Above, she was vaguely aware of the tug sending ripples of tension across the web, but she held her concentration, gripped hard with her hands and feet, and began to climb.

By the time she reached the main web, her shoulders were screaming. She clambered onto it gratefully, climbing upward more easily now, as though it were a ladder. Foxpaw was near the center and, when she drew level with him, he wriggled frantically until his cocoon spun to face her. The silk was thickly wound but thinner around his head. Through the opacity, Twelve could see a small face with enormous golden eyes staring at her.

"Are you really going to do this?" he whispered.

"Of course," Twelve said, more impatiently than she'd meant to sound. "I haven't climbed all the way up here just to chat."

He gulped audibly as Twelve pulled her knife from her belt.

"I'm not going to hurt you," she said, trying to sound reassuring, "but I have to cut through this webbing."

Foxpaw tried to nod and a shivering vibration spread outward along the shining silks. Twelve paused and tracked the movement with her eyes as it vanished into the canopy high above. She suppressed a shiver of her own, hoping the deathspinner was nowhere nearby to feel the disturbance in its web. She set to work, cutting carefully through the sticky mass.

"Be quick!" Six called from the ground. Twelve nodded, her tongue poking out between her teeth and a frown of concentration on her brow.

She was so intent on her work that she didn't feel the first vibration quivering back toward them.

# CHAPTER
# TWENTY-NINE

Twelve was cutting through the side of the cocoon, hoping she could make an opening big enough for Foxpaw to squeeze out of. She didn't dare try to slice through the thinner webbing over his face for fear of cutting him.

"Did you feel that?" Foxpaw asked suddenly, his voice even more muffled than normal as he twisted his head in his casing, trying to see above them. "Is it coming back?" His voice was laced with panic.

Twelve paused and looked around. Below, Six, Widge, and Dog gazed up at her while Five lolled senselessly on Surefoot. There was nothing on the web with them besides the other disturbing cocoons.

"We're fine," she said, trying to sound soothing as she hacked through a particularly tough thread.

"Uh . . . Twelve?" Six called. There was something in his voice that made her heart miss a beat. "Might . . . uh . . . want to pick up the pace a bit?"

A frightened squeak sounded from next to her. Foxpaw wriggled so hard that the cocoon began to spin. The area she'd been working on rotated out of reach.

"Stop that," she hissed, glancing up fearfully.

One of her arms was hooked securely around a web silk. With the other, she pulled the cocoon back, digging her blade into the sticky white mass more firmly, trying to work faster. Slowly, Foxpaw's fingers emerged, tugging desperately at the ragged edges of the hole, trying to enlarge it.

"Don't leave me!" he begged, his golden eyes fixed on Twelve's sweating face.

"I don't intend to!" Twelve snapped, wiggling the blade furiously, cursing how sticky everything was. "Although a few minutes ago you were asking us to kill you."

"Yes, but I didn't realize then that escape was an option," he whispered. "I thought Hunters were only interested in themselves. We are taught never to approach them, let alone ask for help."

"Oh," Twelve grunted. "Well, like Six said, we're not proper Hunters yet." The web was vibrating unmistakably now. An icicle dropped with a *thwump* into the snow beneath them and an ominous rustle sounded in the canopy above.

"Hurry!" Foxpaw whispered and then yelped as Twelve nicked him with her knife.

"Sorry," she winced.

The gap was big enough now for Foxpaw to shove an arm and a shoulder out. He strained with all his might to force his way through, only to pull back, panting. "I can't— it's still too small."

Cursing, Twelve hacked violently at the edges and succeeded in extending the gap with a furious upward slash.

"Twelve!" Six called, his voice high-pitched. "It's coming!" Beside him, Widge squealed, his tail flicking frantically.

"Move, Twelve!" Dog barked at the same time.

Above her, a leg emerged from the canopy, probing for the nearest silks. It was enormous; as long as she was tall, heavily armored, and the grubby white of a maggot. An ominous clicking reached her and the web shuddered as it took the spider's weight.

Beneath her, Dog and Six began shouting in earnest, yelling for her to climb back down. Widge raced to the rope, still hanging from the branch, and began climbing. With growing dread, Twelve slashed at the cocoon while Foxpaw shivered with silent terror inside.

"Nearly there," she panted.

Foxpaw threw himself into the opening, forcing his head and one shoulder through. Twelve sheathed her knife and grabbed his hand, pulling as hard as she could until he squealed in pain.

"It's working," he gasped. "Keep pulling!"

With an unpleasant sucking noise, he suddenly tore free and would have plunged to the ground but for Twelve's hand gripping his.

"Grab the web and climb down," she cried, swinging him onto the sticky filaments.

He nodded dumbly, his golden eyes focused over her shoulder, wide with horror. The vibrations were growing stronger every second and, even without Foxpaw's expression of terror, she knew the deathspinner was very close. She looked up and immediately regretted it. The spider was monstrously large and creeping across the web toward her. Its foot-long fangs clicked with excitement. Mirrored eyes reflected her dire predicament eightfold.

With a strangled curse, Twelve tried to scramble away only to discover she was stuck fast. She had wrapped her arm so tightly around the web filament that the glue had worked its way into the furs at the crook of her elbow. She twisted and tugged, but to no avail. The spider slunk closer.

Dog and Six were frantic. Six began firing arrows that bounced harmlessly off the deathspinner's armor.

Twelve took a deep breath, tried to wrench herself out of her bearskin. Her knife belt and axe slings tangled around her and, in a moment of hopeless clarity, she realized there wasn't time to escape. The spider was almost upon her and she didn't even have her axes in her hands.

Had she really just escaped an Ygrex's illusion only to be immediately devoured by a deathspinner? There was time for a moment of outrage before the spider's fangs filled her vision.

With her free hand, she ripped one of the axes off her back and tried to remember what *A Magical Bestiary* had said. Something about joints? None of them were within reach, so she swung instead for the nearest marble-shiny eye. To her satisfaction, the axe sank into it with a horrible squelch. A thick, gelatinous substance oozed out and the spider flinched back with a shriek.

For an instant, it looked as though it was retreating, scuttling away from her across its web. Then it stopped and the clicking began again, even faster now. There was no expression in its eyes, but Twelve got the distinct impression she'd made it angry. The feeling was mutual.

She adjusted her grip on the axe and watched carefully as the spider positioned itself directly above her. Twelve leaned back as far as she could to face it, hoping the stickiness at her elbow would hold her.

This time when it flew at her, she managed to twist to one side at the last minute, using her trapped arm as a pivot to swing up and slice between the armor plates on the creature's front leg. She felt the axe connect with something soft, but instead of pulling back, the spider spun to face her again immediately. Its fangs were far too close to Twelve's face for her liking. She picked another of the thing's eyes and raised her axe to strike. There was a flash of blinding light, a pop like a soap bubble bursting, and suddenly the deathspinner was no more. Not dead, simply vanished. Twelve twisted on the web, peering in every direction, but the spider was gone.

Six was halfway up the rope to help her and Widge had reached the bottom of the web. Dog was still on the ground. All were staring around, slack-jawed, looking every bit as bemused as she felt.

"Uh . . . what happened?" she called down uncertainly. "Where'd it go?"

Foxpaw cleared his throat from the branch he was clinging to. "Sorry! That was me!"

He shrugged shyly at their collective amazement. "It was the least I could do after you risked yourself for me. Can you see it though? It should still be up there somewhere."

Twelve swallowed a yelp as she stared around wildly.

"Oh, it shouldn't be able to hurt you," Foxpaw added. "I think I shrank it. If you see it, can you bring it down? The others at home aren't going to believe me otherwise."

"You *think* you shrank it?" Six repeated.

Foxpaw shrugged, looking embarrassed, then indicated

how one of his front paws was holding on to the tree. "My magic is unpredictable at the best of times, and I need two hands free really. There are a lot of gestures involved."

Twelve stared at him. A "weak latent magical ability" *A Magical Bestiary* had said of moxies. They needed to update their information.

Twelve couldn't see the deathspinner anywhere so she set about painstakingly cutting herself free from the sticky web. She was assisted by Widge once he reached her and had licked every part of her face in ecstatic greeting. Beneath them, Six was helping Foxpaw to the ground. Even from high above, Twelve could see the moxie looked utterly exhausted. His limbs were trembling so hard he could barely stand and he alternated between apologizing and expressing wild gratitude to everyone.

When Twelve finally slipped down the rope to join them, Widge immediately leaped from her shoulder to investigate Foxpaw. For an awkward moment, she thought Six was going to hug her again, but he just grinned, the relief plain on his face. Dog looked like he couldn't decide whether to berate or praise her. He settled for a noncommittal nod, then changed his mind and butted her gently with his nose.

Foxpaw straightened up and came over to her. To Twelve's amazement, Widge was on his shoulder, chirruping happily. Her squirrel had never taken to anyone so fast before. She took a moment to examine Foxpaw properly. He was small, only as tall as her chest. His skin was tawny and his eyes molten gold, with honey-colored hair sticking up in wild tufts. He was wearing simple overalls of a deep green fabric that left his arms uncovered, but the cold didn't seem to bother him in the least. His bare feet hardly left a trace in the snow. The grin on his face was dazzling. There was something about him that inspired trust, an openness and curiosity that Twelve immediately warmed to.

"Flit won't believe this when I tell him," he beamed. "Except . . . Oh!" His grin grew even broader as he reached up to pluck something from Twelve's hair. "He'll have to now!"

Twelve's eyes grew wide as she stared at the tiny white spider in his palm. It was no bigger than her thumbnail. For once, she was speechless.

Foxpaw rummaged around in his voluminous pockets and pulled out a small desert-glass box. He slid the lid open, dropped the unwilling spider in, and returned it to his pocket with a happy sigh.

"Are you injured?" Dog asked the moxie, sniffing him inquisitively. Foxpaw seemed to see Dog for the first time and stared at him, openmouthed.

"You're the Guardian!" he spluttered, his eyes drinking in Dog's stone fur rippling in the cold wind. "What are you doing outside the lodge? Flit says the Guardian never leaves!"

"Flit is wrong," Dog said.

While Six was rummaging for some dried fruit for Five and Foxpaw, Dog explained all that had happened over the last few days. Foxpaw's golden eyes grew wider and wider as he listened avidly and chewed hungrily.

"Unbelievable!" he murmured when Dog fell silent. "Strange events in strange times. . . ." He shivered suddenly. "I can't find the trail for you, I'm afraid," he said. "But I might know someone who can, and I think I can help your friend." He nodded at Five.

"Really?" Six gasped. Twelve's heart leaped. Five wasn't even speaking anymore. Whenever Six tried to feed him, he bared his teeth.

"Yes," Foxpaw said slowly. "We call your cliffcrawlers by another name, but I'm sure they're the same thing. Their venom is powerful. It devours its victims from the inside out until there's nothing left."

His words chilled Twelve to her core. "Can you reverse it?" she asked. Widge saw her concern and bounded back to her, his familiar warmth a comfort.

Foxpaw stood up, looking determined as Five growled at him. "There's only one way to find out."

# CHAPTER
# THIRTY

Foxpaw returned a short while later, wrestling with a length of strangler vine.

"It used to be hard to find," he panted as Twelve helped unwind it from around his waist. "Now it's everywhere."

"Strangler vine is going to help?" Six asked doubtfully. While Foxpaw was gone, they'd pulled Five off Surefoot with difficulty. He now sat on a fur, hands still bound, hissing at anyone who came too close.

"I hope so," Foxpaw said, pulling a bowl from his pocket and stripping the twitching fronds into it. "The magic in its leaves can be a powerful antidote if prepared correctly." He took an amber stone from another pocket and began to pound the leaves into a paste, adding woundwort and a few drops of a fragrant oil as he worked.

Moxies were healers too? Twelve stared at his crouched form, fascinated. How was it that the Hunters knew so little of these creatures?

"I think I'll need your help," he said to her a minute later, eyeing Five's bared teeth apprehensively.

Together, Twelve and Six tried to pin Five's arms. He thrashed furiously beneath them, writhing like an eel, foam bubbling at the corners of his mouth. With a sudden, vicious twist, he kicked Twelve hard in the side, throwing her back into the snow. Her yell was half pain, half surprise.

"Enough," Dog said, leaping forward to place a paw firmly on Five's chest. "Let the moxie do his work." He looked back at Twelve scrambling painfully to her knees. "Are you all right?"

She swallowed a curse and nodded grimly. Widge's claws dug hard into her shoulder as she grabbed hold of Five's flailing arm again. "Do it now," she said, turning to Foxpaw. "Quick as you can."

Five fought harder than ever, but it was useless against the three of them.

With a grateful nod, Foxpaw darted forward. He painted the paste over Five's wound in a complicated pattern, then wove his magic with quick, fluid hand gestures, mesmerizing in their complexity.

Twelve stared, fascinated, her expression mirrored on Six's face.

"That's it?" she asked as the moxie sat back. "That was . . . magic?" Widge's bright-eyed chirp reflected her wonder.

Foxpaw nodded, smiling. "If it works, it will do so quickly," he added, wrapping a clean dressing around Five's head. "We'll know soon."

Six nodded, his pale face desperately hopeful. "Thank you."

Five's eyelids drooped. He seemed exhausted after fighting all of them. Foxpaw kept a close eye on him as he built a small fire in the snow.

"Do you really think your friend can help us find the goblin tracks again?" Twelve asked, warming her hands over the flames. A restless feeling itched through her, reminding her that every second they delayed, Seven was being whisked farther away.

"Not a friend," Foxpaw said slowly, sitting beside her. "There's a very ancient tree here, one of the forest's Heart Trees. Oakhammer. He was planted by my ancestors and sometimes he remembers his allegiance to us."

Twelve thought of the forbidding faces in the trunks and shuddered, despite the warmth. Widge nudged her cheek in agreement.

Foxpaw shrugged apologetically. "He's always unpredictable, and now things are changing in the forest, which may make him even more so. It's not as safe here as it once was."

Twelve couldn't help but snort a laugh, gazing point-edly up at the empty web. "Safe?"

"For those with enough respect to learn its ways? Yes," Foxpaw said firmly. His tone chastened Twelve enough to stop her laughing.

"How does the forest change?" Dog asked, keeping his voice down so as not to disturb Five.

"There's a balance here," Foxpaw said, "between light and dark. This place has always been a battleground for them, but, since what you call the Dark War, the balance has been maintained. Now it's shifting again, as it did then."

His words were an icy breeze and Twelve shivered under them. Dog whined, a soft, pained sound in the back of his throat.

"He's waking up!" Six cried suddenly. He gazed wild-eyed at Foxpaw as Five groaned and shifted beside him.

They hurried over and Foxpaw laid a small hand on Five's brow. "His fever is dropping," he said with relief. "We'll leave the dressing on for now, but I think it's safe to say the wound is healing and your friend is recovering." He sat back on his heels, looking inordinately pleased with himself.

Twelve, Six, and Dog huddled around Five, hardly dar-ing to breathe as his eyelashes fluttered and finally opened. For a moment, his eyes seemed unfocused, then they set-tled on each face in turn.

"What are you all staring at?" he croaked, looking surprised. "Have I got food on my face or something?"

Six gave a wordless shout of delight and grabbed Five by the shoulders, pulling him into a hug. Twelve rocked back on her heels, her relief so strong she felt light-headed. She wanted to laugh and cry at the same time. Widge spun in a circle on her shoulder, tail flicking madly with delight.

When Six set Five back down, Twelve punched him gently on the arm. "It's good to see you awake. Really good." Her voice cracked a little and she swallowed. "You gave us quite a scare." She scanned his face quickly. The whites of his eyes were back again and the terrible grayness was receding from his skin.

Five blinked at her, looking decidedly nervous. "Why are you talking like that?" He peered around, his expression becoming progressively more worried. "And where *are* we?"

"What do you remember?" Dog asked gently.

Five bit his lip and struggled to sit up. His eyes widened as he caught sight of Foxpaw bent over the fire. From yet another overall pocket, he'd produced a teapot that he was filling with snow and fragrant herbs.

"Uh . . . what in Ember is that?" Five whispered, lowering his voice.

"That's Foxpaw," Six grinned. "He's the moxie we rescued from the deathspinner web. He's the one who healed you."

"The who that we rescued from the . . . ?" Five trailed off and shook his head. "What *are* you talking about?"

The smile faded from Six's face.

"How much do you remember about what happened after we met the cliffcrawlers?" Twelve asked, echoing Dog.

"Cliffcrawlers," Five murmured. He nodded. "Yes, I remember them. They killed Charger." He shook his head slowly.

Twelve and Six exchanged a worried glance over Five's head.

"What else?" Dog pressed.

"Ugh, it's all fuzzy," Five said, scrunching his eyes as he thought. "I remember Twelve telling me it was just a scratch," he said eventually. There was accusation in his voice as he glared at her. "You were *obviously* lying!"

"Well, I didn't want to scare you," she admitted.

Five snorted. "How kind of you. Now will *someone* tell me where we are?"

The amazement on Five's face grew as Six filled him in. He couldn't believe that they were in the Frozen Forest or that they'd fought off an Ygrex and a deathspinner without him. Six didn't mention that Five had attacked him, or the form the Ygrex had taken, and for that Twelve was infinitely grateful. The more Six spoke, the more worried Five looked, until Foxpaw came over with a cup of tea for him.

"Ginger and honey," he said, his golden eyes scanning Five's face and noting the improvement. "I've also added a pinch of dreamroot to sharpen your memories."

"Thank you," Five said uncertainly, taking the cup. "And, uh, thank you for healing me."

Foxpaw inclined his head. "It was a debt owed and willingly paid. Your friends saved my life."

As Five sipped his tea, the color began to return to his cheeks, and it wasn't long before the group were back on their feet. Five needed a lot of help to climb onto Surefoot, but then they were moving again, trotting to keep up with the moxie.

"What is this Oakhammer tree?" Five asked, his eyes wide as he stared around.

"Not 'what' but 'who,'" Foxpaw corrected him quickly. He slowed down and rubbed his chin thoughtfully before turning back to them. He lowered his voice to a whisper. "The Heart Trees are unimaginably old and Oakhammer can be . . . uh . . . *aloof.*" Foxpaw glanced around, nervous. "He has a great deal of power, but very little patience. For all our sakes, don't do anything that might insult him."

"Insult a tree?" Five snorted. "Why would anyone bother doing that?"

Foxpaw flinched. "Saying something like that, for instance, would not go down well. We're just specks in time to him, nothing more. You must ask your question politely and, if he refuses to help, walk away." Foxpaw looked at each of them in turn. "Can you do that?"

Twelve nodded, intimidated and intrigued. The others nodded too.

The forest changed around them as they hurried on. The tree trunks got wider and the canopy even higher, but a feeling of claustrophobia grew steadily in Twelve. The farther they traveled, the more imposing and darker the woods became. Widge pressed himself against her throat, then thought better of it and disappeared into her bearskin. Eventually, Twelve took the moonstone from her pocket to light the way. Its clean, bright light eased her discomfort, but Five yelped when he saw the slumbering tree-faces illuminated.

"Shh!" Six hissed, prodding Five. "You don't remember them either?" Five shook his head, eyes wide.

Foxpaw stared at the moonstone, his golden eyes almost green in its glow. "That's a rare treasure you have there," he said quietly. "It's a very long time since a moonstone like that has been seen in these parts."

"It's not mine. I'm just looking after it for someone," whispered Twelve, her voice catching. The air had developed a strange weight, prickling her skin as if she was being watched. It made her want to shrink into herself and disappear. Beneath her, Dog slowed. "Do you feel that?" she murmured to him.

"Definitely," he growled. "I like this place even less than the rest of the forest."

"We're approaching the Heart Grove," Foxpaw whispered to them. "There are defenses around it. Walk *exactly* where I do and don't stop."

The group exchanged glances, but this was their only chance of finding Seven's trail again. It didn't seem they had much of a choice.

Twelve followed Foxpaw as closely as she could—making sure she only trod where he did. Inside her furs, she could feel that Widge had curled himself into the smallest, tightest ball possible and was shivering with dread.

She couldn't help but wonder if he knew something she didn't.

## CHAPTER
# THIRTY-ONE

When Twelve looked back, she saw without surprise that they were no longer leaving footprints. The cold was absolute and not a breath of air stirred. A tight feeling was choking her chest and the hairs on the back of her neck were standing up. She saw Six whisper something to her, but couldn't hear anything, neither the beating of her own heart nor Widge's fearful squeaks.

She took a slow, deep breath and tried not to give in to panic, her eyes fixed on Foxpaw's back. The moxie was walking more slowly than before, his shoulders hunched down as though battling against an invisible wind.

Then suddenly it stopped. Foxpaw straightened up and turned to them with a smile. Sound returned and the heaviness about them dissipated with a pop. The relief was indescribable.

The group found themselves in a small, round clearing bounded by nine truly enormous trees. The trunks stood so close together they almost touched, while overhead their canopies were tightly entwined. There was something otherworldly about the grove, a sense that it stood outside time. And the feeling of being watched was stronger than ever.

The bubble of silvery moonstone-light flowed up the straight trunks, throwing nine faces into sharp relief. Forbiddingly regal, five women and four men slumbered in the bark, their mouths downturned, their brows creased into frowns.

Foxpaw beckoned them over to stand before one of the male faces. Twelve held the light up higher and the group regarded him in silence.

"Oakhammer?" Six guessed and Foxpaw nodded.

"Unsafe," Dog growled, looking around. His hackles were raised and Twelve could feel tension rippling through him.

"I . . . I have spoken with him before," Foxpaw whispered.

"Is that supposed to reassure us?" Five muttered.

"It's our only chance of finding Seven's trail," Six whispered. "We have to try, or all this has been for nothing."

Twelve caught his eye and nodded her agreement. For Seven's sake, they had to do this.

The bark of the great tree was twisted to form long, untidy ropes of hair and a great bushy mustache. The tree-face's twiggy eyebrows sprouted in profusion, but beneath them the features were sunken and wasted. His cheek-bones and nose were as sharp as razors and his eyes deeply recessed beneath a prominent brow. He looked ill.

"He doesn't always look like this?" Twelve guessed, seeing dismay flash across Foxpaw's face.

The moxie paled at her words and glanced fearfully at Oakhammer, before glaring at her. Belatedly, she remembered his warning about not saying anything that could give offense. Wincing, she gestured that she'd be more careful.

Foxpaw turned back to the tree and began to speak, his words rolling into a chant that made Twelve's ears tingle.

"Oakhammer, Great Tree Spirit and Ninth Keeper of the Forest, Wanderer of the Frozen Wastes, Watcher of Beyond and Keeper of the Balance, I beg you in the name of my ancestors to awaken."

Nine times he chanted it and, with each repetition, the tension in the clearing increased.

Then, so suddenly that Five yelped, the eyes above them flickered open and the mouth stretched wide to draw a deep, rattling breath.

Oakhammer was awake.

# CHAPTER
# THIRTY-TWO

Something invisible knocked them all back a step, a release of energy too deep to have sound, but that reverberated through them warningly.

Oakhammer gazed down on them, his eyes gleaming like the night sky, all darkness and starlight.

"Moxie!" Oakhammer said, focusing on Foxpaw. "Why have you woken me?" His voice was the slow growth of old wood, the creaking of branches, the passage of time in an untouched glade.

Foxpaw gulped as he bowed before the tree. "Great Oakhammer, I owe my life to these humans and the Guardian who accompanies them. They have lost their way and seek to regain the path. I have brought them to you, knowing you may choose to help them."

Icy wind, as sharp as a blade, cut through the clearing, making them all flinch. Twelve and Six exchanged worried glances.

"Wonderful," Five muttered under his breath. "What have you got us into now? I've *barely* recovered from my last near-death experience."

"Shh." Six hushed him, seeing Oakhammer's focus was now on them.

"Who are you?" the Heart Tree asked. A simple question, but his voice made Twelve's teeth chatter. Her tongue slithered uselessly in her mouth. Six was the first to gather himself enough to speak. He cleared his throat nervously and told Oakhammer their tale.

"So, we're tracking Seven," he finished a few minutes later, "but the trail vanished in the forest. Please will you help us find it again?"

The starlight grew brighter in Oakhammer's eyes and his mouth creaked slowly into a smile. "How could I refuse such a polite request, especially from huntlings?"

"Really? You'll help us?" Six asked, a delighted grin spreading over his face.

"Of course," Oakhammer said. "Although I will ask for something small in return."

Foxpaw suddenly looked worried. "Oh no."

"We don't have much with us," Six admitted, "but whatever you want is yours if you'll help us."

Twelve shot him a sharp look. "As long as we all agree," she added, throwing back her head to look Oakhammer in the eye. "We're in this together after all."

He laughed gratingly and the sound filled Twelve with irrational fear. Widge was shaking so hard she worried he'd fall out of her furs. She willed him to stay still, not to show himself.

"All I ask for in return is truth." Oakhammer spoke quietly now, his words falling like dead leaves around them. "A few questions each, answered honestly. I do miss honest conversation; it can be surprisingly hard to find."

The starlight in his eyes burned brighter and the band around Twelve's chest tightened.

"This is *clearly* a terrible idea," Five hissed. "Let's get out of here." For once, Twelve was in total agreement with him.

"We'll answer your questions truthfully," Six called, averting his eyes from the others' shocked expressions. "It's our only hope of finding Seven," he whispered to them, his face pale. "We don't have a choice."

"Wonderful!" Oakhammer rasped.

Twelve shivered at how pleased he looked.

"So, boy, why are you here?" Oakhammer asked Six.

Six swallowed his confusion and spoke respectfully. "As I told you, we're here to find Seven."

"And who is this Seven?" Another smile scratched over Oakhammer's face.

"She . . . she's a fellow huntling," Six said, stumbling over the words.

"Hmm," Oakhammer said thoughtfully. "Part of the truth only, I think."

Twelve could hear Six's hoarse breathing beside her as Oakhammer's attention slid away from him and onto her. She stiffened her spine against a lurch of fear, reminding herself she was doing this for Seven.

"Girl," Oakhammer said, his eyes narrowing as he gazed at her. "So much fire in you! Tell me about this revenge you dream of?"

Five and Six shot puzzled glances at her, but Twelve kept her gaze on Oakhammer, trying to squash her rising fury. "Since you seem to know so much about it, why don't you tell me?" she called, struggling to keep her voice even.

Oakhammer laughed and Twelve's skin crawled.

"Very well, I'll try you, then." Oakhammer turned to Five, his expression predatory. "Why do you want to be a Hunter?"

Five flinched. "We . . . uh, we aren't allowed to speak of the past."

"Oh, but I insist," Oakhammer said smoothly. "If you refuse, I will have to find a way to encourage you. Maybe I'll kill that boy next to you."

A deathly silence fell across the clearing.

"I'm so sorry," Foxpaw gasped, his eyes wide with

shock. "I thought—" His words were cut off as roots tore themselves from the ground to wrap around his mouth. Dark soil spattered across the pristine snow.

Twelve made to move toward him, her hands already reaching for her axes, but the moxie caught her eye and shook his head, his eyes pleading. Beside her, Dog began to growl.

"Now," Oakhammer said, ignoring everyone but Five, "answer my question."

Five stared helplessly at them and then shrugged. "My father exiled me. I'm not chief material apparently, but my little brother is. He told me if I didn't disappear he'd find a way to make my death look like an accident. . . ." He trailed off and shrugged again. "So I ran." His cheeks were burning, his gaze firmly on his feet.

"I see," Oakhammer said ponderously. "What an insightful man your father was. Now tell me of the boy next to you. What is he to you?"

Five raised his flushed gaze to Six. "He's Six—he's my friend."

"Ah, your *friend*."

Fear flashed across Five's face. Twelve suddenly had a very bad feeling about this.

"Yes," Five whispered.

Silence hung over the clearing and Oakhammer smiled knowingly.

"Five?" Six asked uncertainly.

There were two bright spots of color on Five's cheeks, but otherwise he was paler than when he'd been sick.

Six's expression shifted through bewilderment and surprise to arrive at understanding. "You . . . you like me?" he asked. "Not just as a friend?"

Five's eyes were on the ground, refusing to meet Six's gaze. Twelve felt his pain and discomfort as though they were her own.

Above them, Oakhammer roared with laughter and Twelve squeezed her axes tighter, fury boiling through her with every beat of her heart. Dog's growling intensified.

"That wasn't your secret to tell!" she yelled at Oakhammer, her voice shrill. "Why are you doing this?"

"Because I can," he sighed contentedly. "You asked for my help and agreed to the price." His black-eyed gaze shifted to her and his smile sharpened behind his beard. "Now tell me, why did *you* join the Hunting Lodge?"

Twelve's teeth ground together so tightly a muscle in her jaw spasmed. She wasn't going to tell him anything. Beneath her furs, Widge dug his claws into her skin, his terror vibrating through her.

"Oh, come now," Oakhammer chided. "Do I have to encourage you too? Very well."

Beside her, Dog began to howl, his legs giving out beneath him as he fell writhing into the snow.

Twelve ran to him, horror coursing through her. "Stop it!" she screamed. "What have you done to him?"

"I've granted his heart's desire," Oakhammer said modestly. "He wishes to be real. What is more real than pain?"

The sight of Dog yowling, his limbs contorted, was almost more than Twelve could bear. Her hands clenched convulsively around her axes as tears prickled her eyes.

"Dog and I will think it very selfish if you don't answer me soon," Oakhammer prompted. "I would have thought you'd try harder to protect him. But then you're not very good at protecting the ones you love, are you, *Starling*?"

Fingers of icy cold crept up Twelve's spine. Six mouthed her name in amazement and Five stole a glance at her before squeezing her arm in solidarity. He released her quickly, as though he thought she'd pull away.

A sudden sadness gripped Twelve. That he should reach out to her now, when she was about to make him hate her again—by telling the truth.

"Starling?" Oakhammer crooned. "I'm waiting."

Behind her Dog yelped and Twelve knew she would have to speak, maybe even tell the truth, for the first time. It would condemn her, change the way they saw her; maybe force the group to leave her behind.

But, if it saved Seven, it was worth it.

# CHAPTER
# THIRTY-THREE

"I came to the lodge after my family died, to train as a Hunter," Twelve said coldly, staring into the swirling depths of the old tree's eyes. She doubted it would satisfy Oakhammer, but it was worth a try.

"Aha," he cried. "So close to the truth, and yet so far." He went on sadly. "Dog seems like such a nice Guardian, but I wonder if it won't be difficult for him with only three legs?"

"Stop!" Twelve cried. She couldn't bear the thought of Dog being maimed—and maimed because of her. "I came after my village was slaughtered by the cave clan. I wanted to learn the skills of a Hunter."

Oakhammer smiled darkly. "Do you want to *be* a Hunter?"

Twelve took a deep breath. "No."

Five and Six shifted beside her, but Twelve didn't look at them; she could already feel their shock and disappointment. She hardened herself against it.

"Why do you need to learn their skills, then?" Oakhammer asked.

Twelve hesitated. Oakhammer flicked his gaze over to Dog and back to her. The implication was clear.

"To avenge my family," Twelve said, pleased her voice sounded strong, despite the hammering of her heart. She had never spoken of her plan aloud, nor had she wanted to, but Dog's howls were so piteous she couldn't stay silent. "The cave clan killed them. I intend to return the favor." Twelve met Oakhammer's eyes unblinkingly.

"I see," Oakhammer said, feigning surprise. "A blood feud. Someone hasn't been paying attention to their Pledge. Well, what do you think of that, Six?"

Like a searchlight, Oakhammer's attention slid off Twelve onto Six, leaving her feeling scorched and breathless. Dreams of revenge had driven her since her family died, but speaking them out loud left her feeling strangely empty, diminished. She turned away from the sensation, not wanting to examine it more closely.

"I—I don't know," said Six.

"Yes, we come finally to the Boy Who Lies," Oakhammer said softly, his pleasure evident. "I've saved the best for last."

Six was very pale and ramrod straight. She hated herself as soon as she acknowledged it, but a small part of Twelve was intrigued.

"Why did you seek the Hunting Lodge, Boy Who Lies?"

Six took a deep breath and sighed it out before speaking. "My parents were killed too." He glanced at Twelve and she startled at the desperation there. "I didn't feel there was a place in my clan without them, so I left and came to the lodge."

"Hmm." Oakhammer nodded thoughtfully. "I see. Why were your parents killed?"

"*Why?*" Six cried, unable to keep the anger from his voice. "How should I know? They were good people!"

"Of course," Oakhammer murmured. "Well, perhaps you are in the same boat as Twelve; perhaps your parents were murdered by the cave clan?"

"I . . . no," Six muttered, his shoulders slumped.

"How can you be so sure?" Oakhammer asked silkily. "Starling's whole village was wiped out. It sounds like they're capable of anything. Were you there when they died?"

"No."

"So how do you know it wasn't the cave clan?"

The starlight was sparkling in Oakhammer's eyes as he pinned Six with his gaze. Six said nothing, but the look he gave Twelve was full of fear and regret.

There was a little voice whispering in the back of Twelve's mind: Six knew a lot about moonstones. The cave clan mined moonstones. And then there was that stupid, apologetic look he was giving her.

Blood roared in her ears as horror and disgust flooded her. Six who had saved her life. Six who had been good-humored even when she was at her worst. Six who she'd begun thinking of as a friend. Cold fingers of despair gripped her by the throat and her breath juddered as she met his eye.

"I'm sorry," he whispered. "But . . ."

"Cave-creeper!" Twelve hissed and her heart twisted violently in her chest. Six said nothing.

"I'm not done with you, Boy Who Lies!" Oakhammer's inhuman voice silenced them.

"I'm not answering any more of your questions!" Six cried, his face like chalk.

"Oh? But I thought we had an agreement?" Oakhammer cocked an eyebrow and the earth at Twelve's feet shifted. Roots sprang up to coil around her legs and drag her to her knees. Before she could even swing once with her axes, they were wrapped around her wrists and neck as well, wrenching her back into an impossible position until she could barely breathe.

"Watch out, Starling," Oakhammer chuckled, "the cave clan might yet kill another member of your family."

Six squeezed his eyes shut and shook his head. "Stop it—leave her alone!"

"With pleasure," Oakhammer smiled. "Once you have answered my last question."

Six bowed his head in resignation.

"Who is the girl you seek?" Oakhammer asked.

"Seven," Six said dully.

"And what is she to you?" Oakhammer's eyes gleamed. "Why have you come after her?"

Six took a deep, shuddering breath and raised his gaze to meet Oakhammer's. "She's my sister," he said.

# CHAPTER
# THIRTY-FOUR

Five gave a yelp of surprise and Twelve closed her eyes in despair. It made perfect sense: all the times Six had pushed them to go faster; the fact that he'd avoided Seven at the lodge, but then tried to rescue her when she was taken. The pieces fit together and Twelve was left with the ghastly realization that she'd set out on a mission to rescue a cave clan girl, had thought of a cave clan boy as a friend. The wrongness of it sickened her.

Oakhammer laughed in delight. "Ah, it's been many years since I've met such an ill-matched group!"

"Twelve," Six whispered, trying to get her to look at him.

The roots binding Twelve and Foxpaw retreated. She stood up slowly.

"Twelve," Six said again.

She wasn't sure which of her swirling emotions would rise to the surface if she met Six's eye, so she hurried instead to Dog. He was still on the ground, dazed.

"She's your sister?" Five asked numbly. "Why didn't you *tell* me? You could have trusted me with that at least! I've followed you out here blindly, nearly died, and you obviously know far more about—"

"Enough," Oakhammer creaked, his laughter fading. "I'll keep my word and deliver you to the goblin stronghold so Boy Who Lies can rescue his precious sister. Or you can tear each other's throats out, whichever you prefer."

He smiled genially down on them and Twelve grabbed her axes where she'd dropped them. Before a conscious thought had formed in her mind, Foxpaw was beside her, restraining her with surprising strength.

"I'm sorry," he whispered, his golden eyes swimming with tears. "He's never been like this before. Like I said, the forest is changing. But please, if you want to live, control your temper."

Ragged breaths shook her, but she managed a tiny nod.

"Gather in front of me," Oakhammer boomed. "Moxie, stop your mutterings, and Guardian, get up. You're made of stone—there's no need for you to be quivering on the ground like a pup."

With a snarl, Dog staggered to his feet, leaning against Twelve so hard she nearly fell.

"Good," Oakhammer purred as Surefoot ambled cautiously over to Six. "Now I will open my mouth and you will walk in."

"What?" For a moment, the group was united in disbelief.

Above them, Oakhammer opened his mouth. Inside, the same shiny blackness as was in his eyes greeted them.

With a shudder, Five drew back. "You've *got* to be joking. You actually think we're stupid enough to just walk into your mouth?"

Oakhammer didn't answer. His mouth yawned wider and wider. His lower jaw unhinged like a snake's and the gaping darkness slid down the broad trunk until it touched the ground in front of them.

"I know it seems unusual, but he is telling the truth," Foxpaw stuttered, seeing none of them make a move toward the trunk. "I've traveled in this manner myself once. It's not uncomfortable. You should hurry though; go, before his patience runs out." With herding motions, Foxpaw tried to get them to move toward the tree. All resisted him.

"No," Five said simply. "This has gone far enough. You're both liars and I'm not traveling a *single* step farther with you. Not without trust."

"Trust?" Six asked darkly, eyebrows raised, his mouth pressed into a line. Spots of high color returned to Five's cheeks.

"Aaargh!" Foxpaw cried, dancing from one foot to the other. "He's closing the door—you must go now, or never find your friend's trail."

Sure enough, in front of them, Oakhammer's mouth was closing, his eyes narrowed to dangerous slits.

"Forgive me," Foxpaw cried, "but I can't let you waste this opportunity when you've come so far." He raised his hands, quickly sketched a bewildering profusion of patterns in the air, then shouted a word that slipped through Twelve's senses and vanished. Before any of them could object, or even make a sound, the whole group was flung bodily into Oakhammer's mouth, leaving Foxpaw alone in the Heart Grove.

Twelve tumbled through absolute darkness, her heart drumming a frantic rhythm. Desperately, she tried to find something to grab on to, but there was nothing. Then suddenly she was facedown on the ground, her nose and mouth filling with powdery snow, Widge's claws digging into her painfully.

A scream dragged her to her feet, her senses reeling. Six was on his knees a few paces in front of her, his shoulders shaking. Twelve staggered forward and froze, unable to comprehend what she saw.

The group was on a snow-covered ridge. In the distance, its red stone walls unmistakable, stood the Hunting Lodge.

Oakhammer had tricked them.

They were back where they'd started.

# CHAPTER
# THIRTY-FIVE

"I . . . I don't understand." Five's face was a sickly white.

"Oakhammer lied to us," Twelve snarled. "After all that, after . . ." Her voice wobbled and she stopped speaking. Widge crept out of her furs. Even his whiskers were trembling.

Six was still on his knees, shaking his head silently.

Dog went to him. "Get up, Six," he said, his voice gentle. "Grab my fur." Six stood, as unsteady as a newborn frost-deer.

"Are you all right?" Dog asked, nudging him with his nose.

Six turned staring eyes onto the Guardian. "She's gone, isn't she?" he whispered, desolate. "We'll never find her now."

Twelve ground her teeth and looked away. She reached

up a hand to comfort Widge and tried to concentrate her thoughts on the frightened squirrel. She didn't care about Six's pain—she *wouldn't*. A cave clan boy and his sister. She hated them both. *Murderers*. She thought of Seven, how the girl's smile had reminded her so much of Poppy. For a moment, their faces wavered, mingled. Twelve swallowed a rush of bile. Seven was not her friend, was not her sister. Rescuing her wouldn't have changed a thing. If anything, it would have been a betrayal of her family, of their memories. Not that it mattered now anyway.

The group stood in silence for a long time. Overhead, the sun dipped and the temperature began to drop. It was only then that Dog stirred.

"We must return to the lodge," he said heavily, turning to look at the others.

"What? No!" Six cried, looking up. His movements were suddenly quick and eager. He rushed to Surefoot. "We just have to go back to the forest!" he gabbled. "We'll follow the tracks and find another way to pick up the trail again. Maybe we can . . ."

He trailed off when he saw Five shaking his head. "No," Five said. His voice was very quiet, shaking with suppressed emotion. "I won't do it. By the frost, I won't go through that again for you. I thought we were friends. I thought you trusted me, but you've kept *so* much back. I almost died, Six! Would you even have cared?"

"Trust," Six said, his fingers knotting themselves in Surefoot's fur. "That's the second time you've mentioned that. Where was your trust of me? You should have told me how you felt about me."

"Why?" Five asked. "What difference would it have made?" His voice twisted as he glanced at Twelve. "Oakhammer used her instead of me. That makes everything clear."

Twelve shifted, uncomfortable despite herself. "What?"

Five was breathing hard. "When he was forcing answers out of me, he threatened Six to make me talk. But, when he was questioning Six, he threatened *you*. Not me."

The jealousy was unmistakable and Twelve laughed humorlessly. Five's fury spilled over. "And you, Twelve! You're no better. You've lied to everyone at the Hunting Lodge, stolen food and training from those who actually want to be Hunters and believe in the work they do. You disgust me."

"I really don't care what you think of me," Twelve said, lacing her voice with as much venom as she could manage. Her anger burned hot inside her.

"Stop it, both of you!" Six cried. "Oakhammer played us against one another. We're letting him win."

"I'm fine with that," Twelve said. "I'd rather he won than you."

"What does that even mean?" Six asked shakily.

"Stop this," Dog growled, trying to step between them. Twelve darted around him.

"Do I really need to spell it out?" she hissed. "You're cave clan. Your kind killed my whole family, murdered my village even down to the animals. It took me three days to bury them all. Three days of mud and sweat, of blood I wished was mine. Three days of fending off carrion crows. Do you really think I would have tried to rescue Seven if I'd known she was one of *them*? No! I hope she's already dead."

A sickened silence fell. Twelve wanted to take the terrible words back, but they'd already flown, more destructive than anything her axes could do.

She saw a deep shudder run through Six and, when he spoke, his voice trembled with emotion. "How can you say that? She's still the same person you knew. She gave you Widge."

Twelve couldn't move, couldn't speak. Widge was like a statue on her shoulder.

"Give me her moonstone," Six said, his voice harsher now, his breathing ragged. "She made a mistake giving it to you."

"The moonstone is Seven's?" Five asked wonderingly.

Surprise mingled with shame as Twelve pulled the stone from her pocket and half flung it at Six, startled at the wrench she felt to let it go. Its light had been a reassuring certainty for the last few days.

"Yes, it's hers," Six snarled, snatching it up and cradling it.

"Another thing you could have told me," Five said coldly, recovering his composure. "Exactly how much more is there that you've kept to yourself? Do you know why she was taken?"

"What does it matter now?" Six asked bitterly.

"You do know!" Five exclaimed, his voice rising to a shout. "And you didn't think fit to share it with us? Quite happy to use us, but *clearly* no need to trust us!" He shook his head and wrapped his arms around himself, his misery obvious.

"Six?" Dog asked, turning to him, a dangerous light in his eye. "Is this true?"

"The Hunters don't even let us keep our names!" Six cried, his eyes wild. "You think they'd let me keep my sister?"

A salt-stained memory snatched at Twelve: Elder Hoarfrost, true to his name, unmoved by her pleas and tears as he carried her father's axes away. She shook herself furiously.

"Seven insisted we had to go to the Hunting Lodge together," Six said. "I begged her to choose somewhere else, but she said no. She must have known this was going to happen, but she never said anything. She gave her moonstone to *Twelve* and I don't understand why!"

The blank look on Five's face gave way to doubt, then

outright confusion. "How could she have known this was going to happen?"

Twelve felt sure her expression mirrored Five's and Dog's. She tried to tell herself she didn't care, that none of this mattered, but her curiosity burned bright.

"I don't know!" Six threw up his hands and groaned. "It's . . . it's hard to explain. She just knows things."

"You *really* need to do better than that," Five hissed, his anger barely in check.

"All right," Six said, rubbing a hand across his face. "It . . . it started when she was little. Sometimes she would have these dreams that came true. As she grew, it became more complicated though. Instead of simple outcomes, she saw paths, routes to possible futures and all the ways that led to them. Now she sees them everywhere, in everything, even when she's awake."

Twelve tried to make sense of what Six was saying and failed miserably. Beside her, Dog was stiff and still. "She can see the future?" he asked eventually.

"Yes," Six said, burying his face in his hands and drawing a shaky breath.

Something clicked into place for Twelve. "That's why they took her," she said, finding a dark satisfaction in the mystery being solved.

Five whistled softly. "That is quite a power." He stiffened suddenly. "Wait, that *is* a power!" he said again,

250

his eyes wide as they sought Six's face. "Something like that . . . doesn't it make her a witch?"

Goose bumps broke out on Twelve's arms and she scratched Widge's ears, more to comfort herself than him.

"I don't know," Six said sadly. "Our cave paintings tell us that Icegaard always claims a witch born into the clans. We waited and waited, but no one came. After our parents were murdered, Seven said we had to come to the lodge. She never said why though, and she never said anything about this happening." His voice shook.

"I never even saw you speak to each other," Five said wonderingly. Some of the tension had left his shoulders.

Six shivered. "We didn't. We said goodbye to each other before we got to the lodge, then I went ahead so we wouldn't arrive together. We knew we'd have to do a convincing job of not knowing each other and the easiest way was to avoid one another completely."

An unexpected anger fizzed through Twelve. Seven had always seemed so alone—the other students had mocked her, laughed at her, and the only person who knew her, her own brother, had ignored her. He'd even let his best friend pick on her.

"So, this is how the cave clan looks after its own?" Twelve said coldly. "That explains a lot."

A vein pulsed in Six's neck. "You don't know anything about us," he growled. "And you're not the only one to have lost people. My parents were murdered for nothing. Nothing. Just because of our clan. They weren't even robbed, just left in the dirt like rubbish." His breathing grew ragged. "All the clans hate us, and because of what? Stupidity, that's what. Fear based on ignorance and history hundreds of years old."

His lip curled as he stared at Twelve. "Look at you: a few hours ago, we were friends. I'm still the same person, but now you hate me because you know I'm cave clan. And you think I'm the monster?" He shook his head in disgust.

"Monster?" Blood was pounding in Twelve's ears. "Not a monster," she said carefully, picking the words that would cut the deepest. "Just a terrible brother."

A sharp intake of breath. "I'm a better brother than you were a sister."

Twelve felt her fist hit Six's cheek hard, saw the moonstone fly from his hand. His fingers raked her face, trying to push her off as she flung herself at him. Widge squealed and darted away as Twelve rained blow after blow onto any soft part of Six she could reach, cursing the furs that were protecting him. A fist came out of nowhere, connecting solidly to her jaw, and her head snapped back.

Five was yelling and Surefoot surged away, but Twelve barely noticed as she fended off more blows from Six and threw in a few of her own.

252

"Stop this!" Dog barked, the snow groaning beneath his weight as he leaped forward to drag them apart. Twelve screamed as his teeth sank through her furs and into her shoulder. She tore herself away from him as his jaw slackened.

Blood slid down Twelve's face from a split eyebrow and Six's nose was gushing red down his chin.

"Twelve!" Dog yelped. "I am sorry! Are you all right?"

Her shoulder throbbed painfully in response and she couldn't look at him. Six spat a mouthful of blood onto the bright white ground and Twelve felt her rage crystallize into icy determination. She'd already decided she was no longer part of Seven's rescue mission. There was no reason to stay a moment longer.

She grabbed her pack, summoned Widge to her shoulder and, in a moment of blistering malice, stooped to sweep the moonstone into her pocket. Then she began to walk away.

She didn't look back. With every step, a boiling anger pulsed through her, pushing out rational thought. She had helped the cave clan and betrayed her own family in the process. Twelve wrapped her arms around herself and walked faster, wishing she could outpace her raging thoughts. On her shoulder, Widge was stiff, silent with shock as her feet carried them back to the lodge.

The sun was diving behind the mountains, the light fading to a warm, orange glow. In the distance, Twelve could see figures on the skybridges, lighting the braziers. The familiarity of the sight warmed her in spite of herself and she walked even faster.

She couldn't say what it was that pulled her up mid-stride, but some primal instinct made her look again, more carefully. Her eyes scanned the looming walls and skybridges more urgently until she saw it: the fire in the braziers was green. Like goblin fire.

Twelve had only half worked out what that meant when something hit her hard on the back of the head and everything went dark.

# CHAPTER
# THIRTY-SIX

She was being dragged by the ankles, her head rasping painfully across uneven ground. Senseless images flared blindingly, then faded to darkness.

A great gate swung open silently.

Walls hemmed in the darkening sky.

Down. Each step cracked painfully on the back of her skull.

Stillness.

Cold.

Silence.

When Twelve next woke up, she had no idea where she was or how long she'd been there. Arcs of pain shot through her, radiating from her head along every nerve in her body. Her shoulder still throbbed where Dog had bitten her, and her mouth tasted of old blood. With a groan, she curled into a tighter ball.

What had happened?

She was lying on scratchy straw at the back of a cell. A single candle burned low between the bars of the door. She was unmistakably in the Hunting Lodge's dungeons. For a confusing instant, she wondered if everything had been a dream until her head gave a particularly powerful throb and her fingers found a wet, sticky warmth there.

She pushed herself up, ignoring the pain screaming through her, and squinted around.

"Widge?" she called, her voice barely a croak. "Widge, are you here?"

She strained her ears for any sound from him, but everything was ominously silent. Twelve's heart twisted agonizingly when she realized her squirrel really wasn't there. Looking around her prison, she saw it wasn't only Widge that was missing—her bag, axes, and the moonstone were also gone.

Slowly, quelling her rising panic, Twelve tried to remember what had happened.

Foxpaw. Oakhammer. The terrible fight.

Where was Widge? Where were the others? Were they looking for her? Did she even care? Shame gnawed at her over the things she'd said. She had an irrational urge to apologize to Six, which she pushed away. She hoped he and Five would forgive one another and in the next instant she hoped they wouldn't. Confused emotions raged back and forth inside her until she wanted nothing more than to escape from her own head.

If only she hadn't found out that Six and Seven were cave clan. The thought was almost a longing. She'd been starting to think of Six as a friend. And Seven was so like Poppy. Saving her would never have brought back her little sister, but it would have been something. Something good. Now everything was ruined—Six was a liar and Seven . . . Seven was gone.

Twelve shook herself; she shouldn't care about her enemies like that. If she did, then where would it end? Would she forgive the people who'd killed her family, stolen her life away? Would she let them live happily ever after when they'd denied her that? Of course not: she had to put her family first, honor their memory.

Miserably, she pulled her knees to her chest and hugged them. Even with her arms wrapped tightly around herself, she felt chilled without Widge's soft warmth pressed against her. Where was he? Was he all right? Her fear for him made breathing difficult. A cold tear rolled down her cheek as she rested her forehead on her knees, trying to fend off thoughts as dark as the dungeons.

She'd almost had friends and she had attacked them, abandoned them. She'd lost Widge. Now she was truly alone. Perhaps it was what she deserved.

*"That's just not true, Starling."* Her ma sounded tired, a little impatient.

*"It is!"* Starling's voice, angry. *"She did it on purpose! She broke off both Staggy's antlers. That doesn't happen by mistake!"*

Twelve blinked, colors shifting in and out of focus, the present and the past mingling, until the scene settled before her.

And her mother, sitting on a low stool, a lifetime ago.

# CHAPTER
# THIRTY-SEVEN

*B*ehind their home, her mother sat, stirring the contents of their very largest pot, suspended over flames. A basket of lavender, flowers carefully picked from the stems, sat next to her. The day was warm and the fire hot; her mother's dark, wild hair stuck to her face in damp tendrils. She stirred with one hand and fanned herself with the other, gazing at her older daughter all the while. Starling stood in front of her, cheeks flushed, rigid with righteous anger.

"Oh, Starling," her ma sighed. "Fine. Fetch Poppy."

Starling looked fit to burst. "Why? Don't you believe me?"

"I believe you," her ma said, threads of a warning tension in her voice. "But I'll hear her side too. I can't leave the soap"—she nodded at the steaming pot—"so go and get her, please."

259

*Twelve crept closer, breathing in the familiar scents of Poa: woodsmoke, grass, warm animals. She ran her fingers over the lacquered walls of their home, eyes never leaving her ma's back. She wanted to see her face but, as she moved closer, Starling stomped away, brows thunderous, bawling her little sister's name. Twelve had no choice but to follow.*

*"Poppy?" Starling bellowed, striding past the house toward the green. "POPPY! WHERE ARE YOU?"*

*"Stop tha roaring," cried Old Skylark, leaning out of the window next door. "There are babbies and oldies tryna rest!"*

*Somewhat chastened, Starling ducked her head and apologized. "Have you seen her though?" she asked, raising her eyes to the old man's face hopefully.*

*"Aye," he sighed. "She went to the cow barn 'bout ten minutes ago. Looked mighty upset."*

*"So she should," Starling muttered. "She's in big trouble."*

*"Is that so?" Old Skylark mumbled, disappearing back into the coolness of his dimly lit house.*

*The girl hesitated, looking across the green at the cow barn, then she jutted her chin and marched toward it. Twelve followed a couple of paces behind, unease rising in her with every step.*

*"Poppy! I know you're in here!" Starling called, throwing open the door a minute later. A snuffling sound from the hayloft confirmed it. Poppy's dark head poked over the ledge, gazing down with red-rimmed eyes.*

"I . . . I already said sorry," she hiccuped. "I'll fix Staggy, I will!"

"You can't and you know it," Starling said with sudden despair. "You broke his antlers off. He's ruined."

"I didn't mean to," Poppy whispered. "I'm sorry."

The younger girl's face was blotchy, filled with regret. For an instant, it seemed Starling would soften, her fingers twisting behind her back, as she gazed up at her little sister. Then anger resurged and she scowled again.

"I told you not to play with him! You're always so clumsy. Why are you so stupid?" The last word came out as a shout and Poppy began to sob again. Then, lightning-fast, she darted down the ladder, past Starling and out into the bright, blazing heat of the afternoon.

"You can't run away from me forever!" Starling shouted after her, as the small figure fled across the green. "Ma wants to talk to you!"

Muttering angrily, she stomped back to the house.

Twelve followed the other girl closely now, hungry for another glimpse of her ma. Starling circled around the house to where her mother was still stirring the soap, now adding handfuls of lavender.

"She won't come," Starling snapped without preamble. "She ran away again."

"Goodness, I wonder why," her ma said, pushing her hair back from her face.

The sarcasm was not lost on Starling. "You and Da always take her side!"

Twelve ignored Starling and stared at her ma, drinking in the beloved features. Longing, as fierce as she'd ever felt it, rose in her. She moved closer, until she could have reached out a hand and touched the familiar dark hair.

"That simply isn't true," her ma said calmly, taking a deep breath of the sharply fragrant air. She caught Starling's scowl and sighed. "Bring that over and sit with me." She nodded to another stool in the shade of the house.

Moodily, Starling obeyed even though the heat of the flames was almost unbearable and set her blood throbbing.

"Look at me," her ma said. The command in her voice was impossible to disobey. "You remember Redfern? Your da took you there once when you were little."

Starling nodded.

"Well, many years ago, they tried to grow greenmeal there." Her ma paused to scoop another handful of lavender into the soap. "It's a delicate plant, difficult to cultivate. Always brings a good price as a result though. But Redfern was unlucky that year—there was a great spring storm that flattened the young crop. Undeterred, they replanted the next year. Again, a spring storm came and ruined their efforts."

Starling listened, a trickle of sweat working its way down her temple. So did Twelve.

"In the third year," her ma continued, "there was a village

moot to discuss what was to be done, and they decided to plant maize instead. Spring came and went with fine weather and the maize crop was a success. The next year they planted it again, and the year after that. For five years running, there were no spring storms, but they never tried to grow greenmeal again."

Her ma nodded, satisfied with her telling. "Can you see what I'm saying, Starling?"

Starling stared at her blankly. "Uh—" She paused, then brightened. "That if Poppy would stop destroying my things, I could have nice things . . . ?"

"No!" her ma exclaimed, startled.

"Well, why don't you just say it straight," Starling muttered. "I never understand your stories."

Her ma's bark of laughter was sudden and loud. "So like your da," she grinned. "Fine, I'll tell it plain. You are like the storm in that story, Starling."

"What?" Starling sputtered. "I'm not the one always breaking things!" She crossed her arms. "This is what I mean. You and Da do always take Poppy's side!"

"Enough!" her ma cried, soap splashing out of the pot to hiss in the flames. She took a deep breath. "Your sister is clumsy, we all know that. But the way you react . . ." Her ma cast her eyes skyward as though the clouds might explain for her. When she next spoke, she said the words slowly, choosing them carefully. "Your reaction, your anger, is as destructive as

Poppy's carelessness. Maybe more so. Have you thought about that?"

"No." Starling's shoulders were slumped, her face sullen. "That's not true anyway."

"She breaks something you care about," her ma said, "and so you shout at her, and keep going until she cries. Don't you see that you're breaking something too?"

Starling shrugged.

"Do you think your anger will magically fix your broken toy? Turn back time?"

"Of course not," Starling scowled, stirring the dusty earth by the fire with her toe.

"Then . . . why do it?" her ma asked.

"It's her fault!" Starling burst out. "I wouldn't have to be thundery with her if she didn't make me so angry all the time."

To her surprise, her ma laughed. "You sound like you think there's no choice in the matter."

Starling shrugged again and her ma's face grew serious.

"There is always a choice in how you behave toward people, Starling," she said. "Getting angry is not the only response to feeling angry." She paused expectantly, but Starling's eyes remained resolutely on the flames. "Do you ever think about forgiving her instead?" she asked quietly. "What would it really cost you?"

Starling's shoulders hunched and her brows furrowed. "You mean pretend I don't care. Let her get away with it?"

"Forgiveness is not the same as indifference," her mother sighed. "In some ways, it's the opposite."

"Seems the same to me."

A sniffing sound alerted them both that Poppy was approaching. She appeared in front of them, clutching her favorite straw doll, Min. Ma had stitched a tunic for it, identical to Poppy's own.

Starling stared at her little sister's face and Twelve saw the sudden shame there, the realization that, although she might have been the one wronged, it was Poppy who had been more hurt. By her.

"I . . . I know I did a bad thing," said Poppy, a tear leaking down her cheek. "I can't fix Staggy, I tried." She took a shaky breath. "I ruined him." Another tear. "But I know how I can make it right."

With a sob, she threw Min into the flames, covering her face so she didn't have to see her catch fire.

Their ma leaped up with a cry, but Starling was faster. Snatching the stirring stick from her mother's hand, she reached into the fire and flicked her sister's doll out, falling on it and patting out the flames furiously.

"Why did you do that?" she cried, spinning to face Poppy.

Tears were streaming down her little sister's face again. "So . . . so you'd know for sure that I'm as sad as you," she wept. "And that I'm sorry. For real sorry."

"Oh, Poppy," their ma groaned, pulling her into a hug.

*Starling stared at the doll in her hands. Despite her quick reaction, the straw was black and crumbling, the tunic ruined.*

*Twelve watched as confusion chased guilt across Starling's face.*

*"Now do you see, Starling?" her ma sighed.*

In the darkness of her cell, Twelve's eyes opened, a cramp in her leg waking her. She staggered to her feet, sickened and shivering, her ma's question echoing through her.

*Now do you see?*

She hadn't. Not then. The words had been a puzzle. Now, in the darkness of the dungeon, and the deeper darkness of her despair, they whispered themselves over and over.

*Forgiveness is not the same as indifference.*

*There is always a choice. . . .*

# CHAPTER
# THIRTY-EIGHT

Words warred in Twelve's aching head. She stood at the front of her cell, fingers wrapped around the bars, eyes fixed on the dwindling candle.

Six was a liar.

Seven was gone.

It didn't matter. Both were cave clan anyway, so she wouldn't care. Their kind had murdered hers. She would avenge them, not be tricked into rescuing a lost cave clan girl. She would honor her loved ones.

But *was* she honoring them? a treacherous voice whispered to her. Was this what her family would have wanted for her? Would they feel venerated by the hatred she carried inside her?

*Think about the person you want to be.*

Words Silver had said to her down here in the dungeons.

Words her da had said to her years before on a starry night.

They came back to her now, clearer than ever, pressed upon her by the teasing darkness.

What did it all mean? Twelve buried her face in her hands, wished more than anything that Widge was with her to keep the terrible loneliness at bay. What she would give to feel his paws on her shoulder again.

What would Six give to have Seven back? The thought took her by surprise, but she already knew the answer: anything. He'd give anything, do anything, *say* anything, because Seven was his sister. Just as she'd do anything to have Poppy back, or Widge, because she loved them. He might be cave clan, but in this there was no difference between them.

What was it all for, then? Years of carefully planned revenge and the first cave clan people she met . . . she liked? Wild laughter and grief swooped through her and her ma's voice whispered again:

*Forgiveness is not the same as indifference.*

Could she forgive him? It was the first time she'd considered the possibility and the thought almost tore her in two. He was cave clan. He'd lied.

But he had almost been a friend. Twelve longed for her

ma with every fiber of her being, for her calm eyes and wise words. She would have known what was right.

Her ma would have hated her dreams of vengeance. Twelve knew it suddenly and so completely that it winded her. She would have been horrified to know the black things Twelve had imagined for the past two years. So would her da and Poppy. Twelve had avoided this hard truth by pushing away every thought and memory of her family. Everything they had stood for was the opposite of what she'd planned to do. She had allowed anger and hatred to poison her, to turn her into something they wouldn't have recognized.

It was a conclusion Twelve couldn't ignore. It shifted the axis of her world and stopped her in her tracks. And with it came fresh grief as memories she had drowned in dream milk resurfaced. She missed her family. She wanted to talk to them again, to tell them her fears, to be comforted by them and offer comfort in return. She wanted to go back and be a better sister to Poppy—how different their relationship would be if she had another chance.

A cold weight settled in Twelve's stomach. Pointless thoughts. There was no going back. No chance to apologize. Her family were gone forever, and nothing could change that.

And yet, something whispered, *were* they truly gone? She still carried the memory of them. Couldn't she keep them alive in other ways? They'd taught her so much, shown her what goodness was. If there was any tribute worthy of them, wasn't it that?

She could be a better person. For them. She *would* be.

Although the darkness around her was weighted with terror, Twelve felt suddenly lighter. The relief was indescribable: for the first time in years, she thought of her loved ones without shame or agony or despair. Her da, who had believed in her, inspired her to be better. Her ma, who had taught her to forgive, shown her the quieter type of strength it took. And Poppy. Poppy, who had looked up to her, imitated her, infuriated her. Twelve thought of her family now with a burning desire to do right by them, and the simple certainty that she could.

She bit her lip and forced her thoughts into order. She was going to make everything right; it wasn't too late. Somehow she had to help Six find his sister, even if it took years, even if he hated her now. But first she had to get out of here and discover what had happened to the lodge.

The memory of the green fire nagged at her. Were there goblins here again? It was impossible; the Hunters would have collapsed the tunnel by now and been on high alert for another attack. Still, something was clearly wrong. She had probably broken a hundred lodge rules in going after Seven, but a Hunter would never hit her over the head and drag her unconscious to a cell. They would take her to see Elder Silver. No, not Silver, Twelve reminded herself sharply, another flash of grief searing through her.

A distant sound stiffened her spine. Footsteps were approaching quickly and, with them, the glow of a torch. Twelve resisted the urge to slink to the back of the cell and instead pushed her face against the bars, straining to get a better view down the dark corridor.

"Who's there?" she called, relieved that she sounded confident, imperious even. "Why am I locked up down here?" Beneath the bars, she twisted her fingers into trembling fists.

"Shh," someone hissed back. "Do you want them to hear you?" The voice was familiar.

"Victory?" Twelve asked, her heart leaping as a figure appeared. "Is that you? What's going on?"

The weaponsmaster's face appeared outside Twelve's cell, the torch casting deep shadows under her eyes. She looked awful: pale and disheveled. A far cry from the perfectly controlled Hunter who Twelve was used to seeing.

"They've taken the lodge," Victory said, without preamble.

"What?" Twelve gasped. "Who?"

Victory went on as though she hadn't heard. "There must have been more tunnels. A lot more. I managed to get down here and lose them in the passages, but we won't be—"

"Victory!" Twelve gasped, pushing her hand between the bars to grab the Hunter's shoulder. "Who? Who attacked the lodge?"

"Goblins," the weaponsmaster whispered. "Lots of them."

*Goblins.* Shock sealed Twelve's lips. So Oakhammer had kept his promise after all. He *had* sent them to the goblin stronghold. It just hadn't been where they expected.

Victory's eyes were wild, but they calmed as they settled on Twelve's face. "You were right," she said. "Hoarfrost was a fool not to heed what you saw down here. We've got to fetch help. I have a plan, but I heard them bring you down here and knew I had to get you out."

Twelve's heart leaped as Victory refocused her attention on the lock.

"Did . . . did you see Widge when they brought me down?" she asked, half afraid of the answer.

"Who?" Victory asked.

"My squirrel."

"Ah, I'm afraid not." Victory didn't look up, her brow furrowed as she worked.

Twelve nodded, swallowing the lump in her throat. Widge would be safe somewhere and she'd find him. The alternative was unthinkable.

A moment later, the lock clicked and the door swung open. To Twelve's amazement, Victory pulled her into a short, fierce hug. "Can you walk?"

Twelve's vision was swimming, but she took a couple of tentative steps and nodded. "I've felt better, but I'll keep up."

Victory's face broke into a rare smile. "You're a fighter. Come on!" Taking her arm, the Hunter pulled her through passage after passage until suddenly they were at the foot of the spiraling stairs. Without hesitating, Victory began to climb, dragging Twelve after her.

The weaponsmaster was brave, but this seemed mad, even by her standards.

"What are we doing?" Twelve whispered. "We can't just pop up in the training ground."

"Why not?" Victory said grimly, continuing to climb. "It's the last thing they'd expect. We'll have the gate open before they even know what's happening."

"But we don't have any weapons!" Twelve hissed, pulling back against the Hunter's insistent tugging.

"Leave that to me," Victory said, glancing back at her. "Where are the others? Where's the Guardian?"

Twelve barely heard the question as she stared at the weaponsmaster's back. This wasn't like Victory: she was usually calm to the point of icy, totally in control. The shock of the attack must have affected her judgment. Twelve dug her heels in and pulled Victory around to face her, nearly sending them both careering back down the stairs.

"We can't just stroll into the training ground without weapons," she said, trying to keep her voice level. "If there are goblins up there, we'll be dead before we've taken three steps. You said they came through more tunnels—let's find those instead. If we get out, we can buy more time, plan a counterattack. What about the original tunnel, the one the first attack came through? Is that still open? I know how to find it if so."

Victory shook her head and resumed her climb. "I told you, I have a plan. You'll have to trust me."

Twelve nodded. Of course she trusted Victory . . . but at the same time every bone in her body was crying out that this was a terrible mistake.

"You never answered my question," Victory reminded her. "Where are the others?"

"I left them," Twelve puffed, the exertion making her head swim. "Six and I, we had a . . . we . . . we fell out."

"What about the Guardian?" Victory's back was still to her, but there was a new stiffness in her shoulders. "Was he with you? Where did you last see him?" The questions came quickly, the Hunter's voice eager. They were nearly at the top of the stairs. The door was open a crack and Twelve could see more torchlight gleaming through, shapes moving in the training ground beyond. Panic filled her.

"Victory, please—"

"Just tell me," Victory snapped, whirling to face Twelve as they crested the last step. Her face in the torchlight was a twisted mask of fury. "Tell me where that infernal Guardian is *right now*!"

Twelve stared at the Hunter, pain dulling her thoughts.

The door was tugged open and a small figure stood silhouetted against the light in the training ground. A ball of green fire flared in his hand, illuminating cruel features and gleaming armor. When he spoke, his voice was low, rasping, and strangely familiar. This was the goblin mage from the earlier attack on the lodge, Twelve was sure of it.

"I thought I told you to leave the interrogation to us, Victory," he said. "It's our specialty, after all." His grin revealed teeth filed to a point.

Twelve cried out, expecting the weaponsmaster to lunge for the goblin's weapon, try to push him down the stairs, *anything*, in short, other than what she actually did.

"Morgren," Victory sighed, laying a hand on his shoulder. "I had to try. Simply asking is much quicker and much less messy."

"Hasn't worked though, has it?" Morgren's eyes fixed on Twelve and his grin widened. "Besides, I like messy."

# CHAPTER
# THIRTY-NINE

Twelve stared between Victory and Morgren, struggling to make sense of it. The weaponsmaster's wild, disheveled appearance had vanished. She stood straight and tall, a little more bedraggled than usual perhaps, but otherwise her normal self. She didn't seem the least bit surprised to find a goblin mage standing in front of her—if anything, she seemed pleased to see him.

Victory turned back to Twelve and took her by the arm, pulling her forward into the training ground. Twelve's bewilderment only increased. The sky was dark above them, the lodge both familiar and strange. Torches burned with green flames, the sickly light distorting the shadows of hundreds of scurrying goblins. To one side of the octagonal space was a gaping hole, another tunnel entrance. Small figures crisscrossed the training ground from it, ferrying crates from its depths to the council house.

"What have you done?" Twelve cried, struggling against Victory's grip. "Where are the other Hunters?"

In an instant, the weaponsmaster twisted Twelve's arm behind her back, making her gasp with pain as Dog's bite reopened.

"Don't fight me, Twelve," Victory whispered. "This can be easy for you or very, very difficult." Her grip tightened. "I have to say, I'm a little disappointed. How many times do I have to say it? Constant vigilance. I shouldn't have been able to surprise you like that."

Twelve tried to wrench herself away and Victory twisted her arm even harder. This didn't make any sense. Victory was part of the lodge, central to it. She and Silver were . . . The thought of Silver brought Twelve up short. Suddenly she was back in the training ground during the Grim attack, watching Silver and Victory fight the creature side by side, perfectly in sync . . . until Victory tripped, accidentally throwing Silver off balance.

Had it been an accident though?

Twelve couldn't breathe. Her chest felt impossibly tight. "Silver," she gasped, "did . . . did you . . . ?"

Victory's grip loosened a little. "Silver was very dear to me for a long time," the Hunter sighed, then her voice hardened. "But she was getting soft in her old age and I outgrew her. She would never have accepted this new era of the Hunting Lodge. I saw an opportunity and I took it. She died as she would have wanted, her swords in her hands."

A strange numbness had fallen over Twelve, but Victory's words burned through that. Anger flooded her, red-hot and as bitter as ash. "Died as she would have wanted?" Twelve spat. "Betrayed by her closest friend?"

"Well," Victory allowed, "maybe not *exactly* as she would have wanted."

Twelve redoubled her efforts, kicking out at the weaponsmaster, ignoring the pain as she tried to pull her arm free. A spine-tingling sound brought her up short. Morgren was watching them both and he was laughing. As he doubled over with mirth, his handful of green fire blazed all the brighter. His rasping chuckles resounded around the training ground and other goblins began to join in. They sounded just like crows.

"Oh, Victory," he gasped. "This is the one you spoke about? Are you sure?"

"Very," Victory said grimly, her grip tightening until Twelve cried out.

Morgren wiped tears from his eyes and straightened up, his expression serious again. Twelve swallowed down her fear as he stepped forward, examining her. Up close, she could see his eyes were violet and his hair long and dark, tied back in a ponytail. He was taller than the other goblins by a head and much better dressed, a long fur cloak trailing from his shoulders.

"And yet she didn't tell you anything," he murmured, his eyes flicking to Victory. "Not very cooperative. Although I'm sure I can . . . loosen her tongue. We need to know where that Guardian is—he could ruin all our plans."

The smile that spread over his face sent chills down Twelve's spine. She forced her face to stay blank and jutted her chin at him. Appearing frightened, she thought, would be fatal.

"Ah, she has spirit though," he grinned. "I admire that." His eyes met Twelve's and his smile became wolfish. "I do hope you aren't planning on cooperating too quickly, huntling. It's been so long since my last interrogation."

Twelve squeezed her hands into fists to stop them from shaking as he reached inside his cloak and drew out a blade. It was short and squat, an ugly thing, but the edge caught the ghastly green light and gleamed, its sharpness beyond doubt.

"This is a family heirloom," Morgren told her, his fingers caressing the hilt. "It's called Skin and it has flayed some of the greatest names in history. It almost seems a shame to use it on someone as insignificant as you, but . . ." He shrugged carelessly and touched the icy blade to her cheek. Twelve's breath caught at the touch of the metal. "No point in me sharpening it if I don't use it," he whispered. His eyes blazed with a sickening excitement.

"Stop it, Morgren," Victory tutted, jerking Twelve backward and away from the blade. "I'll get the answers we need. In the meantime, remember she wasn't alone. We should collapse the tunnels to be on the safe side."

"As soon as we've emptied them," he growled, glaring at the scurrying goblins behind him.

"No, now," Victory said firmly. "The Guardian is probably nearby. If he regains entry, all of this was for nothing."

"*Probably* nearby' is not good enough for such drastic measures," Morgren said. He pointed his blade at Twelve's eye. "She knows for sure where he is. Let me take over the questioning."

"No," Victory said evenly. "I'd like to keep her in one piece if at all possible."

Morgren smirked and inclined his head, then raised his voice to a shout. "Where is the Croke?"

A breathless goblin appeared by his side instantly. "Expected any moment, my lord," he gasped.

"Good," Morgren said. "See what you can do, Victory. The Croke can take over when it arrives."

Victory made a noncommittal sound and shoved Twelve toward the council house.

"No!" Twelve yelled, fighting in earnest now, wishing more than anything that she had her axes. "You traitor, how *could* you? What have you done with the other Hunters?"

Victory's fist connected solidly with her temple, making Twelve see stars. Her knees buckled. She felt Victory drag her up the steps and into the Great Hall.

# CHAPTER
# FORTY

By the time she could see properly again, she was tied to a chair in the middle of the cavernous room. All around the walls, goblins were stacking crates. A rough wooden scaffold had been thrown up and, high above her, more goblins were prying the moonstones from the ceiling with wicked-looking blades. Green-flame torches gave the scene an underwater, otherworldly quality.

Twelve drew a shuddering breath and stared at the weaponsmaster sitting in front of her. Victory looked perfectly calm and composed in the midst of the devastation she had wrought.

"I trusted you," Twelve whispered, shock hammering through her. "I looked up to you. I . . . I wanted to be like you." The thought made her sick now.

Victory smiled. "That's because we're the same, Twelve," she said gently.

Twelve shook her head so hard it throbbed in protest. "Where are the other Hunters? The other huntlings? What have you done to them?"

Victory narrowed her eyes. "You mean the Hunters who did nothing but complain about you? Failed to see your potential? The huntlings who despised you?"

Twelve's mouth felt like it was filled with sand. She didn't trust herself to speak.

Victory's lips pressed into a thin line. "I didn't kill them, if that's what you mean. Not yet anyway. The Croke will tell us which will bend to our cause. Those that won't will be . . . disposed of." A smile ghosted across her lips. "A thousand years of history, hundreds of attacks repelled, and the lodge finally falls. To me." The smile spread into a grin that didn't reach the Hunter's eyes. "So much attention focused outward, but none inward. In the end, it was easier than some of the hunts I've been on."

"What did you do?" Twelve asked again, her voice shaking. The ropes were tight around her wrists and ankles. She was losing feeling in her fingers and she wriggled them desperately.

"I drugged the water." Victory shrugged. "Can you believe something so simple would be their downfall? That the great and powerful Hunters are all locked up, awaiting their fate, simply because they quenched their thirst?" This time the smile did reach her eyes.

"But why?" Twelve whispered.

Victory's face remained impassive. "An opportunity arose and I took it," she said. "In the lodge, we are slaves to that ridiculous Pledge; it shackles our every move. I've shaken off those ties with the help of Morgren. Now, finally, my skills will earn me the respect I deserve."

"You *had* respect," Twelve said, loathing rising in her. "You'll be despised for this." Her eyes swept over the mutilated council house, desperation growing in her. How was she going to get out of this? The ropes cut into her wrists, brutally tight. Victory clearly wasn't taking any chances with her. If Widge had been there, he would have gnawed through her bonds. She feared for him so intensely that it made her feel shaky.

"You're thinking too small, Twelve," Victory sighed, folding her arms and leaning back in her chair. "This is only the beginning. The plans we have . . ." Her eyes scoured Twelve. "No. First, tell me where the Guardian is."

Twelve's mind whirled. She pushed away thoughts of Widge and forced herself to concentrate. "The drug wouldn't have worked on Dog," she said slowly. "And even a hundred goblins couldn't get past him."

Victory nodded, almost seeming to approve. "You've always been a bright one. Go on."

"You had to find a way to get him out of the lodge." She paused as the enormity of it sank in. "But that would mean the Grim attack, the kidnapping of Seven, it was all just . . ."

". . . a diversion," Victory said, her smile wolflike. "To draw away the Guardian. Yes. Well, sort of," she amended. "If the information I have is to be believed, then Seven also has an extraordinary ability. She may actually be useful." Victory's lip curled. "I can't really believe I'm saying that about such a pathetic failure of a person."

"But we followed her tracks," Twelve said, her confusion growing. "We followed them all the way to the Frozen Forest. We . . ." She stopped talking, a terrible thought creeping over her.

She looked at Victory and the Hunter nodded slyly, the corners of her mouth lifting. "I think you have it."

Seven was kidnapped because they needed to get the Guardian outside the walls. But once that had been accomplished—

Twelve wanted to howl in horror. Hadn't she followed Seven's footprints to the sleds herself, seen that the last tracks were facing the wrong way, that Seven had been barefoot? Her prints at the goblin campsite had been booted again, but few in number and so shallow. Too shallow really, for someone of Seven's size and weight. Suddenly Twelve was certain that it hadn't been Seven wearing those boots, but another goblin.

Which meant it had all been a trick.

"She was never in the sleds," Twelve gasped.

"No," Victory said, her pleasure evident. She cracked the joints in her fingers, one by one. "The finest plan I've ever come up with. There was a hairy moment when that ugly Guardian tried to refuse to go after her, but I'm nothing if not persuasive."

Twelve felt sick, remembering how furious she'd been at Dog for not wanting to leave the lodge. He'd been right all along. With a lurch, Twelve thought of him, Five, and Six, outside the walls, oblivious to the danger they were in. Whatever happened, she promised herself she'd say nothing that would give them away.

"She's alive, then?" Twelve asked. "Seven is here?" Hope blossomed inside her in spite of herself.

"Yes," Victory smirked. "Morgren used his magic to erase their trail back from the sleds, brought her to one of the other tunnels. They waited there until I had . . . disabled the Hunters, then they emerged. This will be our base for now. Seven will remain alive for as long as our master believes she's useful."

"Master?" Twelve whispered, a clammy coldness creeping over her. There was a fanatical light in Victory's eye that was terrifying.

"Yes," Victory said. "He'll like you, Twelve. You're just like me—filled with darkness. I saw it as soon as you arrived."

Nausea roiled in Twelve's stomach. She shook her head. "No," she whispered, "I'm not. I'm nothing like you."

Victory laughed then. A full-bellied, happy sound at odds with the grim situation. "Liar," she snorted. "You have the same rage burning inside you, and the same fierce lust to use it. Tell me that when you practice in battle class you aren't imagining using your axes to really hurt someone. Why do you think none of the others wanted to partner with you? They see it too."

Twelve shook her head mutely and a cloud crossed Victory's face. "You don't ever have to hide that side of yourself from me, Twelve," she said, leaning forward, suddenly earnest. "With me, you can give in to it, be the greatest version of yourself you can be."

"No."

"Yes. I meant what I said in Silver's study. You have so much talent with those axes, more than I had at your age, and I do not say that lightly. With me, you'll be unstoppable."

Twelve's thoughts had been muddled, chaotic, but, when Victory mentioned Silver, they settled with a cold, crystal clarity.

"Don't talk about Silver," Twelve spat. "Her name does not belong in your mouth. You murdered her. I'm nothing like you."

A look something like hurt passed across Victory's face before a great crash made her spin on her seat.

"Careful, you idiots!" she cried. "It took years to make all those." Two of the hurrying goblins had dropped the crate they were carrying. Its contents spilled out, rolled across the floor toward Twelve and Victory. Arrows, hundreds of them. One came to a stop against Twelve's foot and she peered down at it, a frown on her brow.

The shaft was made of very dark wood, a slice of night against the floor. And the fletching was bat wing.

Twelve jerked away from it with all her might, almost tipping her chair over in the process. Horror coursed through her. She hadn't seen one of these since her last night in Poa. What did it mean?

Slowly, Twelve's thoughts ordered themselves.

Victory and the goblins were making arrows—perfect imitations of the cave clan's distinctive design. The exact design she had seen in every arrow in every body of every person killed in her village. Her mother. Her father. Her sister. All slain by these very arrows. She'd been able to examine them in great detail.

After all, it had taken her a long time to bury all those bodies.

Breathing felt very difficult and ice crept down Twelve's spine. Everyone blamed the cave clan for the massacre of her village, because of those arrows. *She* blamed the cave clan.

But was it possible that her family's killer was right in front of her?

# CHAPTER
# FORTY-ONE

"Was it you?" Twelve gasped, her voice cracking. "Did you attack Poa?"

"Ah." Victory frowned, her gaze flicked from the arrow to Twelve and back again. "This is . . . unfortunate. I was planning on telling you a little later, when you'd see the whole picture more fully. Understand everything a little better."

A sob of horror broke from Twelve's lips. "*No.*"

"You have no idea of the shock you gave me when you first arrived here and I discovered where you were from," Victory said, sounding almost apologetic. "I thought you'd seen something and come to make trouble. I should have trusted myself; we're always extremely thorough."

Twelve was fighting against the ropes binding her, all

her fear and pain forgotten. The only thing that mattered was feeling her fingers wrapped around Victory's throat.

The Hunter watched her.

"Please don't, Twelve," she said. "I know it's a shock—we changed the course of your life that day, but undoubtedly for the better. You must see that. Do you think you'd be happier wasting your life away in a little nothing-place like that, learning how to grow crops?" Victory snorted derisively. "We saved you from mediocrity."

"You killed everyone!" Twelve screamed, feeling tears streaming down her face as she fought her bonds with all her strength. "Everyone I loved! Everyone I ever knew! My sister was only seven years old. And then you hide behind prejudices. Pin your crimes on the cave clan! Is that why you trained for so many years? Is that why you think you deserve *respect*?" Twelve spat the word. "You—you disgust me. You're a monster!"

Victory pressed her lips together.

"Well," Morgren drawled, appearing behind the weapons-master, "it doesn't seem like she's joined our cause."

"She will," Victory said darkly.

"The Croke will determine that, not you," Morgren reminded her.

Victory gave a low grunt. "If your idiot soldiers hadn't dropped those arrows all over the place, it would have been much easier. She knows about Poa."

"Why?" Twelve cried, her voice a strangled croak. "Why did you do it?"

Morgren's violet eyes raked over her impatiently, barely seeming to see her. "Our master required it of us," he said. "Anyway, your village wasn't the only one."

The shock was a physical blow to Twelve. Poa hadn't been the only one?

Morgren was still speaking. "The more violence, the more chaos and destruction, the stronger he grows." A crooked smile flashed over his face. "He chose well when he favored us, Victory." His eyes settled on Twelve again and this time she saw disapproval there. "I think you might be deluding yourself over this one though."

The Hunter shrugged, her eyes still fixed on Twelve. Her expression was hard to read.

"We're collapsing the tunnels," he went on. "The next phase of our plan begins with the Croke's arrival."

Victory shook herself and rose from her seat. A fierce, ugly excitement flashed across her face. "Let it start with Seven and Twelve," she said, her voice hard. "Then it can work through the Hunters at its leisure."

"My thoughts exactly," Morgren agreed.

Behind him, two figures pushed through the doorway, dragging a third between them. The slim, slumped form was topped by a mass of vibrantly red hair. Even before the other girl lifted her head, Twelve knew it was Seven. The two girls' eyes met and, despite the pain in her head and heart, Twelve felt a surge of emotion. Everything she'd endured with the others over the last few days had been for her. For this small, deathly pale girl who had been kind to Twelve when she didn't need to be. It shouldn't have been worth it, but somehow it was.

The look on Seven's face mirrored Twelve's thoughts. Hope, delight, and despair flew over her features like clouds across a storm-whipped sky.

"Y-y-you're really here," she said softly, her words swallowed by Morgren calling for another chair.

The guards dragged her closer as another seat was hurried in and set beside Twelve. Seven wasn't able to put up much of a fight as they tied her to it. Her face was chalk-pale and her blue eyes sunken over bruised cheeks and a split lip. She was as weak as a kitten and shivering. Twelve suspected she hadn't had much to eat in the last few days. A comforting rage flared in her chest.

"Yes, I'm here," Twelve whispered. "I wanted to rescue you, but I got it all wrong."

Seven shook her head. "No," she said, "y-y-you didn't. You don't know w-w-what—"

"Quiet," Morgren said. He peeled off his glove and pale fire ran between his fingertips. He held his hand up and stared at it greedily, hardly seeming to believe it was real. Victory eyed it uneasily.

"See how our master keeps his promises," Morgren murmured. "My people's magic will be returned, our territory restored. We will have compensation for our generations of shame." His eyes turned to Seven and his smile showed rows of pointed teeth. "Starting with the caves. They should have been ours years ago. I will stand in the Cavern of Light, pluck every moonstone from its walls." To Twelve's horror, he pulled her moonstone from his pocket. "This is just a morsel of the riches that will be mine."

He set it on the arm of Victory's chair, where it blazed gloriously to life, illuminating the mutilated hall around them. Twelve was surprised at the wrench of guilt and sadness she felt to see it in his hands. It had been given to her by Seven, had helped save her from the Ygrex, and had given her light in some very dark places. Now she'd lost it.

"It will n-n-never happen," Seven said, her fragile form trembling with defiance. "Never."

He sneered at her. "We'll soon know if that's the truth or an idle wish, so-called seer."

A voice came from the doorway behind him, toneless and strange. "The truth is a slippery thing, Morgren. I cannot promise you that, only what lies inside her thoughts and dreams."

The hairs stood up on the back of her neck before Twelve even saw the thing that had spoken. Fear coursed through her, pure instinctive fear, like when—as a child—she had heard wolves howling in the night.

The goblins leaped aside as though poked with spears and even Victory flinched. Only Morgren appeared unfazed and his gaze, when it brushed Seven, was alight with triumphant malice.

"Your timing is impeccable as always," he purred.

# CHAPTER
# FORTY-TWO

Framed in the doorway was a narrow figure swathed in a great black cloak. Its shape was human, but Twelve could see nothing of its face beneath the deep cowl. Even as it stepped into the blaze of moonstone-light, that place remained featureless, shrouded in darkness. No feet emerged from beneath the cloak and there was no sound of footsteps. Twelve's heart was thundering, her palms slick with sweat. Fear seemed to snake around the Croke, infecting everyone with unease. Beside her, Seven shuddered so hard her chair shook.

"Good of you to come so fast," Morgren said. "Your unique talents are very much needed here."

Despite the warmth in his voice, Twelve saw him step back when the Croke drew near. Victory didn't bother to hide her disgust, her lip curling as she moved several paces away.

The voice inside the hood was expressionless. "They often are."

Twelve screwed up her courage and stared into the blackness under the hood, trying to make out the features of whatever lay beneath. The cowl twitched as the Croke turned toward her and Twelve gave a cry of shock. The power of its attention was a physical force, squeezing her, crushing her until she thought her ribs would crack. Black spots danced across her vision.

When the pressure eased, she saw that Morgren and Victory were standing on either side of the creature. The Croke was motionless as the Hunter and the mage talked over each other. For a moment at least, their attention was off the two girls.

"T-T-Twelve," Seven whispered.

Twelve glanced at the girl next to her. Seven's eyes were wide and sweat sheened her forehead.

"I-i-it sees the things we know," Seven murmured. "That's w-why it's here."

"How?" Twelve whispered back, trying not to move her mouth. Dread weighed on her. Somehow this sounded worse than the goblin tortures she was trying so hard not to think of.

"It looks inside your head," Seven muttered. "I don't

know h-h-how, but it does."

Twelve pushed down a wave of nausea. The Ygrex had gotten inside her mind, used what it found there to trick her, trap her. Oakhammer had seen inside her heart, found her darkest secrets and revealed them with malicious enjoyment. What would this new creature do?

"Imagine a w-wall or an ocean," Seven whispered urgently. "Something it can't pass across. Imagine it with e-e-everything you've got."

Seven yelped as the Croke glanced at her before turning to Twelve. There was no time to do anything, no time to plan. The Croke moved closer and an invisible weight pressed around her, making it harder to breathe. It stopped in front of her and two matchstick-thin arms appeared from the folds of its cloak. Even this close, Twelve could still see nothing beneath the hood. Perhaps it simply didn't have a face at all, Twelve thought wildly, the urge to scream becoming almost overpowering.

Slowly and carefully, the Croke removed a long dark glove from each hand. The skin underneath was maggot-pale and cold-mottled, but it was the markings that caught Twelve's attention. Runes drawn in liquid darkness coiled around the Croke's fingers, the patterns writhing as though alive, complex and shifting in the moonstone-light.

Ice-cold sweat trickled down Twelve's back. Before she could organize her thoughts, the Croke was upon her.

Its long-fingered pale hands reached for her face and no matter how much Twelve squirmed, she knew she wouldn't get away; the bonds around her wrists and ankles were too tight. Her last coherent thought was of Silver, how she'd died when a monster touched her.

The Croke's fingers were cold enough to freeze blood. There was a moment of searing, blinding white, as though a flare had gone off in front of her eyes, then images began flitting across her vision. Sickened and dazed, it took Twelve a moment to realize they weren't just pictures, they were her memories.

Her senses were thrown into a tornado; sounds, smells, and emotions buffeted her as her past whirled, settled butterfly-like for an instant, then whirled again.

With growing panic, Twelve tried desperately to draw up a wall, but the Croke broke through as easily as if it had been made of paper. Beneath the torrent of memories, she could feel the thing sliding through her thoughts, pitiless and dark. Then it dived deeper and all Twelve could see was her past.

# CHAPTER
# FORTY-THREE

*S*he and Poppy sat side by side in a sun-dappled meadow. "No, like this," she explained, guiding Poppy's fingers as the younger girl braided grass into a lopsided bowl.

Their ma sat by the fire, brushing Poppy's cloud of hair until it crackled. Irritation fizzed in Starling's chest; Poppy had been there for ages—surely it was her turn now?

She was walking through a barren landscape. Perhaps she'd make it to the Hunting Lodge, perhaps not. There were holes in her shoes and the wind pushed her cruelly on. Her heart was broken and the future was a vast, gaping emptiness.

Silver bent over her, questions falling from her lips like shattered stars. Twelve was so tired she couldn't hear, couldn't move, couldn't feel. Silver's eyes were infinitely gentle as she gathered Twelve up off the ground.

*Five offered her an apple after a training session. Her arms were trembling from the strain of wielding her axes and Five's grinning face filled her with an inexplicable fury. She threw his apple into one of the braziers. The skin blackened and split.*

The memories swirled faster and Twelve sensed the Croke's impatience. These weren't what it was looking for.

*The group stood before the gorge of cliffcrawlers. Five made jokes, despite his shaking hands, Six and Dog as steady as ever. Together they tried to think of a way to get through safely.*

*In the Ygrex nest, Six tossed her axes to her, relief written over his face as Dog faced off against the creature.*

*Oakhammer leered down at them and the group stood before him, their fledgling trust in one another shredded.*

*"I hope she's already dead." Resentments surged with the lodge in sight. Dog leaped between them.*

Twelve felt the Croke's concentration grow sharper and the whirling thoughts slowed. Twelve relived again her fight with Six, wincing beneath the remembered blows and Dog's misjudged bite. The Croke pored over this until the pressure in her head was so great, Twelve felt sure her skull would crack. Then, abruptly, it began to ease. The flow of images slowed to a trickle as the Croke made to slip out of her mind. A final image of Sharpspark, the firesprite, speaking to her rolled past. *"You are different from them,"* he said.

Something about this caught the Croke's attention and suddenly it was back in full force, examining her memories of the firesprites. It rolled them back and forth like marbles until it found what had happened in the cliffcrawler gorge. Again and again, it replayed that scene; Six screamed her name, Sharpspark threw a handful of flame at her, and burning gold sparks appeared from nowhere to engulf him. Her fingertips throbbed with heat, and the rage she had felt flooded her again.

The Croke's attention shifted. Seemingly random memories flashed before her, emotions washed through her until she was sure she would vomit and then, just when Twelve thought it couldn't get any worse, the Croke found what it was looking for.

*A fire burned and she sat silently before it on the grass, legs crossed, back ramrod straight. The moon shone down coldly and a breeze swept through Poa. Doors creaked and shutters rattled. She hadn't bothered closing any of them: there was no one left to care.*

*Behind her, a great mound of fresh-dug earth stood sentinel. Her arms still shook with the effort she had expended in digging, moving the occupants, filling in the cold earth again. She hoped it was deep enough. Black dirt streaked her face and crusted thickly beneath those of her fingernails that were left. The mound whispered for her to look at it, but she resisted,* tried not to think of the soil weighing on eyelids, filling mouths. She shivered in spite of the fire and wondered if the tales about wraiths were true.

She was exhausted but sleep was unthinkable. Her fingers toyed ceaselessly with one of the arrows and she examined it again by the firelight, taking in the taut leather fletching. She placed it carefully on the fire and watched it burn.

Her da's axes lay beside her and she stroked the hafts, smoothed by his hands over years of use. With trembling fingers, she lifted them, the weight heavier than she'd expected. She knew she should get up, leave this haunted place, but she couldn't move, could barely breathe.

As the moon rose higher, anger broke through her shock. It grew and grew, an infinite pit of rage and hatred. With every breath, it gathered force, expanding inside her, pressing outward, threatening to tear her at the seams. It hurt; it was too much for a single body to hold and she struggled to breathe.

Everything should suffer like this. It wasn't right that houses still stood and wheat still rippled in the breeze when really the world had ended. She wanted to slash the moon out of the sky and rip down the calm, beautiful plane trees. The feeling scorched her. Her fingers tingled and heat spread through her. The flames of the fire curved toward her and brushed her knee, burning through her torn leggings and blistering her skin.

Somehow the fire awoke something inside her that she'd

*never noticed before. There was a window of sorts, and if she opened it . . .*

*Rage blasted out of her across the village and the fire rode it joyously, tearing through house and crop alike. She didn't hear herself screaming and, when she opened her eyes, she didn't understand where the wall of flames around her had come from.*

*She didn't care. It seemed right. Nothing mattered anyway.*

The Croke drew back.

Twelve slumped forward, wrung out.

"I think," the Croke said in its flat, expressionless voice, "that we had better put out the torches."

# CHAPTER
# FORTY-FOUR

"What's this rubbish?" Morgren snapped. "Where is the Guardian?"

A muscle flickered in Victory's jaw and her brow furrowed as she stared between Twelve and the Croke. "What did you see?" she asked.

The Croke spoke again. "Put out the torches. Immediately."

Twelve heard their words from a great distance, her mind fogged and stunned. Disgust rolled through her. The Croke had pawed over her memories like secondhand clothes on a market stall. But it had also shown Twelve something vital that she hadn't wanted to remember. Somehow she had done something that last night in Poa. Something impossible.

She thought of the cliffcrawler gorge and how, out of nowhere, flames had engulfed Sharpspark. Had she done that too?

The goblin guards were dousing the torches in a bucket of water while Victory and Morgren looked askance at the Croke.

Beside her, Seven shifted. "Are you a-a-all right?"

Twelve stared at her, half stunned, and was surprised to see tears rolling down the other girl's cheeks.

"I'm s-s-sorry," Seven whispered. "There's so much that isn't clear, the paths are so tangled, but I've always known that you had to find out h-here, like this. I wanted to tell you before, but you n-n-never would have believed me."

Twelve stared dumbly at her, barely able to take in her words.

"She is an elemental," the Croke said to Victory and Morgren. Did Twelve imagine it or was its voice not quite as emotionless as before?

Victory shrugged impatiently and Morgren looked blank.

"A type of witch," the Croke said. "A very rare one. The last ones on record were killed during the Dark War."

Twelve felt a dull thud of surprise. *A witch?*

"Powerful?" Morgren asked. He stared hard at Twelve. She didn't even have the energy to look defiant. "Perhaps she could be of use, then."

"Powerful, yes," the Croke said slowly, "but she will never join our cause. Her path is set against ours."

"No." Victory's voice was rough. "She isn't a witch. She can't be! I've known her for years and I would have seen if she carried that kind of contamin—" She stopped talking abruptly as Morgren stepped closer. "There will be a way to make her see," she said more quietly, a strange pleading tone in her voice. "She just needs time. Perhaps when she meets our master . . ."

Twelve looked up. So the Croke was not their master? She shuddered. If the master was more terrifying than the Croke, then she was in no hurry to meet him.

Morgren scowled. "When has the Croke ever been wrong, Victory? If this child has power and sets herself against us . . . you must see we can't allow that to happen." He drew Skin from its sheath and stepped forward. "I will make it quick and clean for your sake though."

He raised the knife and slashed at Twelve's throat in a deadly, sweeping arc.

Seven screamed and Twelve pushed against the chair with all her might, toppling it over backward. She felt the blade shiver through the air a hair's breadth from her neck, then she was falling, praying the chair would break. If she could just get one limb free . . .

With a curse, Morgren stepped forward again. Another scream tore through the hall. This time it came from the training ground outside. Everyone froze. A wet, tearing sound reached their ears. Twelve's stomach churned. Someone had just died horribly.

Morgren's and Victory's faces told her they had come to the same conclusion.

"Guards, to us!" they roared together, their voices mingling into one.

"Barricade the doors!" Morgren yelled, the green fire flaring bright in his hand.

One of the arms of the chair had cracked and Twelve worked at it frantically, feeling it give a little more. The Hunter and the goblins had their weapons drawn and were arced around the doorway, waiting. And something was definitely coming. Twelve could hear it now, huge and approaching fast, the floor vibrating beneath her.

She managed to rip her arm free and started undoing the rope around her other wrist, keeping one eye on the door.

"You can do it! You *w-will* do it," Seven whispered breathlessly, her eyes wide and fixed on the goblins' backs.

Twelve's numb fingers worked frantically at the knots. Then her second arm was free and she turned to her ankles as something enormous smashed through the doors, sending goblins and splinters of wood flying.

Nearby, someone shrieked, a keening sound of agony that was abruptly cut off, then the room was full of shouted commands and the scream of steel. Frantically, she tugged at the ropes, praying she could get herself and Seven free before anyone remembered they were there. Finally, the rope came apart, and she stood shakily.

"TWELVE!"

So loud the ground shook with it.

The voice was so familiar, she was afraid to look in case it wasn't true. But she forced her eyes upward.

Her breath caught in her chest.

A mud-streaked Dog stood in a circle of goblins, looking supremely unconcerned by all the weapons pointing at him. On his back were Five and Six, looking even muddier, and a lot more worried, but holding their weapons steadily nonetheless. Even more amazingly, they looked happy to see her.

"You dropped these *again*!" Six called, pulling her axes off his back and tossing them over the heads of the goblins.

## CHAPTER
# FORTY-FIVE

There was a lump in Twelve's throat that made breath-ing difficult and speaking impossible. But she caught the axes, heart pounding with adrenaline and disbelief.

Six was the only one with a bow and he put it to good use, taking down one of the goblins who turned toward Twelve as she sprang up.

Victory threw herself out of the way as Dog leaped forward. Morgren hurled a handful of green fire at the boys and Five deflected it neatly off his sword back at him. The mage flung himself aside with a muffled shout.

Twelve made short work of the ropes holding Seven. She hauled the girl to her feet, feeling her sway danger-ously, her eyelids fluttering.

"Stay with me," Twelve whispered, resisting the urge to

pull the girl into a hug. Seven nodded.

Steel shrieked on steel as a goblin lunged for Five. His sword would have found its mark if not for Dog leaping gracefully to the side. His jaws latched on to the goblin's shoulder and he tossed him away as easily as if he'd been a doll.

Awe and fear rose in Twelve. She'd become so familiar with Dog that she'd almost forgotten why he was so big, why his teeth were so sharp. He'd been created to fight and never had that been more evident than now. His hackles stood up in ridges and his lips were drawn back in a vicious snarl. Twelve wasn't sure she'd ever seen anything so magnificent or so terrifying. The goblins were at a loss: their weapons just bounced off him. In a single bound, he was by her side and suddenly, unbelievably, Six's hands were pulling her onto his back while Five grabbed Seven.

"Where are the Hunters?" Dog snarled.

Twelve's brain whirred. Victory had said she hadn't killed them, that they were locked up. But where? Not down in the dungeons, that was for sure. In that dripping silence, you could hear rats scurrying. It was impossible that there could be hundreds of Hunters trapped down there without her hearing even a scuffle. "The huntling dormitories," she gasped. "It must be—they're the only rooms with locks on the outside!"

"Then that is where we go!" Dog roared, springing

forward and barging through a crowd of goblins trying to block him at the door. He sent them flying as he sped through. Victory's and Morgren's screamed orders mingled behind them as they emerged into the cold night air.

"Aim for the boys," Twelve heard Victory shriek. "The Guardian we can only subdue!"

Hatred bubbled through Twelve at the Hunter's words and her hands tightened around her axes. She had never been so happy to feel their familiar weight.

"How did you get in?" she cried, glancing back at Six and feeling her heart swell.

"We found your axes. Saw the goblin fire," Dog snarled, bounding across the training ground toward the resthouse, plowing through more goblins. "It was clear what had happened."

"We got lucky with the tunnel," Five called. "The mage hadn't erased the footprints at the entrance. We were almost in the training ground when the goblins tried to collapse it."

Behind her Six shivered. "We were nearly buried alive. Dog dug us out."

Ahead of them, the door to the resthouse loomed. Just in time, Twelve realized Dog had no intention of stopping to open it. They crashed through and shards of wood flew past as Twelve buried her face in her arms, clinging on to Dog with her legs.

Inside, it was obvious that Twelve had been right. Muffled yells and banging came from each of the dormitories: the sound of hundreds of Hunters trying to force their way out.

"Quickly!" Dog barked. "Set them free. I will guard the door." As he spoke, several arrows pinged uselessly off him. He nudged the damaged doors closed and leaned his weight against them. There were gaps where they'd splintered, but they offered some protection.

In the training ground, Twelve could hear the surge of feet and Victory shouting. "They will be unarmed!" she yelled. "Form up in front of the armory. Without their weapons, they're helpless."

Twelve tried not to think about what was coming next as she scrambled off Dog's back with the others. There were two corridors on either side of a central staircase, one for boys and one for girls. Ghastly green fire burned in the torches here as well.

Twelve darted into the boys' hallway with Six and they began pulling back bolts and throwing the doors open. Bewildered, bedraggled Hunters emerged, and, with a sinking heart, Twelve realized whatever Victory had used to drug them must have been powerful. They were awake enough to know what had happened and to try to escape their prison, but their eyes were glazed, their movements sluggish. They spilled out into the passage, taking in the green light with horror, slapping their cheeks and shaking their heads, trying everything to make themselves more alert.

As they poured out of the rooms, no Widge appeared alongside them. Twelve pushed down her rising dread, told herself that just because he wasn't there didn't mean he was dead. But there was a cold fist of fear in her gut, hard to ignore, growing all the time.

Shouted questions overwhelmed Twelve and hands grabbed at her as the Hunters sought an explanation. She twisted away furiously and rushed to the last door, the one from which the loudest shouting came. When she drew back the bolt, Elder Hoarfrost burst from the room, his tall frame almost filling the doorway. White hair poked out wildly from under his helmet and keen black eyes darted about, taking everything in at once. Unlike the other Hunters, he seemed fully alert and in control. One look at him and Twelve's heart began to lift. She might not like the man, but the Hunters uniformly feared and respected him. Perhaps there was hope for the lodge after all.

Hoarfrost's gaze took in the situation at a glance: Dog guarding the door, the dazed Hunters trying to push past him into the training ground.

"Scuttling skryll! Shut it, all of ye!" he roared. "Guardian, report!"

In as few words as possible, Dog sketched out the situation. Twelve saw the Elder's face pale when Dog explained

Victory's betrayal but, when he next spoke, his voice rang with authority.

"First things first," Hoarfrost boomed. "Huntlings, upstairs now! Take shelter in the Elders' rooms on the top floor an' barricade the ruddy doors." The students rushed for the stairs. Twelve, Seven, Five, and Six stayed exactly where they were. Hoarfrost noticed this with only a slight narrowing of his eyes. "Next, weapons," he called. "What do we have?"

When the goblins moved the unconscious Hunters, they'd stripped them of any weapons they could see. But every Hunter worth his or her salt carried at least one concealed dagger, and these appeared now: long, short, curved, and serrated, but all extremely sharp. With a weapon in their hands again and their Elder shouting orders at them, the Hunters were starting to look more alert, and, Twelve noticed, much, *much* angrier.

"Guardian," Hoarfrost called, forcing his way through the crowd to Dog. "What's the situation out there?"

Dog stepped back to allow Hoarfrost to peer through one of the ragged cracks in the door. Twelve seized her chance and darted forward as well, pressing her eye to a gap. Her heart sank. The training ground glowed green in the goblin-light, enough to see hundreds of goblins amassed in front of the armory, Victory and Morgren among them. Swords, axes, and armor glinted. Twelve gulped—suddenly the Hunters' daggers looked much less impressive.

Hoarfrost blinked as he noticed her crouched next to him. "Well," he growled, "what do you reckon?"

She wasn't sure where it came from, but the words that emerged from her mouth weren't those she intended. "Are you sure you don't want to hear from one of your more *reliable* students?"

Did she imagine the slight twitch at the corner of his mouth?

"You'll do," he said dryly.

Twelve bit her lip. "We need to get to the armory and they know that," she whispered.

He nodded, his eyes hawklike on her.

"There's no way in other than across the training ground," she went on, thinking hard. "Victory will defend it with everything they've got."

"That snake!" Hoarfrost spat. He took a deep breath, "Go on . . ."

"But we have Dog," Twelve whispered fiercely. Dog had lowered his head to listen and a low growl sounded from him. "The first attack, when Seven was taken, was all just a decoy to get rid of him."

"What?" Hoarfrost whispered, his horror obvious.

"Victory told me herself," Twelve said grimly. "They fear Dog more than anything else. He could break through their lines, clear a path for us to the armory." She glanced at Dog for confirmation and the growl grew louder.

"Of course I can," Dog said, a fierce fire in his eyes. "It is what I was made for. And I could smash into the armory itself. Widen the doorway for faster entry."

Hoarfrost nodded once and stood, his back very straight. Quickly, he relayed the plan to the Hunters and they fell into formation behind Dog, tension humming through them. Six, Five, and Seven pushed their way to the front to stand beside Twelve.

"Ye four clear off upstairs with the others," Hoarfrost said. "Ye'll only be in the way out there."

For once, Twelve's anger felt controlled. Hoarfrost wasn't the enemy here. "We're the only ones with proper weapons," she pointed out.

"Without us, you'd still be locked up," Five added.

"We stay," Seven said, her voice carrying a finality that made Hoarfrost stare. She linked her arm through Six's and met his gaze levelly. "W-w-we have to."

"They have surprised me," Dog growled, his eyes flicking away from the door. "They have faced cliffcrawlers, an Ygrex, and a deathspinner. They have been Blooded. They have earned their place."

Twelve felt a warm glow inside her.

Hoarfrost hesitated, before nodding. "All right," he said finally. "Ye'll have to watch each other's backs out there though. Ye may be Blooded, the Guardian speaks for ye on that, but there'll be more blood spilled tonight."

# CHAPTER
# FORTY-SIX

Hoarfrost turned to the silent crowd of assembled Hunters, his eyes scanning each face in turn. Under his gaze, Twelve saw spines straighten, chins raise, hands grip daggers more tightly.

"Beyond these doors lies the fight of our lives," Hoarfrost called. "Our weaponsmaster has broken faith with us, led the enemy right into our ruddy training ground. She reckons she can undo in one night what has taken a thousand years to build, but I say she blimmin' well can't."

A ragged cheer sounded from the Hunters and Twelve felt hope swell in her. Seven's hand found hers and squeezed hard.

Hoarfrost spoke again. "I know ye're battered an' I know ye're bruised, but tonight we gotta fight as never before. Will ye fight for the safety the lodge has given us? Will ye fight for the names we've earned here an' the loved ones lost gaining 'em?"

A ripple of energy spread through the assembled Hunters, the growl of a great beast rousing itself.

Hoarfrost's voice rose to a roar. "Will ye fight with me for those we protect? For justice? *Will ye fight for our home?*"

There was nothing ragged about the sound that erupted now. Every Hunter's battle cry filled the hall and their feet stamped a slow, threatening rhythm on the floor, shaking the walls.

The hairs stood up on Twelve's neck and her chest felt tight again. Nervously, she adjusted her grip on her axes and turned to Dog. His full attention was focused on what lay beyond the door, tension vibrating through him. His teeth were bared in a snarl and he looked larger than he ever had. In the ghoulish green light, he was the stuff of nightmares. Twelve ached with pride.

She raised her hand to her shoulder to touch Widge, to reassure herself with the warm softness of his fur.

Then she remembered, with a sickened jolt, that he was gone.

"The f-f-fox must stay muzzled," Seven whispered, her breath warm on Twelve's ear.

"What?" Twelve frowned, pushing away thoughts of her squirrel. "What does that mean?"

"I . . . I don't know," Seven muttered, her voice anguished. "B-b-but it's important."

There was no time to question her, no time to think.

"Ready?" Hoarfrost asked, gripping one side of the door. Dog's only answer was a snarl.

Twelve gripped the other door and pulled at the same time.

Dog exploded out of the resthouse with the Hunters surging behind him. Battle cries roared in Twelve's ears as she raced forward, the ground shaking under her feet, her axes in her hands.

Across the training ground, Victory raised her sword, the tendons standing out on her neck as she screamed, "ADVANCE!"

# CHAPTER
# FORTY-SEVEN

Twelve was racing toward a wall of goblins, their weapons raised, sharpened teeth bared. They looked formidable, unbeatable, and for a moment her heart quailed.

"Hold the line!" Victory shrieked, her determination evident in every syllable.

One glance at the weaponsmaster and Twelve felt herself harden, felt her feet fly faster. She could *never* let that monster win.

With an ugly roar, the two sides clashed in the center of the training ground. Steel screamed as swords met; daggers and bodies slammed into each other. Dog barged ahead through the lines, sending goblins flying as their weapons bounced off him uselessly.

"Hunters, *to the armory*!" howled Hoarfrost. He blocked a deadly goblin sword-sweep with his dagger and elbowed another in the face, forcing his way forward.

Seven, Five, and Six pulled closer to Twelve, and together they rushed into the fray. Six's arrows were deadly, clearing goblins out of their path before they were close enough to strike, but suddenly three goblins filled the space in front of them. They were all small, only reaching as high as Twelve's shoulder, but their movements were quick and lithe, their faces set and merciless.

"I know they have swords, but I'd take these over cliff-crawlers any day," Five muttered.

"Definitely," Six agreed on Twelve's other side.

As one, the three of them stepped forward and Twelve's world narrowed to the axes in her hands and the ground under her feet. She deflected a blow from one of the goblins and dealt him a hard kick in the stomach, knocking him back a pace.

"Duck!" Seven cried from behind her.

How Twelve knew the girl was talking to her, she didn't wonder. She ducked, felt a blade whistle over her head, and whirled to meet her attacker. He lunged at her and Twelve knocked his blade aside, slamming the haft of her other axe into his temple, knocking him out cold.

Beside her, Five and Six were fighting a third goblin together, but, when Twelve turned to Seven, her heart almost stopped. The first goblin had wrestled Five's dagger from the girl's hand and was advancing, his grin triumphant.

Twelve sprang between them, fury pounding through her as his smile faded, to be replaced by an angry hiss. He easily blocked her first wild swings and nearly caught her out with a deadly downward slice. She threw herself back just in time, almost colliding with Seven.

He was good. The realization frightened her, but she pushed it away as they circled each other. Fear now would only get her killed. Taking a deep, calming breath, Twelve reminded herself that she was good too, more than good. With a yell, she leaped forward. The goblin feinted left before driving Seven's dagger straight at her stomach. Twelve's crossed axes slammed over the blade, knocking it from his hand. A swift, hard kick knocked him back a step, and his hand reached for the sword sheathed at his hip. Its pommel was a beautifully carved fox.

*The fox must stay muzzled.*

The memory of Seven's whispered words filled her with sudden certainty: something awful would happen if she let him draw his sword. Tamping down her terror, she surged forward, her axes a whirling blur that drove him back and threw him off balance. She lunged again, slicing through his sword belt, sending his weapon tumbling to the ground. His yell of fury was deeply satisfying, but, before Twelve could make her next move, an arrow came out of nowhere to embed itself in his shoulder. With an agonized scream, he dodged away from her and was swallowed by the battling crowd. Twelve turned to see Six with his bow raised.

"Thanks!" Twelve gasped, a rush of adrenaline making her hands shake.

"We're nearly there!" Five cried, pointing to the armory.

He was right. Dog had almost cleared a path and the Hunters were right behind him, fighting their way through the goblin lines. Twelve almost cheered, then she noticed something that made her voice catch in her throat. The Hunters were bunched up behind the Guardian, and the goblins were circling behind them, surrounding them.

"Hoarfrost!" Twelve yelled, but it was no good. He'd never hear her over the cacophony of battle noise.

"This could get extremely nasty," Six muttered, seeing what she was looking at. "If we don't break through to the armory soon . . ."

"Dog will get us there," Five said with confidence, pulling them forward, back into the tide of Hunters.

The Guardian was unstoppable, surging back and forth through the goblin lines, knocking them aside as easily as if they were dominoes. He threw himself into the fray to defend a Hunter who had nearly been overwhelmed by her opponent and then bounded away to do the same for another.

Victory's voice rose over the training ground. "Bolases prepare!" she roared, springing out of the way as Dog raced past her.

Twelve felt a whisper of doubt as she tried to remember what a bolas was. An old weapon, very much out of fashion: a chain with two weights at either end. What could Victory possibly want that for?

Twelve realized a moment too late.

"Dog, no!" she cried, horror searing through her. He had sprung out of the press of bodies into an open space to see where he was needed. Victory seized her chance.

"Now!" she screamed, her face contorted.

With a crack, three wooden contraptions fired from behind Dog, and three bolases tangled themselves around his legs. A look of horror passed over the Guardian's face as he tried to move and found that he couldn't.

Yelping, he lost his balance and crashed to the ground.

# CHAPTER
# FORTY-EIGHT

A triumphant roar sounded from the goblins and Morgren's voice rose above them. "The day will be ours! The Hunting Lodge will be ours!" The mage flung a spell at Dog and it sizzled against the Guardian's side, leaving a blackened mark. Dog's howl was heartrending.

"No!" Twelve cried. That wasn't right; Dog wasn't supposed to feel pain.

"Come on," Five yelled over his shoulder at them. "We *have* to get those chains off him."

The four huntlings raced toward the fallen Guardian, but the closer they got, the tighter the press of Hunters. The goblins had fully surrounded them and were inching closer, sensing their advantage. Twelve stared around in

326

alarm—the Hunters were in disarray. Half of them were still trying to force their way to the armory while the other half were fighting their way toward Dog.

"The armory!" Hoarfrost's voice boomed, seeing what was happening. "Hunters, stay with me!"

It was impossible, Twelve realized with horror. They would never make it. Under Victory's direction, rows of heavily armed goblins had re-formed in front of the weapons store. There were too many of them. Morgren stood there too, green light pooled in his cupped hands, his face monstrous.

Twelve watched the mage, foreboding prickling through her. His lips never stopped moving and the magic in his hands was responding, feeding out of his fingers in shimmering threads. It arced up and over the heads of the embattled Hunters, weaving itself together until a shining net hung ominously over them. It writhed, crackling faintly and shedding a sinister light onto the fight below. The Hunters were now surrounded on all sides *and* menaced from above.

"STOP!" The mage's triumphant voice was magnified to a hundred times its normal volume. "OR I WILL KILL EVERY ONE OF YOU." His finger pointed at the shimmering net and his eyes gleamed fanatically.

An uncanny silence fell over the fighting groups,

weapons stilled and breaths held. Everyone's gaze turned upward. The few goblins caught in the crowd of Hunters desperately tried to force their way out from beneath the magic net, their faces terror-filled.

Hoarfrost's sharp gaze took this in. "It ain't just my Hunters you threaten with this abomination, you dundering dolt!" he called.

"You think I won't sacrifice my own brethren in order to take this lodge?" Morgren sneered.

As if to make his point, one edge of the net dipped, brushing the arm of a goblin under it. He fell to the ground, screaming, the smell of burnt flesh filling the training ground.

Victory faced the crowd. "Drop your weapons!" she called. Her eyes narrowed at their hesitation. "Now!"

Hatred bubbled in Twelve's chest at the sight of her. Without thinking, she swung the axe in her right hand back and flung it as hard as she could. It cartwheeled straight at Victory, but the weaponsmaster's sword came up at the last moment to send it clattering to the ground. Her eyes met Twelve's and the girl saw hurt and surprise there.

"Nice try," Six muttered sympathetically.

"She said 'drop' them," Morgren shouted. "Not 'throw.' Do you want to get everyone killed, little girl?"

Across the training ground, Hoarfrost caught her eye and nodded once. Her blood pounding, Twelve let her remaining axe fall to the ground as the Hunters set down their daggers. Behind her, Five, Seven, and Six did the same.

Morgren smiled as his eyes locked on to Seven. "Seer, come to me of your own free will and the rest of the Hunters may leave the lodge unharmed." Twelve shivered at the cold glint in his eyes. The net writhed, crackling malevolently.

Seven's breath caught.

"I don't know why, but I have the strangest feeling he's not telling the truth," Five whispered, stepping closer to Seven.

Six caught her hand and pulled her back as she made to move toward Morgren. "No," he hissed, "I've only just found you!"

From the ground, Dog's voice rose in a howl of fury. "Leave now, mage! Remember I cannot die. I will hunt you to the ends of Ember."

Morgren raised an eyebrow, his eyes darkly triumphant. "You were made by magic and you can be unmade by it as well. I will find out how, you can be sure of it." Raising his voice, he turned to the Hunters. "Give me the girl and the lodge and I will let every one of you live. Resist me and you will all die." The net hissed above them, alive with murderous intent. "What choice do you have? You have no weapons, no Guardian, no hope."

Twelve gazed around, despair and disbelief flooding her. It was over; they had lost.

But then a lone voice rang out from where the fighting had been the most intense, quavering with exhaustion.

*"I pledge my life to the Hunting Lodge."*

For an instant, it seemed the night held its breath, and then, as one, hundreds of voices joined in.

*"I vow to serve all seven clans as my own,*

*To protect them from what lies beyond."*

Twelve reached behind her to squeeze Six's hand, hearing her own voice rising with the others'. The words echoed off the walls, growing in volume and power until Twelve's heart sang with them. It was the first time she'd ever spoken the Pledge and truly meant it.

*"I forsake all blood ties and blood feuds,*

*To offer up my name and my past."*

A movement above the shimmering net caught Twelve's eye. Three sparks whirled against the darkness, growing larger as they swooped beneath the skybridges. She stared in disbelief. The firesprites. What were they doing back at the lodge? Around her, the Hunters' voices grew to a roar.

*"The Hunters are my family now and always.*

*I swear before them that I will never lower my weapons*

*In the face of darkness,*

*Nor allow tyranny to rise."*

Slowly, Twelve bent low, and picked up her axe again.

# CHAPTER
# FORTY-NINE

Like darts, the three sprites streamed down into the training ground. To Twelve's horror, Brightfire and Burnfoot grabbed the sinister net. Flames plumed spectacularly from their wings as they touched the threads of magic and wrenched them up, away from the Hunters beneath. The net fought back, huge compared to them, wrapping itself around them, crushing their wings as they sent great gouts of fire coursing across it.

"What in Ember are they doing?" Five gasped.

"Looks like they're saving us," Twelve said grimly, unable to tear her eyes from the firelit battle overhead.

Morgren swore furiously and began to throw spell after spell at the sprites, hopelessly tangled and fighting above him. But the net was shaking, falling apart, and it was clear

Morgren was struggling to maintain it.

"Hunters, ADVANCE!" Hoarfrost's voice boomed, seizing the opportunity. All around him, Hunters dived for their daggers.

The rows of goblins in front of the armory raised their weapons as one, their faces as blank as death masks.

"We'll never break through!" cried Six. "Not without Dog." Around them, the Hunters surged forward, carrying the little group with them.

"We have to try," said Twelve simply, readying her remaining axe as the rows of goblins loomed closer.

They were brought up short by Sharpspark appearing suddenly in front of Twelve, his face fierce and furious. "What are you doing?" he shrieked, his tiny hands scrunched into burning fists. "Why do you not use your power?"

"I . . . What?" Twelve gasped, as Hunters poured past them, battle cries streaming from their lips.

Above them, Brightfire and Burnfoot sent the last and brightest of their fire zinging along the threads of the net before vanishing with it in a flash of violet light. Morgren roared his fury.

Sharpspark reeled where he flew, would have fallen to the ground if Twelve hadn't stuck out a gloved hand to catch him. For a moment, his fire dimmed to nothing and he appeared impossibly fragile, slumped in the palm of her hand. His wings were gossamer, his skin almost translucent.

"Are they . . . ?" Twelve didn't know how to finish the question.

"Gone," Sharpspark whispered. "Returned to the Great Flame."

"I'm so sorry," Twelve said.

Fire began to flow over Sharpspark again as he flew off her hand, his teeth lengthening in anger. "Sorrow is useless," he hissed. "We promised to serve you, and we are."

Twelve swallowed her confusion as he swooped closer to her. "Enough playing with axes," he hissed in her ear. "Now you must fight."

She just had time to feel annoyed before he landed on her shoulder and pressed his burning palm to her cheek. Pain blossomed across her face, but she couldn't pull away. Like a rabbit caught in torchlight, she was frozen by what he conveyed through his touch. Fire flowed between them, restless and hungry. And there, at the center of it, was the catch to the window that she'd found accidentally in Poa.

Except now she could see it clearly and it seemed laughably simple to open. How had a firesprite known that when she hadn't?

*Hiding from yourself.*

Twelve was almost certain the pointed thought had come from him rather than her.

Somewhere far away and behind her, the Croke's voice, barely recognizable, shrieked out the danger.

"Now!" Sharpspark whispered, and she saw he was right. Morgren had stormed away from his soldiers and stood apart. Light swirled in his cupped hands as he whispered a new horror into being.

Twelve bit her lip. In Poa, it had been a formless fury that had caused such destruction. This time was different: people were relying on her, people she cared about. If she did this right, perhaps she could save them. She needed to concentrate, just as she had focused on the sprites in the gorge, otherwise she might incinerate them all.

She thought first of Poppy with all her stolen laughter. Then of her parents and all her friends in Poa; of Seven, so pale and weak after her ordeal; of everything they'd been through to try and get her back; of Skin and the pride Morgren had taken in the wounds it inflicted . . .

"Enough!" Sharpspark gasped, his palm still burning on her cheek. "More than enough!"

Heat was building and spreading through her. She could feel thick ropes of it twisting in her veins. Faster and stronger it flowed, winding itself through her emotions and building in intensity. Her fingers throbbed painfully and, without thinking, Twelve ripped off her glove and raised her hand, pushing open the mysterious window at the same time.

And with it came the fire.

# CHAPTER
# FIFTY

She had known what was going to happen, but the sheer power of it still surprised her. Flames blasted from her fingertips in a golden, writhing burst. They rushed over the heads of the Hunters and goblins as Morgren released his newly formed spell. The two magics met in mid-air and Morgren's was hurled straight back at him. It hit him squarely in the chest, slamming him to the ground. Twelve's fire tore past to explode against the lodge walls.

A wave of energy blasted from Twelve that knocked everyone to the ground and shook the lodge mercilessly. The light was blinding white and the heat searing. It sucked the air out of her lungs with a whoosh as the blaze mushroomed across the walls. Twelve and Sharpspark were the only creatures still standing and, through the glare, she saw the unthinkable happen. The walls—walls that had stood strong for a thousand years—began to fracture. Fiery cracks cobwebbed across the stone with a sound like whip-lashes.

Sharpspark took his hand off her face. With their connection broken, Twelve resurfaced as though from underwater. She sucked in a heaving breath and fell to the ground, her limbs like jelly, her heart sluggish in her chest.

"They have a mage!" a goblin screamed nearby, his panic audible.

"Where is Morgren?" cried another.

The world faded in and out of focus as Twelve struggled to stay conscious.

She saw Seven, Five, and Six plant themselves solidly around her, their weapons back in their hands.

She saw the Hunters rally to Hoarfrost, swords wrenched from goblin hands, Hunters pouring into the armory with the Elder in the lead.

She saw the stables catch fire, panicked snagglefeet fleeing, strands of burning hay floating over everything.

Then she saw nothing.

# CHAPTER
# FIFTY-ONE

*L*eaves were rustling in a warm breeze and the air was laden with the heady scent of cloudflower. A strip of cloth, worn soft with use, was tied loosely over Twelve's eyes, but she felt sure she knew where she was nonetheless.

Nearby, there was a muffled giggle. A twig snapped as light footsteps circled closer, then away again. Twelve turned slowly on the spot, following the sound. She knew she wasn't supposed to remove the blindfold, but suddenly her curiosity was too strong to resist, and she pulled it off, blinking in the light.

It was as she had thought. She was in the clearing, the one that had been their place. The bushes around her drooped under the weight of white blossoms, the air alive with the hum of nectar-drunk insects.

*"You always peek!"*

A small figure emerged from the explosion of white, moving hesitantly at first, then with more confidence, coming closer until Twelve could finally see her clearly.

Slight build. Gray eyes. A cloud of dark hair.

"Poppy," Twelve whispered.

She looked around for Starling, who always pulled her through these dreams, but there was no one else, just her and Poppy.

"She's not here," Poppy smiled, stopping in front of her. Her favorite blue dress rippled in the breeze. "This time it's my dream, not yours."

"I don't understand," Twelve said. For the first time, a flicker of uncertainty crept through her and she took half a step back.

"I'm not an Ygrex, if that's what you're thinking," Poppy said. She sounded faintly hurt. "It copied me, not the other way around! I won't let it take this place from us though." Her small fists pressed to her sides, her chin jutting out with determination.

Twelve looked around again and thought she understood. This had been one of their favorite places to play, the dense branches perfect for hide-and-seek. The Ygrex had used that, twisted those memories into its cruel trick.

"You hardly ever think of me," Poppy said, stepping closer and slipping her hand into Twelve's. There was no accusation in her voice, no malice, just sadness. "You're letting yourself forget all this, forget us. I wanted to remind you."

Twelve's chest ached so much she could barely breathe, but the little hand in hers squeezed encouragingly, giving her the strength to speak. "It hurts to remember," Twelve whispered. "I have . . . so many regrets. I broke everything." Her voice shook.

"You didn't, Starling." Twelve startled to hear her old name. "We may have fought at the end, but it wasn't anyone's fault."

"It was," said Twelve. Said Starling. "It was mine. And, if I'd taken you with me, you would never have been . . . have been . . ."

"And, if the traitors hadn't attacked our village, no one would have died at all. We fell out, as sisters sometimes do—but you were only being yourself. You didn't kill me. You have to forgive yourself."

"I don't know if I can."

"You can," said Poppy firmly. "You only think of the end. But you must remember that we were happy too. So often we were happy."

There was a telltale prickling behind Twelve's eyes, the pressure of tears building. "Sometimes I can only think about how much I hurt you, about how much I miss you," she said. "Were we really? Happy?"

"Of course we were, silly!" Poppy's laughter was high and fluting. "We fought each other cruelly and loved each other completely. We were sisters. You must know that?" Her laughter faded at the uncertainty in Twelve's face. "Don't forget us, Starling."

*She said it quietly, the ghost of a plea in her words.*

*"I won't," Twelve whispered.*

*"Good," said Poppy. "I love you. I'll always love you."*

*Something dark and thorny loosened in Twelve's chest, something she had carried so long she'd forgotten the terrible weight of it. Hot tears spilled over her lashes as she nodded, unable to speak.*

*Poppy pulled her into a hug. Twelve closed her eyes and breathed her in: lavender and meadowsweet. "It's not too late, you know, to be the person you want to be."*

*Poppy's words were so quiet it was as though the breeze had murmured them and, for a glorious moment, everything was right. Her sister was beside her and Twelve felt at peace.*

"Twelve, can you hear me?" Six's voice sounded as though it was coming from a long way away.

The scene dissolved around her, and Poppy was gone—but also *not* gone. Not like she had been before. There was a warmth in Twelve's chest, a calmness that stayed even after her little sister disappeared.

"Twelve?"

She opened her eyes to find Six leaning over her, his face full of fear and hope.

"You're awake," he yelped. Then, raising his voice even more, he bellowed, "She's awake."

Twelve flinched and groaned, pushing him away, trying

to hold on to the dissipating threads of the dream.

*Not too late . . .*

Something moved over her chest. She felt two paws on her chin and suddenly her vision was filled with a little copper face, bright eyes examining her beadily.

"Widge!" she gasped, raising her arms with difficulty to stroke him. "You're all right! I thought . . . I thought . . ." She couldn't finish the sentence, couldn't say it out loud. Tears prickled behind her eyes. She sank her fingers gratefully into his fur, the cold knot of fear inside her finally relaxing. He was safe.

"He's a real survivor," Six grinned. "They must have been keeping him in the kitchen." He frowned and shook his head. "Let's not think about why. But, when it collapsed, he suddenly appeared. He ran straight to you and no one's been able to get him off since." His smile wavered. "I think he's been really worried about you though. He's been chewing your hair again. Quite a lot."

Widge looked abashed as Twelve raised a hand to her head. Her hair *did* feel significantly shorter on one side than the other. She found she didn't really care; it didn't seem important. Not after she'd spent so long thinking she would never see him again.

"It'll grow back," she said, to her squirrel's obvious relief. With a gentle chirrup, he nestled into her neck, content just to be with her.

"Wait." Twelve frowned suddenly, wincing at a sharp pain in her cheek. "Six, what do you mean 'when it collapsed'?" She looked around and her confusion only grew; they appeared to be in some sort of tent. She was lying on a cot with furs piled high over her. "Where are we?"

"Ah." Six's face grew somber. "Well . . ."

He was interrupted by a canvas flap being pulled back as several people rushed in. In the lead was Seven, her smile as bright as snow, then came Five and Elder Hoarfrost. Dog was too big to fit in so made do with poking his head through the entrance.

"I knew y-you'd be all right," Seven said. The relief on her face told another story though.

"Course she is," Six grinned.

"She's *obviously* as indestructible as Dog," Five added, punching her none too gently on the arm.

"Ouch." Twelve grimaced. It felt like she had bruises all over her, but somehow she was alive. It seemed nothing short of a miracle. She stared at the others, drinking in their faces hungrily, unable to believe that after everything that had happened, all the awful things that had been said, they'd still come for her. She held Widge close and let a warm feeling of certainty wash over her.

She was among friends.

# CHAPTER
# FIFTY-TWO

"Glad to see you awake, Twelve," Hoarfrost said gruffly, pulling a stool from the corner of the tent and sitting. The others followed suit. "This lot have filled me in on as much as they can, but there are still a fair few blanks to my mind."

Twelve edged herself up painfully in the bed and nodded.

Hoarfrost looked exhausted, dark circles under his eyes and a nasty gash across his forehead, but he sat ramrod straight and his gaze was as penetrating as ever.

"Why," he said softly. "Why did Victory do it?"

Twelve's breath caught and a sour taste flooded her mouth. "Respect." The word came out as a hiss. Hoarfrost's eyes narrowed.

Words spilled from Twelve's mouth as she related everything that had happened to her since she had left the others: how Victory had pretended to rescue her from the dungeons, how the Hunter had interrogated her over Dog's whereabouts and allowed the Croke to invade her mind. Then she took a shaky breath and told them about the arrows, about the untold depths of Victory's darkness and deception.

Hoarfrost stood abruptly, knocking his stool over. "Splottering spineghasts! I never woulda believed it if I hadn't seen her there myself. Fighting alongside the ruddy goblins! Victory!"

"She escaped?" Twelve asked, already knowing the answer.

"Aye," Hoarfrost growled. "With whatever's left of that mage an' the thing you called the Croke. I couldn't send a team after 'em, not with everything so chaotic." His eyes narrowed. "We *will* catch 'em though."

Five's face was screwed up as he absorbed everything Twelve had said. "What did Victory mean about a 'master'?" he asked.

"An excellent question," Dog said. "Could she mean Morgren?"

Twelve shook her head quickly and regretted it. Pain jarred down her neck. "No," she winced. "Morgren talked about a master as well and"—she paused and frowned—

"I got the impression that it was this master who had given Morgren his powers." Twelve remembered how the mage had stared at the fire in his hands, the delight and greed and wonder on his face. "I don't think he'd had them very long."

"He should not have them at all," Dog growled. "The witches bound goblin magic."

"What else can you tell us about this 'master,' Twelve?" Hoarfrost asked.

She thought hard. "When I asked about . . . about Poa, about *why*." Her voice shook and she bunched her hands into fists. "Morgren said that their master had required it. He said, 'The more violence, the more chaos and destruction, the stronger he grows.'"

Dog whined quietly. Widge pressed himself against her cheek.

"Those were the exact words?" Hoarfrost asked, frowning.

Twelve nodded.

"A creature that feeds on chaos?" Six said. "I've never heard of such a thing."

"That makes two of us," Hoarfrost said slowly. "But, according to Victory an' Morgren, it's behind all this, an' they would ruddy well know! It's recruited allies, returned banned magic to the goblins, an' managed to gather enough dark critters to attack the Hunting Lodge. Whatever it is, it's strong."

"And clever," Dog growled. "If it feeds off destruction, then it is sustaining itself well."

"You're thinking of the attack on Twelve's village?" Hoarfrost asked.

"Not just Poa," Twelve reminded them, her stomach churning. "Morgren said there were others."

Hoarfrost shook his head. "I can't believe the lodge would not have heard of such a thing."

"In the last few years, the rifts between the clans have grown wider than ever," Five said. "Some places have cut themselves off altogether. The floating villages and desert caravans are always on the move anyway. If this *thing* targeted them, it could be some time before anyone misses them and raises the alarm."

"But when the alarm is raised you can be sure the blame will fall on one of the other clans, not some mysterious, never-before-seen dark creature," Twelve said grimly.

"And so the m-mayhem spreads," Seven said quietly, her expression far away.

"But why?" Six asked. "What does it want?"

"Since when do dark critters want anything beyond their next meal?" Hoarfrost snorted.

"No," Dog growled. "The boy is right. This thing is

not like other creatures. It is clever and organized. It has already achieved a lot. It has a plan. A final goal."

Silence fell and Twelve shivered. The others looked every bit as worried as her.

"How can we stop it?" Six asked eventually.

Hoarfrost nodded at him approvingly. "That's the spirit." He stood abruptly. "Slickering snaverslakes, sitting here ain't gonna solve anything though!"

His restless energy was infectious and Twelve struggled to her feet, feeling like she'd been trampled by a herd of snagglefeet. Widge trilled his concern, but she shushed him and hobbled over to Dog. He nudged her gently with his nose.

"It is good to see you awake," he said. "And alive."

"Thanks, Dog," she whispered, leaning on him as she ducked out of the tent, wondering what awaited her outside.

The smell was the first thing she noticed: ash and cordite. Before she even saw the lodge, she knew the damage must be serious. What she hadn't expected was that three of the eight walls would have fallen, that the beautiful skybridges would have collapsed and the buildings would be gutted. Charred and smoking stone littered the snow-covered ground. The Hunting Lodge was a ruin.

"How did this happen?" Twelve gasped.

The others had come to stand alongside her.

"One word: you," Five said, looking impressed in spite of himself. "I still don't understand what in Ember you did!"

Dog shot an angry glance at Five but no one contradicted him.

Twelve stared at the carnage with growing horror. "I aimed for Morgren," she whispered, shaking her head. "I never . . . I never thought . . ." She broke off, too shocked to speak.

Looking at the destruction seemed to be physically painful for Hoarfrost and he turned away from it with a grunt. "What you did saved us." He spoke as though trying to convince himself and didn't look at her. "The tunnels were collapsed, the gates locked—there was nowhere for us or them to go. We woulda slaughtered each other if you hadn't . . . done what you did."

"Th-that's true," Seven said, stepping closer to Twelve.

Hoarfrost's eyes flicked between them. "Ye both have some form of magic," he said eventually. It wasn't a question.

Twelve glanced uncertainly at Seven. "Yes," the other girl said simply.

Hoarfrost's gaze swept over the ruins once more and he nodded slowly. "It's been a long time since a witch called the lodge home. Perhaps this is the cost."

"This is not the fault of Twelve," Dog said, the barest

hint of a growl in his voice. "Blame rests with Victory and the goblins."

"You reckon I don't know that?" Hoarfrost snapped.

Twelve couldn't look at the remains of the lodge anymore either—she turned away, taking in her surroundings for the first time. She was standing outside one of hundreds of tents, set a safe distance back from the lodge. Firepits burned at regular intervals and Hunters were building a rough wooden palisade wall around the camp.

"This is it?" Twelve whispered, guilt making her voice crack. "This is the lodge now?"

"Yes and no," Hoarfrost said, his eyes finally resting on her again, his voice gentler than she expected. "The lodge has always been more than its walls, more than its weapons. It's the people that make a place, Twelve." He took a slow, deep breath. "An', on that note, I reckon I should thank you."

Twelve blinked, sure she'd misheard. *Thank* her?

"You faced Victory, released the Hunters, an' gave us a fighting chance. Not one of us perished last night an' I have you to thank for that. Furthermore, you did what was right. You went after Seven when she was taken, did everything you could to recover her." Hoarfrost paused and shook his head. "Crackling crawlers! It shoulda been Hunters out there. I don't know why I listened to Victory when she said it should be Dog."

"She is persuasive," Dog growled.

Hoarfrost nodded as he turned to include Seven, Five, and Six. "Ye all showed great fortitude, huge bravery." He paused and a scowl appeared. "So now I find myself in a tricky position. It's clear that some of the lodge's most important rules have been broken by ye four. Six and Seven, ye're siblings?"

They nodded, their faces wax pale.

"And ye're all aware of one another's clan origins?" he asked.

They nodded in silence. Twelve thought about pointing out she didn't know Five's, but decided against it. Hoarfrost looked particularly fierce at that moment.

His breath exploded out of him in a long sigh. "Ye should all be banished for that! Yet over the last few days ye've proven yourselves to have the qualities of true Hunters. Without yer actions, last night woulda been a very different affair."

"Y-yes, it would have," Seven said confidently. She was rewarded with a thundering glare from Hoarfrost.

"Then there's the fact that three of ye passed through the Frozen Forest. Did so despite meeting an Ygrex, a deathspinner, and whatever manner of creature this Oakhammer was."

"We were lucky," Six said quickly.

Hoarfrost snorted. "Lucky? 'Lucky' he says! To meet

those critters and survive? No. Five, Six, and Twelve, ye've performed a feat reserved for much older students and proven yerselves equal to the task. Ye managed to pass yer ruddy Blooding without even being sent on it."

The little group absorbed this in shocked silence.

"So . . . we're actually Hunters now?" Five asked cautiously.

"The youngest in five generations," Hoarfrost said. He glared at each of them in turn as though they had planned it. "But none of ye will ever, I repeat, *ever* reveal that Six and Seven are related."

Four heads bobbed in agreement. Six was so relieved he swayed where he stood. Seven beamed at him.

"Ye will continue yer studies until ye're ready to hunt for the clans. If this episode is anything to go by, then ye'll enjoy great successes together." Grudging respect fleetingly appeared on his face. "I'll be announcing it to the others tonight. There'll be the usual feast to celebrate."

"There will?" Five asked, looking around the ragged campsite doubtfully.

"Aye!" Hoarfrost glared. "As for these *other* skills of yers," he went on, addressing Seven and Twelve, "I reckon I'll be sending a hawk to the witches. I'm hoping they may be able to identify this unknown 'master' of ours. I'll ask for their advice regarding ye two as well, although I expect they'll respond with their usual silence. Until then though,

I absolutely forbid ye to use these . . . powers."

Seven opened her mouth to speak, but was silenced by a look from Six. Twelve nodded at Hoarfrost, a muscle in her jaw flickering painfully.

"Not going to be a problem," she said tightly.

Hoarfrost stared at her for a moment and nodded once. "Glad to hear it. Any questions?"

They shook their heads.

"All right," he said, his gaze encompassing the others again, "I'll make the announcements. I suggest ye all start thinking about yer new Hunter names." A storm-swept smile flickered across his face and was gone. "Ye've ruddy well earned 'em."

# CHAPTER
# FIFTY-THREE

They made their way to the nearest campfire and sat on the logs around it. Food and hot drinks were pressed on them, but then suddenly they were alone, looking at one another uncertainly. So much had happened and no one knew how to begin to broach it. Feet shuffled, Six became very interested in his tea, Five purposely crammed an enormous handful of cake into his mouth. Dog's gaze moved from face to face, infuriatingly hopeful.

"Th-th-thanks for rescuing me," Seven burst out at last, color rising in her pale face. The food seemed to have given her a new strength and her words tumbled over themselves. "I wasn't sure you would. I did everything I could to make it easier, but that w-wasn't much really." She shrugged and looked at Twelve. "I just gave you the moonstone and h-h-hoped that would be enough."

A cloud crossed Six's face. "Why didn't you say something to me?" he asked. "A warning or . . . or anything! I would have protected you! Or . . . tried to at least."

"I wanted to," Seven said miserably, her shoulders hunched against his anger. "B-b-but, in most of the paths where I did that, you ended up dead. And"—she hesitated—"things have been so d-d-different between us since we got to the lodge. We haven't talked properly since we arrived. I kn-know we only came here because of me," she added quickly, holding up a hand to stop Six's interruption. "But part of me wondered if you were relieved. To not h-have to deal with . . . all this anymore." She made a vague gesture at herself.

Six looked stricken. "That's ridiculous," he said faintly.

Seven nodded quickly in agreement, but her expression was uncertain.

"No," Six said more firmly, pulling her into a hug. "I missed you every day and worried about you. I thought if I spent time with you it would be more difficult for both of us. I . . . I'm sorry. I know it's much harder for you here than for me. I was selfish."

The smile on Seven's face was like the sun, changing her features completely. For an instant, Twelve saw Poppy in her again.

"No, y-y-you were right," Seven said. "Everything is as it should be."

Six blinked in surprise and pulled back from her. "Really? You never say that."

"Yes," Seven said, smiling beatifically. "For once, w-we were in exactly the right place at the right time. Only one path led here—the chances were so s-s-small—but we've made it." The relief in her voice was palpable.

Twelve wondered where the other paths had led, what other fates Seven had seen for them. She shivered despite her hot drink, despite Widge wrapped firmly around her neck. Seven's gift seemed more like a curse.

"I agree," Five said cheerfully. "And the time and the place is perfect for giving Twelve a rollocking!"

"You know I could blast you into oblivion?" Twelve asked, wondering why she felt amused rather than irritated.

"I think I'm safe," Five shrugged. "All right, things we *clearly* need to discuss: your temper, being rude, punching people and, most importantly, running away and abandoning your friends." He ticked each item off on his fingers and shook his head at her. "This isn't how friends treat each other."

Twelve felt shame burn her cheeks, even as her heart thrilled at the word "friend." It was now or never. "I'm sorry," she said, surprised at how easy the words were to say and by how much she meant them. "I said terrible things to all of you and I shouldn't have." She met Six's eyes. "Especially what I said to you about Seven and the cave clan. It was awful of me and . . . and I was totally wrong about everything. I'm sorry."

"I said some horrible things too," Six said quietly. "We were as bad as each other. I'm sorry as well."

There was a stupid lump in Twelve's throat. She decided it was better not to speak so she just nodded, hoping he could see how much that meant to her.

Dog's tail had begun to wag slowly and now it sped up, relief evident in his face. He paced energetically in front of them.

"Are you all right, Dog?" Twelve asked.

"Yes," Five frowned. "I know it's good to focus on the positives, but you're *terrifyingly* cheery right now."

"I know," he said, still pacing, his voice a curious mix of growl and yelp. "I cannot help it. You cannot know what it is like. How could you?"

"What do you mean?" Six asked.

"The walls," Dog said, halting abruptly and turning to face them. "They have fallen."

"That means . . . you can't return to them," Twelve said slowly, understanding dawning.

"Yes," Dog said. "Hoarfrost will rebuild them eventually. But for now I am free. I know dark times are ahead, but I feel . . ." He paused, searching for the right word. "I feel *excited*."

"Now there's something I *absolutely* never thought I'd hear," said Five.

"Hoarfrost has had word from the mountain tribe," said Dog. "They are offering us sanctuary. We begin the journey there tomorrow. For the past millennia, I have only left the lodge to fight. When I traveled, it was to or from battle. Always the oblivion of the walls waited for me. Now perhaps . . ." He broke off, looking confused.

"Now you can live," Seven said gently. "Y-you've already proven you can do more than fight."

Dog nodded, his tail wagging slowly. "Maybe it is time to expand my role," he agreed. There was a light in his eyes that made Twelve's heart sing. "I feel different," he said. "Perhaps what Oakhammer did to me changed something. I *feel* everything more. The wind. The coolness of the snow beneath my paws. I felt the heat of the walls burning. And food." He sniffed the air. "I almost think I can taste it."

Five was the only one who frowned. "And pain," he added. "Morgren's spells shouldn't have hurt you, but they obviously did."

"That is true." Dog nodded slowly.

"We still beat him," Six said, his eyes falling on Twelve. A question hovered on his lips.

"Are you really, *actually* a witch?" Five burst out.

Six, Five, and Dog stared at her, their eyes wide.

Twelve's tongue suddenly felt heavy in her mouth as she struggled to think of how to answer. In the end, Seven saved her.

"She's an elemental witch," she explained, her eyes warm on Twelve. "Her power is clearly over fire. I think Sharpspark helped her understand that."

Five and Six stared at her with slack-jawed awe.

The mention of Sharpspark made Twelve sit up straighter and glance around. "Where is he?" she asked. Widge growled in her ear, his displeasure obvious, but for once she ignored him. She felt an affinity with the sprite that both excited and terrified her. He had shown her how to use her powers and helped to save them all at great personal cost. But she knew without a doubt that he would have delighted in the destruction of the lodge where she felt only guilt and horror.

"Hoarfrost sent him away," Five said darkly. "He enjoyed watching the lodge burn far too much. Might have helped it along a bit too."

"Of course," Twelve said quietly, pushing down a wave of sadness.

"H-h-he'll be back," Seven said with confidence, nudging Twelve.

"Don't say that!" Five exclaimed, recoiling in horror. "Although"—he paused and glanced at Twelve—"I now understand why he liked you so much." He whistled. "An elemental witch."

"I didn't know," Twelve said, color rising in her cheeks. "I mean, the fire thing happened before, but never as powerful as that. I still don't understand what it means." She looked at Dog. "The Croke said the last elementals lived during the Dark War. Do you know anything about them?"

Dog's happy expression faded and his tail tucked itself between his legs. Twelve's heart sank.

"I know a little," he said. He spoke slowly, as though choosing his words carefully. "Their magic was . . . unruly. And they were not born with it. A witch of Icegaard is born with her magic. Elementals rise."

"Rise?" Five asked, wrinkling his nose.

"They are made by their circumstances," Dog explained. "Circumstances that are always unpleasant." He nodded slowly and turned to Twelve. "Elementals appear in times of trouble. Times of great darkness. For centuries, there have been none. Now there is you."

A coldness swept over Twelve, and Widge pressed closer to her.

"Uh, could we just be happy for a second?" Five said, breaking the silence. "I mean, Victory couldn't kill us; goblins couldn't kill us; we're together; we found Seven."

He ticked the items off on his fingers. "By the frost, there's loads to be pleased about there!"

A shout caught their attention. A group of Hunters were trying to position the next section of palisade wall. Dog sprang up to help them.

Twelve moved around the fire toward Five, knowing she had to clear something up between them. Their fight still whispered in her ear like a wraith. His eyes were fixed on Six, whose arm was slung around Seven's shoulders, both of them laughing at something, their smiles identical.

Twelve took a deep breath, and sat down beside Five.

This was the last thing. The final piece to mend.

# CHAPTER
# FIFTY-FOUR

"There's nothing between Six and me, you know," Twelve said quietly, looking anywhere except at Five. Beside her, Five snorted. "Same here!"

The resignation and hurt in his voice was enough to make her look properly at him.

To both their surprise, Widge leaped lightly onto his shoulder. Twelve was sure she saw him give Five's cheek a quick lick. A few days ago, she would have been furiously jealous of that. Now the delight and surprise on Five's face made her laugh.

"He wants you to stroke him," she grinned. "Just be warned, once you start, he probably won't let you stop."

"I'm all right with that," Five beamed. For a minute or

so, he ran his fingers through Widge's fur, his expression thoughtful. Twelve waited for him to speak.

"Six and I, we're still friends," Five said eventually. "But he doesn't feel that way about me."

"Oh," Twelve said cautiously. "Isn't it better you both know where you stand though?"

Five shrugged, but Twelve saw uncertainty beneath the casual gesture. "I hope so. I can't lie about who I am."

Twelve nodded, feeling on more solid territory. "No, you can only be yourself. No one else will do it for you."

"Easier if you know who that is though," Five muttered.

Twelve thought of her da and Elder Silver. *Think about the person you want to be.*

"You get to decide, you know," Twelve said slowly. "I have." A liquid warmth spread through her as she spoke.

*Not too late . . .*

Widge bounced back onto her lap, happiness radiating from him as he gazed up at her.

"What have you decided?" Six called across the fire. "Your Hunter name?" He hurried around to sit next to them.

"*Not* what we were talking about," Five said. "Your Hunter name is obvious though—Hare. Big ears for eaves-dropping."

"And yours should be Shrew, in honor of your bad temper," Six grinned, without missing a beat.

"I was actually thinking of Wolf," Five said with dignity. His face fell as Six burst out laughing.

"W-what about you, Twelve?" Seven asked, sitting next to her. "Any ideas?"

Twelve frowned into the fire and thought. "Not yet," she said, shaking her head. "I never expected to become a Hunter, so I never thought about it."

"How about Scorch?" Five said promptly. "What?" he asked, when they all skewered him with a dark look. "It would be a warning not to mess with her."

"Spark?" Six offered. "A bit less obvious?"

Five rolled his eyes.

Twelve shook her head. "It's an easy no to both," she laughed.

"I h-have an idea," Seven said a moment later. "W-what about Phoenix?"

"Phoenix?" Five scoffed. "That's a magical creature. Hunters never take magical names."

"Twelve *has* magic though," Seven said. "And I c-can't think of a more perfect Hunter name for her—a creature of fire that r-rises from its own ashes."

The others fell silent and a strange electricity ran through Twelve. Phoenix. It would be an unusual choice, a bold one. A title she would have to earn, have to live up to every day. She wouldn't end up like Victory, with a glorious name she didn't deserve.

"Phoenix," Twelve said, tasting the word and liking it. "I'll think about it." Her eyes met Seven's and the other girl smiled.

"So you . . . you will stay with the lodge, then?" Six asked, his expression hopeful.

"Yes, I'm staying," Twelve said slowly. "Everything feels different after what we've done together. I think I could be happy here now."

Happy. The word felt odd in her mouth.

Six nodded, a smile spreading over his face.

"Life will be different now too," Five added, a shiver of excitement passing over him. "I've *always* wanted to meet the mountain clan."

"Me too," Six grinned. "Do you think they really build wings like the ones that were in the council house?"

"Th-they do," Seven said dreamily, staring into the fire. "And soar with them too. Their chief has w-wings made of ice eagle feathers."

"Whoa!" Five said. "How do you know that?"

Seven shrugged. "I dream of them sometimes."

"Brilliant!" Five gasped, his face lit up. He turned to Six. "Do you think they'll teach us how to use them?"

Twelve watched Seven, wondering what else the other girl knew but afraid to ask.

Seven caught her eye and smiled ruefully. "T-trust me, you're better off not knowing. Most of it doesn't make sense anyway. Well . . ." She paused. "It d-doesn't until it does."

"Like keeping the fox muzzled?" Twelve asked, remembering Seven's cryptic warning.

"Y-yes." Seven frowned. "That came to me so suddenly and so clearly that I knew it was important, but—" Her face showed her frustration.

"It doesn't make sense until it does," Twelve echoed quietly. A thought occurred to her. "What would have happened if the goblin had managed to draw that sword?"

Seven shivered and shook her head, her lips pressed into a line. She wasn't going to answer.

A moment later, she reached into her pocket and, to Twelve's delight, pulled out the moonstone. In the daylight, it just looked like a pretty rock, its surface milky and iridescent. "I'd l-like you to keep this," she said, holding it out to Twelve as though it was nothing more than a heel of bread.

"You got it back!" Twelve breathed, running her fingers over its smooth, familiar surface.

"I knew w-w-where it would be if we drove the goblins back," Seven shrugged. "I f-found it for you."

"What? No!" Twelve exclaimed. "It's yours."

"Not anymore," Seven said firmly, brushing aside Twelve's protests and pushing it into her hands. "Just p-promise me you'll always keep it with you."

Twelve stared into Seven's fierce gaze and felt her

arguments die on her lips. There was fear in the other girl's face. Fear and certainty.

"What is it?" Twelve asked. "What do you know?"

But Seven was already walking away. "I already t-told you," she called over her shoulder. "You're b-better off not knowing. Besides, the thing that's important right now is on the other side of camp—dinner!"

Twelve grinned as Five and Six leaped to their feet and hurried after her. Dog followed too, bounding away from the finished section of palisade.

"You coming, Twelve?" Six called back. "Or is it Phoenix now?"

"I'll be there in a minute," she answered, waving him on.

When she and Widge were alone, she pulled her knees to her chest and stared into the flames, feeling an answering echo of heat pulse through her.

"Phoenix," she said thoughtfully, testing it again. She glanced at Widge. "What do you think?"

His dark eyes brightened and his tail flicked with approval.

A smile curved Twelve's lips. "I like it too. That's that, then."

There was a gentle glow in her chest, a sense of belonging. She wanted the hard-won feeling to last forever and she sat quietly with her squirrel, savoring it.

She thought of her family and Silver, of Victory's

treachery, and of all the dangers she'd survived with the others. For once, she didn't have to wonder what her parents would have thought or whether Silver would've approved: she knew in her bones they would have been proud.

The world was darkening, powerful forces were gathering, but, for the first time in a long while, she had friends and a home.

They were worth fighting for.

Phoenix stood, brushed the ash from her knees, and went to join her friends.

# ACKNOWLEDGMENTS

When I started writing Twelve's story, I never dreamed that it would really be published. The fact that it has been is thanks to the hard work and support of a whole host of wonderful people.

My husband Ben supported me in every way possible during the writing of this book. Even as a writer, supposedly with a good vocabulary at my disposal, I can't find adequate words to express how much that has meant to me. He is, quite simply, the best.

My incredible agent, Claire Wilson, is another one whose contribution defies description. She believed in the book from the start and somehow that confidence allowed me to believe in myself as a writer. She is a fiercer advocate and kinder person than I ever could have imagined. I still can't work out what I have done to deserve her—she has changed my life.

My UK editor, Nick Lake, is a wonder. Sometimes I feel that he can actually see inside my head to the story I meant to write and the places I've gone wrong. That's how good his notes are. He is a joy to work with and his input has made *Fireborn* so much better.

My US editor, Kristen Pettit, has had boundless enthusiasm for *Fireborn* from the start and has been an absolute pleasure to work with from day one. I feel blessed to have not one wildly talented editor in *Fireborn*'s corner, but two.

The incredible artist, Sophie Medvedeva, has brought *Fireborn* to life in a way I'd never imagined possible. Seeing her work has been one of the most magical parts of the whole publication process. She is a genius.

HarperCollins has welcomed Twelve rapturously and I am ridiculously grateful to have teams on both sides of the Atlantic who have worked so hard to make the book what it is. In the UK, Tina Mories is a PR wizard, absolutely full of bright ideas. Huge thanks also to: Alex Cowan and Bethany Maher in Marketing; Val Brathwaite, Matt Kelly, Elorine Grant, and Hannah Marshall in Design; Samantha Stewart in Editorial and Carla Alonzi in Rights. In the US, enormous thanks to: Lauren Levite and Aubrey Churchward in Publicity; Nellie Kurtzman, Robert Imfield, and Emma Meyer in Marketing; Clare Vaughn in Editorial;

Mark Rifkin in Production; and Corina Lupp in Design. Extra special thanks to Corina for finding Sophie.

Thanks also to Jane Tait for her copyediting skills and to all the proofreaders in the UK and US—your eagle eyes have prevented many mistakes from making it onto the printed page.

I owe a huge debt of gratitude to all the friends and family who plowed their way through early drafts of Twelve's story and gave me feedback that improved it: Jo, Claire, Sarah, Rich, Cecile, Miguel, Adele, Dad, and Fiacra. You're all Hunter-esque heroes and I'm so lucky to have you.

Special thanks to Iona and Cillian, the two younger readers who volunteered feedback—your thoughts were hugely important and helpful. Huge thanks also to Miriam Tobin for her valuable insight and suggestions, to Mary for the glorious writing afternoons in NYC, and to Phoebe for inspiring me to write again.

And last but by no means least, thank you to my parents, Avril and Max, and to my sister, Adele, for a lifetime of love, support and library visits.